JOYCE MOYER HOSTETTER

Drive

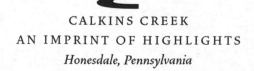

CALKINS CREEK
AN IMPRINT OF HIGHLIGHTS
Honesdale, Pennsylvania

Calkins Creek
An Imprint of Highlights
815 Church Street
Honesdale, Pennsylvania 18431
calkinscreekbooks.com
Printed in the United States of America

ISBN: 978-1-62979-865-3 (hc) • 978-1-68437-145-7 (eBook)
Library of Congress Control Number: 2018933600

First edition
10 9 8 7 6 5 4 3 2 1

Design by Barbara Grzeslo
The text is set in Sabon.
The titles are set in Futura.

For Doris Jean, Nancy Kathleen, and
Joanne Evangeline

Our sisters hold up our mirrors: our images of
who we are and of who we can dare to be.
—Elizabeth Fishel in *Sisters: Shared Histories,*
Lifelong Ties

PROLOGUE
Ellie

Momma says Ida was born ten whole minutes ahead
   of me
and I spent the first years following after her,
doing what she did
and trying to be as good as she was.

Then, when Daddy came home from war
with hurts we couldn't see
and moods he couldn't predict,
the uncertainty hit Ida hardest of all.
She pulled back like a turtle inside its shell,
slowing down while I sped up.
I soon realized I liked running ahead,
hearing people cheer for me.

But sometimes, it was Ida they'd be bragging on.
And when they did,
I always felt that I was losing.
Life became a competition that one of us had to win.

And I was determined that the winner would be me.

1

ELLIE
May 1952

As terrible as it sounds, I wanted to rip the ribbons right off my twin sister's drawing. First place in still life and grand prize in the show!

Ida stood beside me in the hallway at Mountain View School. She wasn't saying much even if she was thrilled—which of course she was. But I knew she felt guilty about *me* only winning honorable mention in my category. For some reason I'd thought a portrait of Dwight D. Eisenhower would help me take first place.

"I'm sorry, Ellie," whispered Ida.

"It's okay," I said. But I had to bite my lip to keep it from trembling.

"Maybe you should've submitted that drawing of the red high heels. It was really good."

"No," I said. "Because that would have been a still life and I wasn't about to compete in the same category as you. But of course you beat me anyway."

Before Ida could try to make me feel better, our best friend elbowed her way between us and linked her arms with ours. "You both did real good," said Vivian, her voice all chirpy and encouraging.

Vivian was trying to be nice without favoring either one of us. After eight years of elementary school together, she knew the competition we felt. And she'd learned a long time ago to let us fight our own battles.

"I guess Ida gets the ten-dollar prize," I said, staring at her picture. "That's her reward for drawing a pile of junk."

Ida gasped, and I knew I'd gone too far.

"I'm not trying to be mean," I said. "But if you think about it, it *is* junk. Ann Fay never uses that leg brace anymore. Or those crutches. And whatever inspired you to include the dust balls under the bed? Or that broken bed slat and the coil hanging loose on the springs?"

If you asked me, it was downright embarrassing to show everybody what things looked like at our house.

"There's a story there," said Vivian. "How your older sister wouldn't let polio keep her down." Vivian stopped all of a sudden because she was starting to come between us after all. "I mean, uh, I'll just look around." She turned and faced the portraits on the opposite wall. "I really do think"—here she leaned my way and lowered her voice—"that *your* Eisenhower is the best one of all."

"Of course," I said. "Ida helped me with it."

"I did not touch your drawing," Ida said. Her blue eyes narrowed. "You did that all by yourself."

It was true. She hadn't touched it, but she did tell me how to get the proportions just right. Ida was great with faces and just about every other kind of drawing. I could draw too, but I didn't do it the way she did—all the time. On any surface she could find—the empty spaces at the sides of the *Hickory Daily Record* and cardboard from the insides of cereal boxes. She always had a pencil tucked behind her ear.

Personally I'd rather be sewing. Or reading. Or gabbing. She could *have* her old pictures.

Maxine came down the hall then. "Hey, twin," she said, "are you the one that won first place?"

I didn't much care for Maxine. By now, she should've figured out how to tell us apart, but she never really tried. Some people just thought twins were too complicated to figure out. And right now, I felt the same way.

"I knew that picture would win. The details are just swell. And look at this one." Maxine grabbed my arm and pointed to a drawing of atomic testing the government was doing out West. "Can you believe that mushroom cloud? Isn't it just glorious? So realistic you can almost hear the blast and feel the earth shake. I watched it on television. Did you?"

I tossed my head and walked away. No. I hadn't watched it on television because we didn't have a television at our house. We listened to it on the radio, and I thought it sounded thrilling. But it was scary too, and it sure shook my daddy. He hadn't been the same since we dropped those bombs on Japan, but for some reason he kept listening to the news about Russia racing to develop the same weapons we had.

Whenever the government tested one, people out West stopped to watch. Or they hurried to picnics and lined up their chairs to see the show. America acted like the atom bomb was the greatest thing since sliced bread. But we were also scared to death of nuclear war.

All day long, students and teachers congratulated Ida on her win. I avoided her so I wouldn't have to smile every time and pat her on the back like a proud family member was supposed to. And also because anyone who bragged on her would feel obligated to tell me how great my Eisenhower portrait was.

To be honest, I could see the problem now—I hadn't captured the softness of the crinkles around his eyes or the way his smile widened his face into that pudgy grandpa look. General Eisenhower's big smile made him seem more like a family member than a hero of World War II.

When the bell rang at the end of the day, it was raining, which suited my mood just fine. Normally I'd be singing *"It's raining, it's pouring"* or some other goofy thing and people on the bus would sing along, but today I watched the rain run like tears down the windowpane beside me.

At our stop, I was all set to run to our neighbors' back porch and wait there for the rain to let up. But Junior

Bledsoe met us in his Chevy. He opened his car door, hopped out, and folded the seat forward so we could climb into the back.

I dashed past Ida to the car and slid across the seat to make room for her. "Whew!" I hollered. "It's raining pitchforks out there." I shook my head like Mr. Shoes, our dog, and when I did, I heard a laugh coming from the front seat. There, sitting smack dab in front of me, was some fellow with wavy black hair. Somebody I didn't recognize—at least not from seeing the back of his head. "I think some of those pitchforks just stabbed me," he said. He swiped at the back of his neck.

I'd just splattered his neck and shoulders with rainwater. "Oops! I'm sorry."

Junior scrambled back into the car. "That's Ida," he said, pointing to my sister. "And Ellie's the one behind you. Ladies, this is Ned Jarrett. I work for his dad at the sawmill."

Yeah, we knew that. And we'd seen Ned around, but it wasn't like we actually knew him. "Hey, Ned." We both said it at the same time.

"Nice to meet you." He turned and flashed a big white smile. He had a handsome face, and I wished I could get a better look—even if he was too old for me and married with a baby boy, which I knew from hearing Junior's stories.

"We've been out looking for car parts," said Junior. He turned around in the Hinkle sisters' driveway. "Ned's

11

building a race car. When that speedway opens, he's gonna show them boys how to drive."

"No kidding?" I asked. It was like Junior had thrown a rainbow across the cloudy sky. "Are you really going to race?"

"That's the plan," said Ned.

"Well then, I'm coming to watch. Did you try Otis Hickey for car parts? He's got a junkyard behind his house."

Junior nodded. "Just came from there."

If Ida was hearing any of this I couldn't tell it. She was looking at Ned but not like she was actually seeing him. More like she was staring right through him—probably still soaking up all that glory from winning the art contest. I waved my hand past her eyes, and she blinked and turned away.

"Guess what!" I told Junior. "Ida won grand prize in the art contest at school."

I don't know why I announced it like that except maybe I was trying to make a good impression on Ned. For Ida and me both. And also—thinking about the races was helping my mood.

Junior woo-hooed and Ned just nodded. For somebody who wanted to drive race cars, he sure seemed like a quiet fellow. Maybe he was shy, like Ida.

By now we were at Junior's driveway—to fetch our six-year-old brother, who stayed with Junior's momma while we were at school. Junior drove right up to their back porch, and Bessie came out the door with Jackie and a big black umbrella. She held it over him while he dashed down the steps and into the car. Ned opened his door and pulled Jackie in on his lap, then slammed the door.

I guess Jackie was a little startled to find himself sitting on Ned's knees. "Bessie said you're the one who drives fast," he told Ned.

"Me? Drive fast? Is that what she told you?"

"Yeah. Her friend was here. She doesn't like when you make all that dust on Finger Bridge Road. You know why? On account of she has to take her clean underpants off the clothesline and wash them all over again."

Ned laughed. "Uh-oh. I see I'm in trouble."

"But now," I said, "he can drive fast on the racetrack. Did you hear that, Jackie? Ned's building a race car. And we're gonna go to the Hickory Speedway and watch him win."

2

ELLIE
May 1952

"Hurry, y'all. They'll start without us." I plowed ahead of my family as we tromped through high grass.

"Wait for me, Ellie!" Jackie caught up and grabbed my hand. The two of us slipped between dusty cars and farmers talking about the weather.

After all our rushing, Jackie and I reached the ticket booth and had to wait on the slowpokes—Junior, Daddy, Ida, and my older sister, Ann Fay. I heard a low roar and knew it was cars in there practicing. I was dying to see what the racetrack looked like. If my family didn't hurry, a fast engine inside of me was about to take off without them.

They finally caught up and I could tell Daddy regretted ever coming. While we bought our tickets he stood back with his hands pressed to his temples—a sure sign of a headache coming on. He got that way sometimes ever since the war. Mostly in noisy places. For a few years he was better, but lately the episodes had started up again.

"I don't know about this," I said. "Why did we think he should come?"

"*We* didn't," said Ann Fay. "Jackie begged him, and just like always, he gave in to that boy."

The words weren't out of her mouth before a car backfired inside the speedway, and Daddy hit the ground so fast you would have thought he was dodging a bullet. He lay there flat on the dirt with his arms shielding his head.

"Daddy!" Ida screamed.

People going past us stopped. "Is he okay? There's an ambulance standing by. I'll get help."

"No!" Ann Fay said. "Thank you, but he's fine. Just spooked. We'll take care of it." She grabbed Daddy's arm. "Daddy, this place is too noisy for you. It'll only get worse once this race starts up. You and me are going home." As the oldest in the family, Ann Fay was used to taking charge. And we were usually glad to let her handle Daddy.

But Junior argued. "Ann Fay, you can't even drive. Let *me* take him."

Daddy was breathing fast and heavy. He got himself into a sitting position and tried to stand up.

"Just rest there a minute," said Ann Fay. "Calm yourself."

But Daddy was too embarrassed to stay on the ground with people skirting around him, staring. He struggled to his feet. "I can walk," he growled. "To Otis's house."

15

"No, you will not. Junior's going after the car and we'll drive you." Ann Fay gripped Daddy's arm to let him know who was boss. I took the other arm and it was quivery. His whole body was shaky.

Ida was jittery too. She stood there with Jackie pulled up against her and both of them trembling almost as much as Daddy was. "He's okay," she was telling Jackie. "He just got spooked, that's all." But I could tell she was trying to convince herself.

Junior brought the car from the parking lot and we put Daddy in the back seat. Ann Fay climbed in beside him. "We'll be back, soon as we get him settled at Otis's house," she said.

Otis Hickey would help him talk it out. He was another war veteran, and for some reason he was the best medicine we'd found yet for one of Daddy's spells. By now, he was almost part of the family.

Daddy kept his head down—probably because he didn't want to know who-all had seen his episode. As they drove away, I turned back to Ida, who was biting her lip, trying not to cry, and Jackie, who was waving at Junior's car turning onto the highway.

"He'll be all right," I said. "We've got our tickets. Let's go on in." Daddy's little spell had taken some of the excitement out of coming to the races, but I wasn't going to let my brother and sister see that. Somebody had to be strong, and with Ann Fay gone, it was up to me.

I hurried them along the dirt ramp into Hickory's brand-new racetrack—a big fenced-in oval filled with smells of popcorn, hotdogs, and cigars. Not to mention car exhaust. "Look at that, why don't you?"

There was so much to see—all those people filling the concrete bleachers with their heads moving from side to side as they followed the cars zooming round the oval.

"Which one's Ned Jarrett?" hollered Jackie.

Ida flapped her hands in front of her face. "Whew! All that dust!" she yelled. "And the noise!"

"Yeah. Isn't it exciting?" I hollered back. "Let's find a seat."

The bleachers were full already so I led them to an empty spot in the grass on the far end of the oval. The noise settled down some because the practice race was over and now the cars started lining up. Most of them were old—about fifteen years old—according to a man in overalls who sat there beside us. "Just a pile of souped-up, beat-up jalopies," he said.

"Where's Ned Jarrett?" asked Jackie.

The man pointed to the cars out there. "Keep your eye on that red-and-white '39 Ford in the infield—No. 99. That's your man."

An announcer came on the loudspeaker. "*Ladies and gentleman, welcome to the grand opening of Hickory Motor Speedway. We are sure proud to bring stock-car racing and NASCAR to Hickory, North Carolina.*

Gwyn Staley, the 1951 short-track champion from North Wilkesboro Speedway, will be racing today. Also Junior Johnson and other fierce competitors, including some amateurs from right here in our neck of the woods."

"Hey," said Jackie. "Why didn't he announce Ned Jarrett? He's the best one."

The man beside us leaned in. "Ned is one of the amateurs," he explained. "This'll be his first race ever. But you watch—next year they'll be announcing his name."

A pretty girl in white shorts cut the ribbon, and just like that the Hickory Speedway was officially open. The man in the press box announced the first heat race, but Ned Jarrett wasn't included. "What?" wailed Jackie. "Where's Ned?"

"He'll get his turn," the man promised. "The heats decide the order for the main race. He pointed to a platform above the first row of bleachers. "Watch the flagman," he told Jackie. "When he drops the green flag, those drivers are gonna take off."

I think everyone at the racetrack held their breath while the cars made a few slow laps around the track. Finally the flagman waved the green flag, and the race was on!

Cars roared around that track so close and so fast I didn't see how they kept from smashing up. Dust and dirt clods went flying, and when the cars passed our end of the track some of it came down on us like a shower of red dust.

Ida grabbed my arm and shouted into my ear. "This is crazy!"

"Yeah," I shouted back. "Crazy!" But in my mind, it was a good kind of crazy. Daddy was probably at Otis's house now—sitting in his junkyard, staring at wrecked cars and telling war stories. The engine inside me revved even higher. I intended to enjoy this race.

"Why are they following so close?" yelled Ida. I could feel her hand trembling on my arm.

"So they can pass, silly."

"Finally!" she said when the first heat was over. "How can you stand it, Ellie? Someone's gonna crash before the day is out."

During the second heat Ned Jarrett drove, zooming around those turns, passing one car and then after a while overtaking the next one. He sure didn't look like an amateur to me. I was on my feet the whole time, screaming for No. 99—"Run, run, as fast as you can! You can't catch me, I'm the gingerbread man!"

Jackie joined in, and soon people around us were chanting it too. In my mind we were pulling him closer and closer to the front of the pack. When the heat was over, he'd earned fourth place in the starting line-up for the main race.

Junior and Ann Fay came back just in time to hear them announce it.

"Woo-hoo!" yelled Junior. He picked up Jackie and put him on his shoulders and then he did a crazy dance while Jackie waved his arms and hollered how Ned Jarrett was the best driver of all.

"Junior Bledsoe, would you sit down?" said Ann Fay. "You're making a fool outta' yourself."

Junior grinned. "Yes, ma'am!" But he danced another little jig. The people around us clapped like he was the one they'd come to watch. One thing I loved about this speedway was how we were all neighbors gasping and cheering together, even if we'd never met before.

Then it was time for the feature race. Whenever Ida didn't have both hands over her ears, she gripped my arm, her nails digging into my wrist. And I declare her eyes were shut more than they were open. All of a sudden No. 15 hit a fence, and just like that we were all on our feet. The car rolled and Ida screamed. I probably did too.

Jackie was so excited I thought *he* would flip. "Whoa!" he hollered. "Did you see that? *Did* you, Junior? Is the driver going to die?"

The flagman waved a yellow flag and the cars started slowing down. "That's Hoover Combs," said the announcer. "Upside down after slamming into the fence."

Ida had her face in her hands. She really should've gone with Daddy—maybe Otis Hickey could have calmed *her* down. "Oh, for Pete's sake," I told her. "Look at him. He just climbed out of the car and he's fine."

We all clapped when we saw that Hoover wasn't hurt. A bunch of men ran onto the track and helped flip his car right side up. Then a wrecker towed it to the pit.

"It appears that Hoover Combs is out of the race," said the announcer.

It was a wild day. The front wheels came off one car, and another one lost its gas tank. But No. 99 ran steady all the way and Ned Jarrett finished in tenth place. He climbed out of the car and his buddy slapped him on the back and Ned just grinned. If you asked me, anyone could see that he'd just discovered what he was born to do.

"That's downright terrific," said Junior, "considering this was his first race ever."

All around us people were picking up empty popcorn bags and Pepsi bottles and leaving. But I just wanted to stick around and watch the dust settle and relive it all in my mind. "That was the most fun I've had in a long time," I said.

"Me too," said Jackie. "Did you see that car flip over? That was the best thing ever!"

"No, Jackie," said Ida. "That was scary." She grabbed my arm then and pulled me around to face her—searching me like I was her mirror. In a way I was—same brown hair and blue eyes, and faces that weren't especially interesting one way or another. "In my opinion that was downright miserable," she said. "My ears hurt and I've got grit in my teeth." Then she laughed. "Your face is dirty." She wiped her finger across my cheek and held it out for me to see. The combination of red dust and sweat turned into mud.

21

"Guess who else is dirty?" I said. I ran my finger down her cheek. "There. Now we match."

I couldn't explain why I loved the race except that it sure made me feel alive. Like every cell in my body was on fire.

But Ida liked things calm and predictable. "Do you think Daddy is okay?" she asked.

I looped my arm through hers. "Yes," I said. "By now, he's probably back to his old self. You know how Otis calms him." But, truth be told, I was convincing myself too. Daddy had been worse lately. I was sure it had something to do with those atom bombs the government was exploding out West. Why else would a car backfiring make him hit the ground like he was right back in the war?

3

ELLIE
June 1952

"*I'm* not the man of the house," said Ann Fay. "Why should *I* go to work every day if *he* doesn't?" She wrapped wax paper around her bologna sandwich and dropped it into a brown paper sack. "Maybe I'll quit. I despise boarding socks anyhow."

Ann Fay dropped another sandwich into the bag—one for Momma. Then she spread mustard on four slices of light bread. "You know what I'm fixing to do? Make Daddy's lunch. And I'll take it in there and show it to him. Maybe that'll get him out of bed."

"I'm going outside to check on the garden," said Ida. She left her cereal half-eaten on the kitchen table and headed for the back door. If there was fixing to be a blow-up between Daddy and Ann Fay, Ida was not sticking around for it.

Momma put her hand on Ann Fay's arm. "Don't start this day with a fight."

"I'm not planning to fight." Ann Fay finished making

the sandwiches while Momma combed her hair in front of the mirror by the back door.

She used a tortoiseshell comb—the kind you wear—to tuck the gray hairs out of sight and to hold them where they wouldn't be so noticeable. I could see her eyeballing Ann Fay in the mirror. "Your daddy had nightmares again last night," she said. "And he has a headache this morning."

"I'll take him something to fix that," said Ann Fay. "Ellie, get two aspirin out of the medicine cabinet."

I could have argued with her, but I didn't. Sometimes Ann Fay could motivate Daddy when Momma couldn't. By the time I fetched the aspirin, she was putting two sandwiches and a slice of rhubarb pie into Daddy's lunch pail.

"Wish me luck," she said when I gave her the aspirin. "And bring him a glass of water." She opened the door to Momma and Daddy's room—just a crack. "Daddy?" All I heard was a grunt. "Daddy, I'm coming in." Ann Fay pushed the door open and went inside.

I filled a glass with water and waited just inside the doorway. Daddy was in the bed with a sheet pulled over him. Ann Fay gave his shoulder a little shake. "I packed your lunch, Daddy. It's time to get up."

"I got a headache."

"Here's two aspirin and Ellie brought you some water." She jerked her head a little to let me know I should come in.

24

"Go away," said Daddy.

"Not till you take this aspirin and get out of bed. It's about time to leave for work. The machines have been breaking down a lot lately and you're Mr. Rhinehart's best fixer. Do you want him to fire you?"

According to Momma, after six years of Daddy being on again and off again, Mr. Rhinehart's patience with him was wearing thin. If Daddy lost his job, what new boss would ever be as long-suffering as Mr. Rhinehart had been? After all, he went to our church, and his daughter, Peggy Sue, was Ann Fay's best friend.

Daddy opened one eye but didn't lift his head. Ann Fay set the lunch pail on the bed right beside his pillow.

"Aspirin don't work."

"It did for me when I had a headache last week. And anyhow, plenty of people go to work with aches and pains. It's what you gotta do." Ann Fay knew all about overcoming. After all, she'd had polio and learned to walk again. And now she even held down a full-time job.

But Daddy argued. "You don't know what a headache is. Not if you think two little white pills are going to fix it."

Ann Fay shook his shoulder again and held out the aspirin. "Take these. Ellie's got the water. Maybe she should throw it on you. That'll wake you up!"

I don't know what possessed Ann Fay to threaten such a thing, because I would never do it. But Daddy sat up real fast. And he took the glass. He stared into it

25

for a long time. Then he reached for those two aspirin tablets in her hand. But he didn't pop them in his mouth. Instead, he dropped them one at a time into the glass of water. He swirled the cup around and watched them dissolve. And then he gave that glass a little fling and dashed the water right into Ann Fay's face.

She jumped back and almost lost her balance. I grabbed her arm to steady her.

Boy! I could sure feel how shocked my sister was. And hurt too. She bit her lip and wiped at her wet face with the back of her hand. She slung her hand toward Daddy so that the water splashed on him. Then she threw back her shoulders, turned, and walked to the door. I could see she was trying real hard not to show her limp from having polio. She stopped and looked back at Daddy.

"Momma and I are going to work," she said. And her voice was thick with anger. "Because some of us have figured out we can do hard things. You used to preach that to me, Daddy. But if *you'd* rather stay in bed all day, go right ahead. Your lunch is sitting there by your pillow. Eating it won't take any effort at all."

Then she turned and walked out the bedroom door.

Daddy watched her go, and when she was gone his eyes moved over to me. He didn't say a thing, but it seemed like he wanted to. Like he'd explain—if he only knew how. But I guess he didn't have the words, because he opened his fingers and let that glass fall to the floor. It landed with a clang and rolled across the boards. He ran his fingers through his hair.

Anyone could see Daddy didn't like how he was behaving. I went to give him a hug, but he stopped me. "Go on, Ellie," he said. "Leave me alone." Then he flopped onto his side and pulled the pillow over his head.

He looked like a scared little boy. I wanted to at least pat his shoulder and tell him there was nothing to be scared of and he should just get dressed and go on to work.

But something was bothering him. Maybe it was that letter on the nightstand—from those people in Connecticut. Daddy served in the war with their son, and for some reason he'd started writing to them. They wanted him to bring his family for a visit. And I really wanted to go.

But it worried me when he got these headaches. Maybe these letters were bringing them on. What if he couldn't face those people after all?

I picked up the glass, went out, and closed the door.

Back in the kitchen Momma hugged Jackie and pecked his forehead with a little goodbye kiss. She blew one to me too. Momma was trying to be cheerful for our sakes, but her smile reminded me of Jackie posing for Ann Fay's camera—saying "cheese" for her even if the sun was in his eyes and he just wanted to go off and play. And Ann Fay's limp seemed more noticeable than usual. Like she was just plain tired. But I knew her feelings were hurt, too. "I'm sorry, Ann Fay," I said. And I gave her a hug. "You didn't deserve that."

She hung on to me for a minute and I felt how Ann Fay might not be as strong as she let on. "None of us deserves this," she said.

Jackie followed them out to the porch when they left. I looked around the kitchen and thought how shabby it was and how stupid I was to dream of getting away from here.

Sometimes I just wanted my life to be like other people's. I wanted a father who didn't get frazzled over a bad dream or loud noises. And a mother who wasn't always aching over her husband. I didn't actually want another family; I just needed to not be embarrassed by the one I had.

Ida and I walked Jackie up to the Bledsoes'. After we dropped him off, we headed for the bus stop. Ida stared into the dirt road and didn't say much of anything. It was the last day of school and we should've both been happy, but knowing Daddy was at home in bed took some of the sparkle out for both of us.

4

IDA
June 1952

This was our last day ever at Mountain View School. I stared at the red velvet curtain on the stage and thought how I never got to pull it open and shut. It was the only job I ever wanted in any play we ever did. But thanks to being a twin, I almost always had to be out front, doing something cute with Ellie and feeling like a country bumpkin in the shadow of a movie star.

And now the principal was calling my name. "Ida Kay Honeycutt."

I did not want to go stand in front of the whole school. "He called your name," said Vivian.

"Go!" said Ellie. She practically pushed me out of my seat. Too bad *she* hadn't won the grand prize in the art contest. She'd be prancing to the front and waving to everybody at the same time.

I took my place beside the other contest winners, and Mr. Lockhart presented me with my prize money. "Better keep it away from that sister of yours," he joked.

Everybody laughed and I glanced at Ellie. She rolled her eyes and gave her head a toss.

"Ida," said Mr. Lockhart, "tell us what inspired your wonderful drawing."

Wait. Nobody told me I'd have to speak. I hadn't prepared a single word. I felt the heat rising around my ears and was sure everyone could see that I was blushing.

"Um," I said. "I draw all the time and I wanted to find something different, so I looked under the bed and found my sister's crutches. And the leg brace she used to wear. I'd never drawn them before, so I gave it a try."

The audience laughed. *What's so funny about that?*

I was done speaking. But evidently Mr. Lockhart thought I needed to say more. "The judges felt there was a powerful message in your drawing," he said. "Tell us about it. Why did your sister need crutches?"

Of course there was a story in that drawing. I'd learned *that* from Norman Rockwell, who painted a story for every cover of the *Saturday Evening Post.* But didn't Mr. Lockhart realize this was me, Ida, the quiet twin? "Um, Ann Fay had polio," I said.

"And?" He stood there like he thought I was going to teach a lesson about how polio could paralyze you. But everyone knew that already. What more was there to say?

But Ellie had plenty to say. She was practically jumping out of her seat in the front row. Mr. Lockhart laughed and called her to the stage. I didn't know whether to cry from humiliation or because my twin sister had to rescue me from my own stupidity, but I felt tears stinging my eyelids. I bit my lip and waited while Ellie squeezed in between Mr. Lockhart and me.

"Some of you are too young to remember the big polio epidemic in 1944," Ellie said, looping her arm through mine. "We were only six years old that summer, and our brother got polio." *Oh, good grief, Ellie. Please don't tell them about Bobby dying or I will cry right here and now.* I jabbed her in the ribs.

Ellie paused, and I reckon she decided not to mention it because she started talking about Ann Fay getting polio. While she talked, I stared at the pinewood floor and traced a knot with the toe of my shoe. "Our sister came home from the emergency hospital on crutches and she had to wear a leg brace," Ellie went on. "But coming to school on crutches wasn't easy, so she went to Warm Springs, Georgia—to President Franklin Roosevelt's place for polios."

Ellie was getting carried away, dropping Roosevelt's name like that. I let out a big breath of air, loud enough for her to hear. But she didn't take the hint; she just kept right on going. "The president inspired Ann Fay," she said. "Even after he died. She learned to walk again and she took that brace off and threw it and the crutches under the bed. And they've been there ever since, collecting dust. I guess you noticed: Ida even put the dust in the picture."

31

The whole school laughed. I noticed Ellie didn't mention the broken bed slat or the dangling coil of the bedsprings. That would be too embarrassing. Mr. Lockhart waited for the laughter to die down, and then he took a deep breath like he was fixing to say something, but Ellie beat him to it.

"The moral of the story," she said, "is something Ann Fay learned at the polio hospital. *It mostly hurts at first. But after a while it starts to feel better.* Isn't that right, Ida?"

I looked up and tried to smile.

"Thank you, Ellie," said Mr. Lockhart. He sent us back to our seats, and when we were settled he said, "I think the moral of the story is, if you need someone to draw a picture, call on Ida, but if you want someone to make a speech, Ellie will be happy to oblige."

Of course the audience laughed again. People always found it amusing to compare us. Like they were trying to convince themselves we weren't the exact same person. We knew they didn't mean any harm by it, but no matter what they came up with, both of us always felt like the other one was the better twin. Or prettier. Or smarter.

I was glad when all the eighth-grade certificates were handed out and Mr. Lockhart moved on to the next topic. "This August," he said, "you will be the first freshman class to attend our brand-new consolidated high school. When you get there, be like Ann Fay Honeycutt. Don't let anything hold you back. The drive to succeed comes from inside you. No one else can give it to you. It's in there somewhere, so dig for it."

I had a feeling he was still comparing me to Ellie—telling everyone she would succeed because she had the drive. And I didn't.

But the minute the school bus dropped us off, I felt lighter. Now I had the whole summer not to think about school or looking stupid beside my own twin. I could work on my art and fill my three-ring notebook with sketches. The only cloud in the sky would be if Daddy got worse. It was hard not to worry about that.

Miss Dinah Hinkle, our neighbor, met us at the end of her driveway. "Hello, girls. Do you have time to come inside? My sister is home from the hospital, and we have a proposal for you."

Ellie and I swapped glances. What was this about?

We followed Miss Dinah. Her sister, Miss Pauline, was sitting in bed, wearing a white satin bed jacket, every hair in place. "Hello, Ida and Ellie," she said. "I'm glad Dinah caught you." Before we could ask about her broken hip, she told us. "I'm doing much better. But of course Dr. Johnson has given me strict orders to get rest, rest, and more rest."

Dinah interrupted. "Might you girls want to earn a little money? With Pauline laid up like this, I could use some help around here."

"You could start saving for the future," said Miss

Pauline. "You do plan to attend college?"

"Yes, ma'am," said Ellie. It was no secret she wanted to get out and see the world. And she always made straight A's. Had to be better than me, and I made B's in arithmetic.

"Would you girls like the job?" asked Miss Dinah.

"Yes, we would," said Ellie.

"Wait a minute," I said. "We haven't even talked to Momma and Daddy."

"Oh, don't be silly, Ida. Of course they'll want us to help. It wouldn't be neighborly not to." Ellie might as well have come right out and called me a bad neighbor. She looked at Miss Pauline and then Miss Dinah. "I'll do it even if Ida doesn't want to."

"Uh . . ." What was I supposed to say to that? *I don't want to?* I looked around Miss Pauline's room. The bureau had a glass tray with bottles of lotion and a jar of Fresh underarm deodorant. Also a hairbrush and a hand-held mirror, but not a hint of dust. No socks on the floor or shoes under the bed.

"We have our maid coming in to clean, but we'll need you to tidy up," explained Miss Pauline.

"Yes," said Miss Dinah. "And to keep Pauline company while I'm in the garden or taking my afternoon nap. We have Scrabble now. It's a word game, and Pauline is extremely fond of it. Perhaps you could play with her."

If you asked me, what they really wanted was companionship. And honestly, playing games with a retired schoolteacher, even one who'd been my neighbor for as long as I could remember, was not how I hoped to spend my summer vacation. I wasn't good with people—especially not sick people. If Ellie wanted to sign up for the job, I might just let her have it.

"We'll be gone the week of July Fourth," said Ellie. "On a family trip to New England. I won't miss that for anything. Do you still want us to work for you?"

"Oh, certainly," said Miss Pauline. "We can manage for one week. New England? My word! That's a big trip."

"Yes," said Ellie. "We never go anywhere, except maybe for a drive in the mountains or to see our grand-parents in Georgia. But Daddy wrote a letter to some people in Connecticut. He fought with their son in the war. And they want us to visit. We might even stop in Philadelphia to see the Liberty Bell."

That was Ellie's wishful thinking. She was jabbering again, giving them details they didn't need. Sometimes she was worse than Jackie when it came to talking.

I waited until we were out of their driveway before I started fussing. "You've got some nerve," I said. "Making summer plans without asking me."

"Hey," said Ellie, "*I* want the job. Look how easy it will be. Wiping down imaginary dust and playing Scrabble. Also, they have a television, for Pete's sake."

"School's out," I said. "In case you haven't noticed. And I don't want to leave home every day if I don't need

35

to. So you can just take that job."

It wasn't that I didn't want to earn money. And I liked watching television as much as Ellie did. Practically the only time we ever saw television was when we went to Vivian's house. But I didn't like Ellie speaking for me. And I wasn't going to take that job just because she said so.

5

IDA
June 1952

The day was sunny, with a breeze. Purple sweet peas by the driveway smelled like sugar. And Bakers Mountain, just ahead, was a mixture of spring green and true blue. I sat on Momma's rocker on the front porch and soaked up the freedom of summertime.

Sitting here on this perfect summer day, it was hard to believe we had soldiers fighting off communism over in Korea. Back when Daddy went to war, you couldn't forget such a thing with all the posters in public buildings, telling us to turn scrap metal and rubber and every extra little thing in to the government so it could be used for the war effort.

Then it seemed like every family had a soldier or two fighting Hitler. With the conflict in Korea, it was different—not as many men being called up, and no rationing of sugar and other products. After almost four years of World War II, people were just tired of giving their all—especially their men and boys. We were ready to get on with our lives.

The news people didn't let us forget about war, though. They kept fretting over the bomb, and about Russia backing North Korea, and North Korea trying to turn South Korea into a communist country like them.

If I could get on with my summer vacation I'd rearrange the bedroom without worrying about Daddy sleeping off a headache in the next room. But I wasn't about to wake him up by shoving furniture around.

Jackie was helping Mr. Shoes sniff out a mole that had dug a tunnel in the front yard. Not because our dog needed help. He didn't, but he sure didn't mind if Jackie cheered for him and made a big deal when he found it. When he did, the dirt would be flying and I would not stick around to watch him shake the life out of that critter.

I flipped through my sketchbook. I loved the one of Ann Fay cuddling with Mr. Shoes, their faces pressed together. Scottie dogs don't sit still for portraits. But somehow I'd captured his cocked head, shiny eyes, and wet nose.

Ann Fay was easier. I was good with portraits. After I learned to get the proportions right, drawing faces just fell into place. Sketch the head shape. Put the eyes halfway down and the tip of the nose midway between the eyes and the chin. No hard lines—just shading.

Tucked in the notebook on a folded sheet of paper was a drawing from my childhood. Ellie and I had blond hair back then. I almost forgot that because it was darker now. The drawing was a family portrait—not much better than stick figures. Momma was holding baby Jackie on one arm. She held my hand and I was holding Ellie's. Daddy had her other hand, and on the far side of him was Ann Fay.

Mr. Shoes was in the picture, too, and for some reason I'd included our old dog, Pete, who was dead before Mr. Shoes came along. He was sitting under the mimosa tree where we'd buried our brother Bobby. Even that picture told a story about how polio changed our family.

By now Mr. Shoes had caught the mole, and nothing or nobody on the face of the earth was going to interfere with that, so I left the porch before I had to listen to the ruckus. Ellie was sitting in the living room reading the *Hickory Daily Record*.

"General Eisenhower is back in the United States," she said. "Getting ready to run for president."

"Yeah, I heard it on the radio this morning. Why do you think Daddy went back to bed?"

She shrugged. "Why does he ever go back to bed? Something upsets him. You'd think he'd want Eisenhower to be president. He was so successful in the war."

"Daddy doesn't like being reminded of war," I said.

"Well, if anybody can get our troops out of Korea, you'd think it would be an army general."

I shrugged. I didn't claim to understand my daddy or why war had changed him so much. It seemed like the upset spells came and went. When he started writing to the family in Connecticut he seemed almost relieved. But then he started dreaming again, calling out in his sleep, and being jumpy about loud noises.

I went into the bedroom and started picking up clutter. Ellie's portrait of Eisenhower was half under the bed, partly crumpled by her school notebook, which she had thrown on top of it. I smoothed down the edges and put it on the bureau. I needed something to weight it down, make it flat again.

There was that wooden carving of me and Ellie that Daddy had made back when we were five. Two little girls in sailor dresses and matching hats. We looked exactly alike and we were holding hands. I blew at some dust that had settled into the crevices. Funny how something as cute as that could sit there for years until we didn't even notice it anymore.

Ellie came into the bedroom and flopped backwards on the bed. "I miss school," she said.

"Ellie, it's only been one day."

"One day is long enough to get bored. July Fourth is almost a month away. I think I'll just die waiting! We need a project. Didn't you want to rearrange the room? Let's do it."

"Not now, Ellie. Daddy's sleeping."

"Good. That means he won't hear us."

"No, it means if he *does* hear us we'll regret it."

"Come on. We'll be quiet. We can do it." Ellie jumped off the bed and started shoving.

"No," I said. "I want our bed on that wall next to the living room."

"Then where would Ann Fay's bed go? There's not room for two beds over there."

"They don't have to be side by side. It could be more interesting this way. More artistic."

Ellie rolled her eyes. "Don't be silly, Ida. It's a bedroom. Not a painting."

"Look, Ellie, if we're on this side of the room, maybe we won't hear Daddy having his nightmares."

Ellie shrugged. "Well, why didn't you say so?" She pushed the iron bedstead, and it made scraping noises on the linoleum.

Yikes! She was going to wake him. "Wait, Ellie. If we put rugs under the legs, they'll move easier and it won't be noisy."

But it was too late. Daddy started pounding on the bedroom wall.

And I declare, it was like he was banging on my heart from the way it got me in the chest. I sat on the rug between the beds and waited. Would he go back to sleep? Or come into our room, threatening to take the noise right out of us?

"Stay here," said Ellie. "I'll check on him."

She could take the yelling for me. After all, she was the one who brought it on. Ellie wasn't scared of Daddy the way I was. She was more like Ann Fay. Bold. Always acting like there was no mountain so tall she couldn't climb it. No race so fast she couldn't win it. And no daddy so mean she couldn't charm him.

But me? *I* was the one he'd slammed up against the wall—back when I was seven and foolish enough to jump out and yell, "Boo!" I'd done it a million times, and nothing bad had happened. But that was before the war. After the war, he wasn't the same daddy we said goodbye to at the train station. He was jittery and sometimes that made him mean, even though I knew there wasn't meanness in his heart.

Momma came to my rescue that day. I could still hear her voice soft as butter in August. But also firm like it just came out of the Frigidaire. "Leroy, it's your little girl. Let her go."

Daddy's hands were shaking, and I was half afraid he would drop me. But Momma slipped her arm around my waist and helped him lower me to the floor. When Daddy went half-running out the door, she pulled me up against her belly that was big with baby Jackie inside. "He didn't mean it for you, honey," she said. "He didn't mean it for you."

She ran her fingers through my hair, soothing me. Letting me know she was going to be there, always standing between me and danger.

And now I heard footsteps coming through the kitchen and then the living room. I just knew Daddy was coming to bless me out and Momma wasn't there to stop him.

But it was just Ellie. "I listened outside his door," she said. "Evidently he settled back down, so you can come out of hiding now. Let's use the rugs like you said. That'll make it quiet. We'll get this furniture moved in no time!"

"No!" I almost hollered it, and then I clapped my hand over my mouth. "You're plumb crazy, Ellie, if you think I'm going to move a stick of furniture while he's trying to sleep in there. Don't you dare get him riled up and then run off to the Hinkle sisters' and leave me here with him."

I grabbed my sketchpad and pencil box and headed outside.

6

IDA
June 1952

Later, while I was sitting on the back steps, sketching Jackie's feet with his toes buried in the sandbox, Otis Hickey came traipsing around the house. "Howdy, miss," he said. "Where's your better half?"

If anyone besides Otis called Ellie my better half I might be annoyed, but Otis wasn't the kind of person to irritate me. And besides, he'd asked Ellie the same question plenty of times. And boy, did she hate it!

"Supposedly she's cleaning for the Hinkle sisters," I said, "but I doubt it, since their house is spotless already. She's probably playing games with Miss Pauline. I suppose you walked over here?"

"That I did."

With all the old cars Otis had in the junkyard behind his house, I was sure Junior and that Ned Jarrett fellow could build a working vehicle for him. But Otis would just as soon walk as ride. So he sold car parts to buy his bread and bacon and relied on his own two feet for getting around.

"Did Momma send you?"

"Stopped by on her way to work," said Otis. He went over to the well and opened the lid. "Said Leroy's been laying around for the better part of a week." He cranked the wooden bucket until it hit water, then reeled it back, reached for the dipper, and took a long, slurping drink. Water dripped off his chin.

"Yeah. Momma's worried. All of us are. Think you can help him?" I started sketching Otis. Thin face. Scraggly hair. Eyes that were slightly wild looking because his glass eye didn't move when the other one did. Wet chin.

"I don't know about helping." He swiped at his chin with the back of his hand. "But your daddy talks to me. I tell you right now, I've heard some stories . . ." Otis stared off into the woods behind our house.

"Like what?"

"Huh?" I could tell Otis had forgotten I was even there.

"Stories. What stories have you heard?"

"Oh—stories." He shook his head. "You don't want to hear 'em. They'd just give you nightmares."

Sometimes I had nightmares already and I sure didn't want any more. "Hasn't he told you all his stories by now?" I asked. "Shouldn't he be over whatever he saw in the war?"

Otis lowered himself onto the edge of the porch and sat with his legs dangling off the side. He pointed to Jackie, who was packing down an oval speedway in the sandbox. "If that scab on Jackie's knee comes off too soon," he said, "there'll be some bleeding."

Otis had a way of saying things that didn't make sense at first, but I figured he was getting around to something, so I just waited.

"Know what I mean?"

I shook my head. "No."

"Your daddy's got war scabs. Sometimes they get scraped off and go to bleeding. But that's part of the healing."

"It is? Are you sure?"

Otis shook his head. "No. I'm not."

I almost laughed except it wasn't actually funny. "I sure do wish he wouldn't bleed all over *us*," I said.

"Sometimes sores have pus in them," said Otis. "And it's got to come out or things just get worse."

Jackie looked up. "Daddy's not bleeding. And he don't have scabs."

I should have known better than to talk about such things in front of Jackie. He was too young to know about all the bad in the world. "Oh, Jackie," I said. "Don't pay us any mind. Otis is just talking in riddles. That's all."

Otis slid off the edge of the porch. "Come on, boy. Let's hoe some weeds. Ida, go tell your daddy I'm here."

"Uh-uh," I said. "I'm not waking him up."

But Otis was halfway to the garden shed and two minutes later he was down in the tomato patch. And Jackie with him.

I went back to shading Otis's face, which was a lot easier than waking Daddy when he was having one of his days.

Behind me the screen door creaked and it startled me so bad I poked my pencil through the portrait—right by Otis' ear. Daddy was awake. He stopped behind me and I could tell he was lighting up a cigarette.

A beetle marched across the step until it came to my foot. It started to go around but I wiggled my toes. It stopped and I imagined his little heart racing. Every muscle in his body tensing.

I looked up finally and Daddy was staring at my portrait. He ran his thumb along the edge of his chin. "Otis has a scar right there," he said. Then he went past me down the steps. He didn't even notice he'd crushed a bug. If he'd seen that beetle, he'd have gone around it. Daddy hated killing of any kind—ever since the war and especially since the atom bombs had dropped on Japan.

He went to the shed and came out with a hoe. It wasn't long until I heard him chopping at weeds so fierce you'd think they were Russian spies invading our backyard.

Daddy was right, of course. Otis did have a scar on his chin. Maybe it was a war wound.

I needed to study Otis some more so I moseyed out toward the garden and settled under the mimosa tree, right beside where our brother Bobby was buried.

But I didn't work on the portrait after all. I just stared at the two of them in the bean patch. Otis had his head to one side, like he was listening with his good ear. Daddy gripped the top of the hoe handle with both hands. When he talked, it jerked around some.

Jackie was sitting in the dirt with Mr. Shoes and the two of them were listening to every word. I doubt Otis or Daddy, either one, remembered my little brother was there.

"Psssst! Jackie, come here."

But Jackie started rolling in the yard with Mr. Shoes. He giggled so much I couldn't catch everything Daddy was saying, but I did hear something about Jackie taking his place. "It should've been me," he said. He slammed the blade of that hoe into the ground. And he turned away from Otis and went back to chopping weeds.

It should have been me? What should have been him? And why was he talking about Jackie taking his place?

7

IDA
June 1952

Daddy stayed outside the rest of the day. Him and Otis working in the garden. Smoking on the back porch. Sometimes talking, sometimes not. I made Jackie stay away from them so Daddy could talk it out and Jackie didn't have to listen to stories that could give him nightmares.

He helped me shove the furniture in the bedroom. "Why're you moving your bed, Ida?"

"Because it makes me happy." For me, arranging furniture was like creating art. It gave me a feeling of control over my own life. I organized the room and dusted the furniture and rearranged the toiletries, the peach-shaped bank that Ann Fay gave us when she came back from Warm Springs, Georgia, and that little wooden carving of me and Ellie. And all of that did make me happy.

Before I knew it Momma and Ann Fay were home from working at the hosiery mill. Momma plopped onto the couch, kicked off her shoes and closed her eyes. "I feel like I've been put through the wringer," she said.

"You look beat," I told her. I pushed the loose hairs away from her face and adjusted her tortoiseshell combs so they'd stay in place. "Thanks for sending Otis over. Last I looked he was still out on the back porch with Daddy."

Momma sighed. "At least Leroy didn't spend the day in bed. I declare some days it's like he's paralyzed."

My poor momma. I wished she could stay home and not have to go to work. But Daddy was unreliable. I pulled her hand onto my lap and laced her fingers through mine. And I leaned my head on her shoulder. From where we sat on the couch we could see right into the bedroom. Ann Fay was in there, shaking her head and grumbling about me moving her bed so that it didn't line up with mine and Ellie's. "It looks wacky," she said. "Why are you and Ellie moving across the room from me?"

"I like it. Don't you?"

"You two'll be over there whispering secrets and I'll miss out. I'll have to holler to be heard. Where is Ellie, anyway?"

"At the Hinkle sisters'. She should be home before long. Come on, Ann Fay. Let's go make supper. Momma, just close your eyes and catch a few winks. We'll heat up some leftovers."

Ellie came home just in time to eat. I heard her out there on the back porch, coaxing Daddy to join us. Sometimes Otis would stay and eat with us but today he headed for home. Daddy came in and kissed Momma and used his handkerchief to dab at the sweat on her brow. She leaned into him and let him hold her. It seemed like Otis had helped to get some of the pus out of Daddy's war wounds. At least for the time being.

I could see on Ellie's face that she'd had herself a fine day. "What's up?" asked Ann Fay. "You're beaming like a flashlight."

Ellie shrugged. "Hurry and say grace, Jackie. I've got some good news."

So Jackie hurried. "*God is great and God is good and we thank Him for our food. Amen.*"

"Next time, slow it down," said Daddy. "You're not at the racetrack."

Ellie dropped a slip of paper onto Ann Fay's plate. "Read that," she said.

Ann Fay put a spoonful of peas on Jackie's plate and then she unfolded the paper. "Who is Norma Sain and why do I have her number?"

Ellie laughed. "Mrs. Sain is a friend of Miss Pauline's. A doctor's wife. And her husband is looking to hire a girl who can type and do filing. He has polio clinics once a week so I told her about you. She thinks you might be perfect for the job. You *would* be, Ann Fay. Of course you would."

"Me? Working in a doctor's office?" asked Ann Fay. She sounded a little breathless.

"Yes, you," said Ellie. "You know you hate boarding socks. And Miss Pauline says you deserve better. She gave you a good recommendation, Ann Fay."

Was Ellie serious? Had she actually gone to the Hinkle sisters' for one afternoon and come home with a new job for Ann Fay? In a doctor's office even?

"I just can't believe it." Ann Fay looked down at the plaid dress she'd worn to the mill. It was faded and even had a small hole in the pocket. "I couldn't wear this to work for a doctor."

"I bet you'll make more money," I said. "*Then* you can afford a new dress."

"We'll sew you some clothes," said Ellie.

We wanted this job for Ann Fay—and I was sure she wanted it too. Instead of sliding socks over a hot board to give them shape, she'd be working with people. Some of them had had polio, like her. "Take the job," I told her.

Ann Fay looked at Momma. "I hate to leave you alone at the mill."

"Alone? I have friends working right beside me," said Momma. "And your Daddy will be there—won't you, Leroy?"

Daddy didn't exactly agree with Momma but he didn't argue her point. He nodded toward the telephone on the little table by the Hoosier cupboard. "Call the lady up."

A smile, big as a bread box, covered Ann Fay's face. "Okay then, I'll call Mrs. Sain tomorrow." But that night, by the time we crawled in our beds, she'd changed her tune. "What was I thinking?" she asked. "You said Dr. Sain's office is in Newton. I don't have a way to get there."

We'd been so busy dreaming of a fine and fancy job that we hadn't thought about transportation.

"Peggy Sue could take you," said Ellie. Peggy Sue was Ann Fay's best friend. She was married and had her own beauty shop in a little building behind her house.

"No, she couldn't," said Ann Fay. "Not every day. She has appointments to keep."

"Hmm," I said. "Well, somebody's got to be going your direction. People catch rides to work all the time." And then I knew exactly how she could get to the doctor's office. "Junior," I said. "He'll take you."

It was quiet for a minute while Ann Fay took that in. "She won't go for that," whispered Ellie.

"I hear you over there," said Ann Fay. "You're right, Ellie. I won't go for that because Junior don't go all the way to Newton."

"So what you're telling me is, you don't want that job after all?" I asked.

"Go to sleep," said Ann Fay. I heard her roll over and I knew what that meant. The discussion was finished. But not in my mind it wasn't. I had an idea and I wanted in the worst way to share it with Ellie but I couldn't because Ann Fay would hear. So I kept it to myself and tried to sleep.

Early the next morning I slid out of bed real quiet, pulled on my clothes, and left the house without making a sound. Mr. Shoes, who spent nights in a rocker on the porch, ran after me. "Come on," I said. "We've got an important job to do."

Even in the dark, it didn't take five minutes to get to Junior and Bessie's. There was a light on in the Bledsoes' kitchen, but I heard singing coming from the barn. When I got closer I could hear it was a song that Hank Williams used to sing on the radio, asking if he'd told her lately that he loved her and wondering if he could tell her again, somehow.

Yeah. You can give her a ride to work. That'll tell her.

Junior didn't sound too good, but I figured the cow didn't mind. I slipped through the barn door and hollered. "Woo-hoo! Junior, it's Ida."

The singing stopped. I peered over the stall. Junior jumped up from the sweet potato crate he used for a milking stool. He squinted—trying to see me in the half darkness. "Ida? What's wrong?"

"Nothing's wrong, Junior. Sorry. Didn't mean to scare you."

He ran his fingers through his hair and even in the dimness of the barn I could see how flustered he was. "Well, if nothing's wrong, what're you doing here at six o'clock in the morning?"

"I need a favor, Junior."

"I guess it don't hurt to ask." Junior was terrible at saying no to people.

"Ann Fay needs a ride. To her new job at Dr. Sain's."

"Ann Fay's working for a doctor?"

"She will be. Isn't that something? She's getting out of that hosiery mill. You know how she hates it,

Junior. But she needs a ride to Newton. That's where you come in."

"I don't go to Newton."

"Oh, come on, Junior. You work at Homer Jarrett's sawmill."

"I'm telling you. It's out of my way, Ida."

"Yeah, but for Ann Fay, you'd *go* out of your way." I turned then and left him there. I figured he could think about it while he milked that cow. He'd come around. I knew one thing about Junior Bledsoe. He'd do anything for Ann Fay Honeycutt.

8

ELLIE
June 1952

"*You* were up early," I told Ida. "Where'd you disappear to?"

Ida shrugged. "I might've gone up to Junior's house. To see about a ride for Ann Fay."

I declare, that twin of mine was not afraid to speak up when it was absolutely necessary. "Yippee! Bully for you, Ida. You know Junior will fall for it."

"Of course he will. And if she doesn't get that job, it won't be because we didn't try. I'm so proud of you Ellie, for telling that doctor's wife about her."

"Oh, so once in a while, it's okay for me to speak for other people?"

Ida grinned and stuck her tongue out at me. "Once in a while," she said.

I knew Ann Fay wouldn't be the only person applying for that job. But I decided to make her a new dress anyway. Even if she didn't get hired at the doctor's office she'd want it when we went to Connecticut. So we pulled out the cloth we'd just bought to make dresses for the trip.

Ida spread the fabrics across the kitchen table. "This blue one with white polka dots," she said. "It'll bring out the color in her eyes."

Ida cut the dress in a pattern we'd made for Ann Fay before. She could try it on when she came home from the mill and if I needed to make adjustments, I would. I declare, I loved the sound of a sewing machine working. And I loved steering the fabric just right under the presser foot, controlling the speed of the sewing—fast on the straight seams and then slowing down for the curves.

I sewed while Ida looked after Jackie. She was in and out of the house with that pencil over her ear, pulling it out to use whenever she got a chance to sketch me at the sewing machine. "What're you doing?" I asked.

"Telling a story," she said. "About Ann Fay getting a new job. And you helping her. There. Hold your head just like that."

"I'm busy. How do you expect me to hold still?"

"Arrgh. You're worse than Mr. Shoes," Ida complained. "Don't you want a good portrait of yourself?"

"What I want is to make this dress. And then one for me and you too. What do you think New Haven, Connecticut, is like anyway? Miss Pauline says that's where Yale University is. We need Daddy to take us to the library so we can look it up."

Ida didn't answer and I knew what that meant. She was too caught up in her drawing to even realize I'd said anything. "Never mind," I said. "I might as well be talking to this spool of thread." But Ida didn't even hear me fussing.

By the time I went to the Hinkle sisters' house, I had that dress sewn together.

Miss Pauline was sitting up in a wheelchair at the kitchen table when I got there. She motioned for me to sit. "You do feel up to a game of Scrabble, don't you?"

"Um, yes, of course." So far, I hadn't done much work for the sisters. But I didn't mind playing games with Miss Pauline. She understood about my dreams to go places. And she wanted better for my sisters, too.

"Ann Fay was planning to call Dr. Sain's office from the hosiery mill," I told her. "Do you think she has a good chance at the job? Have you heard anything from your friend?"

Miss Pauline laughed. "I'm sure *if* she gets the job I won't be the first person to hear about it. So you may just have to wait until your sister comes home from work."

"Well, either way, I'm making her a new dress. We'll need it for the trip in a few weeks. And I'm making clothes for me and Ida too. I can't wait to see Yale University. I'm thinking I might want to attend there someday."

Miss Pauline shook her head. "Yale is only open to boys, you know. But you can still go to college. And you really should begin Latin studies during your freshman year of high school."

Latin? I hadn't signed up for Latin. Ida wouldn't want me to because then we wouldn't have all our classes together. But that also meant I wouldn't always be compared to her. I could have a class that was all my own. A hard one that she couldn't show me up in. "Do you think I could do it?" I asked.

"Of course you can," said Miss Pauline. "And I will help you study."

While we played that game of Scrabble, my mind wasn't on words and scoring points. It kept racing around from not going to Yale to studying Latin to Ann Fay and the new job.

That evening when Ann Fay came home from work she was the one beaming like a flashlight. "You got the job, didn't you?" I asked. "I knew you would. I made you a dress, even. Oh, Ann Fay! I'm so happy for you."

"Whoa, Ellie. Who said I got the job?"

"Boarding socks doesn't make you grin like that."

"It's not definite," she said. "But I talked to the doctor himself. He asked me lots of questions. And he wants me to come in on Monday for a trial period."

"I knew it!" I squealed. "Come try this dress on."

But Momma said to wait because Ida had supper on the table. Fried squash and tomato sandwiches.

After the dishes were finished, Ann Fay came out of the bedroom with that dress on, looking pretty as a party—at least if you ignored the unfinished hem. "Like Ida said, that color is just right for you," I told her. "Bet you'll meet some real nice boy at Dr. Sain's office. With you in this dress, it'll be love at first sight."

"Woo-hoo! Anybody home?" That was Junior at the back door.

Junior stepped just inside the kitchen but he held the screen door open with his foot. "Momma sent rice pudding." He set a crock on the countertop. "Ann Fay, could I speak with you?" He backed out onto the porch.

"Come on in, Junior."

"Could we talk outside?"

Ann Fay frowned but she went to the door. Junior waited for her to come out and when she did, I saw him take a sudden step back. It was as though Ann Fay in that blue dress that matched her eyes had given him a little shove. He stood there and stared for a minute and started to speak. But then he turned away and headed for the steps and sat on the top one. Ann Fay stopped and put her hands on her hips, letting him know she wasn't about to follow him. But he wasn't looking at her so I guess she gave up. Instead of sitting beside him on the step she pulled up a low stool. "Can't get my new dress dirty."

Junior nodded. "It's a real pretty dress. And it looks real good on you."

Ida was over by the sink, on her tippy toes, watching out the window. It's a wonder she didn't have her sketchpad, taking it all down—telling a story about Junior and Ann Fay and her getting a ride to that job in the doctor's office. Ida motioned for me to come closer and she didn't have to tell me twice. We stood by the window and watched.

"So you got a new job," said Junior. "Good for you, Ann Fay."

"Land sakes, Junior Bledsoe. Who you been talking to?"

Junior shrugged. "Word gets around."

"Had to be Miss Pauline. She's the only one who'd know."

Junior didn't agree with her but he didn't disagree either. He was nervous. I could see *that* from the way he kept fiddling with his pocketknife. Opening the blade and clicking it shut again. "I suppose you'll be needing a ride to work," he said.

Ida rubbed her hands together. "Good for you, Junior," she whispered.

I heard Ann Fay fussing on the porch. "Now I *know* you've been talking to someone. And it wasn't Miss Pauline." She hopped off that stool and reached for the door handle like she was going to walk right back in the house. I ducked away from the window and pulled Ida with me. Or tried to anyway. But Ann Fay saw us. "Ida Kay Honeycutt," she yelled.

Ida was trying her best not to bust out laughing. "Yes, Ann Fay?"

"You come here right this minute."

I gave Ida a little push. "You asked for it, Sister!" For once, it was her and not me meddling in somebody else's business. But Ida knew when to take a chance and she wasn't afraid of Junior or Ann Fay either one.

She let out a big puff of air. "Wish me luck," she said and she went to the screen door. "What'd'ya need, Ann Fay?"

"I need *you*. Out here."

Ida just stood there at the door, holding back the giggles until Ann Fay jerked her head in that bossy way of hers. Then she went outside.

"Weren't you the one dreaming up ideas about me catching a ride to work with Junior?"

Ida didn't say yes and she didn't say no. "Did you come up with a better idea?"

"A better idea is for you to mind your own business. Nobody asked you to go traipsing up to Junior's asking him to give me rides."

"What if I didn't?"

"Oh, come on, Ida."

"Oh, come on yourself, Ann Fay. Do you need a ride to work or not? If Junior is offering one, maybe you should take it."

Junior stood then. And when he spoke, Ann Fay surely couldn't miss the hurt in his voice. "Actually I *didn't* offer Ann Fay a ride. I just asked her if she needed one. But evidently she doesn't. So I reckon I'll shove off. Good luck with the new job, Ann Fay."

And just like that, Junior headed around the house, leaving our big sister with her mouth hanging open.

"Now look what you did," said Ida. "Applied for a brand-new job and you've got no way to get to it. Did you think he was gonna stand there and beg?"

9

ELLIE
June 1952

On Saturday morning I asked Daddy if he would take us to the library.

"I've got work around here," he said. "And later I'm going to see somebody about a new tiller."

"That's perfect," I told him. "You can drop me and Ida off at the library. We can do our research and maybe check out some good books and you can come back and pick us up."

"What happened to the bookmobile? You can check books out of it."

"Daddy, I want information about New Haven, Connecticut. And Philadelphia. The bookmobile doesn't loan out encyclopedias."

"You won't be needing that information after all," said Daddy. "I changed my mind about going to Connecticut."

"What?" I yelled it. I know I did. And I saw how my shock hit Daddy in the face because he jerked back like it was my hand coming at him.

Momma was beside us in an instant. One hand on Daddy's arm, the other one on mine. Trying to keep both of us calm. Daddy was shaking his head. "I can't do it, Myrtle," he said. "I can't visit Jackie's family. I'm sorry Ellie. We'll go somewhere else on the Fourth of July."

I butted in. "But Daddy, I don't want to go somewhere else. I had my heart set on New Haven. To see Yale University. Daddy, I'm counting on it. And those people want to meet you. Daddy, it will help you. I just know it will."

I didn't know it. Of course I didn't. It's not like I was Sigmund Freud or any kind of doctor. But Ida had told me what Otis said about the pus inside of Daddy's war wounds. That made perfect sense to me. I knew one thing for sure: if I didn't talk my troubles out, I would bust wide open.

Momma squeezed my arm. "Ellie, go outside. Take a walk. Your daddy and I will discuss this."

"Momma, he promised us. You can't let him back out now."

"Ellie! Go outside!"

"Yes, Momma." I looked at Daddy and I could see in his eyes how much he didn't want to disappoint me. But it was too late. He already had.

I turned and walked out the back door and down past the garden to the creek. Mr. Shoes followed me—he loved the water. Thank goodness our creek wasn't deep, because Mr. Shoes couldn't swim worth a hoot. But he splashed around and barked and carried on like he was the happiest dog in the world. And I carried on like the maddest girl on the face of the earth. "I'm sick and tired of this whole stinking mess," I hollered. "Daddy going through bad spells and Momma and Ann Fay or me talking him through them. Ida disappearing so she never has to hear the explosion. It's not right!"

Mr. Shoes stopped playing and cocked his head, listening to me yell at the trees.

"Ida isn't the only one tiptoeing around," I told Mr. Shoes. "Even *you* go hiding under a chair when Daddy's in a foul mood. Every one of us is allowing him to stay stuck in that war. Pushing away whatever thoughts are coming to the front. Maybe it's time for him to stop shoving them down. I thought he was getting somewhere when he started writing to those people. But now look at him. He chickened out. He's just a big fat fraidy cat. That's what he is."

Mr. Shoes climbed out of the creek and shook himself right at my feet. And of course he splashed water all over me. "Oh, thanks, Mr. Shoes. I was really hoping you'd give me a shower. Good grief! Come on. Let's go. And don't be thinking I'm letting Daddy off the hook. I intend to take that trip to New England."

When I got back to the house Momma was scrubbing kitchen cupboards, a sure sign that she was fretting. She had an old toothbrush and was going around all the hinges and latches on the cupboards, cleaning out every little speck of greasy grime.

Ida was sticking close by. Wiping things down and rearranging canisters and Momma's African violets and cookbooks till they looked like a still life she was fixing to paint. Momma and Ida were the same in that way. They worked problems out by cleaning and making things look neat and pretty.

I guess I was more like Daddy, since I tended to explode when I was upset. Momma gave me a look when I came in, and I knew exactly what it meant. The way she narrowed her eyes and tightened her lips, she was telling me to leave Daddy alone about this trip. But his old truck was gone, so I knew he'd disappeared. He probably went to find himself a tiller and didn't even care if I wanted to go to the library at the same time.

"I can't wait until I can drive myself to town," I said.

"Huh?" said Ida.

"Never mind. Where's Ann Fay?"

"She climbed in the truck with Daddy."

"Oh." That figured. Ann Fay probably went along to have a heart-to-heart with Daddy. I hoped she convinced him he absolutely could not back out of this trip.

But later, Ann Fay came walking in the house and Daddy wasn't even with her. She was so flushed and sweaty that I knew she'd come home on her own two feet. "How'd you get here?" I asked. "I thought you went to town."

"Nope." Ann Fay poured herself a cup of cold water from the Frigidaire and collapsed onto a kitchen chair.

"Ida, I hope you're satisfied," she said. "I went crawling back to Junior, and now he's taking me to work on Monday."

"Whoopee! I'm satisfied," said Ida. She grabbed a kitchen towel and draped it over her head like a bridal veil. "You shouldn't be taking Junior for granted, Ann Fay. Some day he might not be here for you at the drop of a hat."

"Oh, stop it," said Ann Fay.

"I'm serious," said Ida. "Didn't Dudley Walker get drafted into the army and now he's fighting in Korea? They're the same age. Junior could get drafted too."

"Dudley enlisted," Ann Fay pointed out. "And besides, Junior's not likely to get drafted on account of his momma being dependent on him."

"See, you're just taking for granted he'll always be here. But anything could happen."

"Leave her alone, Ida," I said. "You got her riding with Junior five days a week. That should make you happy."

"Huh," said Ann Fay. "It won't be every day. This is just until I find someone nearby who works in Newton."

"Unless she falls in love with Junior and decides to marry him," said Ida.

"Would you hush about that?" asked Ann Fay.

Ida was so sure that Ann Fay and Junior should get together. But I wouldn't have minded if Ann Fay fell head over heels for someone brand-new. Someone who could take her away from this little country life we lived. Not far away, of course, but maybe to Newton or Hickory, where she could live in one of those brick houses with sidewalks leading to the street and English ivy growing up the walls.

Now that she had a better job—who knew? Maybe it could happen.

And me? I was dreaming of going off to college and meeting a rich fellow of my own. But who was I kidding? I couldn't even get out of town on a little family trip.

10

IDA
June/July 1952

Daddy said he was taking us to Rock City, Tennessee, during the week of the Fourth. Not for the whole week, of course—he couldn't afford that. But we'd stay in a hotel for the first time, ever.

Back when we were little and went for a Sunday drive in the mountains, we saw a barn with SEE ROCK CITY painted on the side. Ellie didn't even know what Rock City was, but she begged Daddy to take us right then. Of course he couldn't; he had to work the next day.

Now she was furious. "Why would I want to see a pile of rocks?" she yelled. "We've got those around here."

"It's more than a pile of rocks," Daddy said. "Even you will be impressed."

"I will be impressed with Philadelphia and the Liberty Bell and New England and Yale University."

"Stop talking about Yale University," said Daddy. His voice was sharp, and if I were Ellie standing there in front of him, I'd have been stepping back a few feet. But she stood her ground, hands on her hips and head thrown back real defiant-like. Daddy stepped closer. "You hush about that trip." I could see how he was trying to control himself the way he kept his voice low and talked through clenched teeth. "We're going to Rock City."

Ellie threw her hands in the air and turned away from him. "Maybe *you* are," she said. "But I am not!" She turned and left the room. It was a good thing too, because Daddy reached out to grab her hand. But he missed and just stared after her. I could see he didn't know what to do with her.

For some reason she'd been counting on this trip more than the rest of us had. And I couldn't tell if it was because of Daddy and that family of his soldier friend. I didn't think so. Seemed to me it was more about her dreams of going places. Leaving us behind. Even me.

Sometimes I thought Ellie was getting too big for her own britches. She was ashamed of where she lived and the looks of our house and probably our whole family. That's why she wanted that job for Ann Fay—so our sister could move up in the world.

On Monday, Ann Fay rode off with Junior in his Chevy toward Newton, and by the time she came home it appeared that she had herself a permanent job. "I was a hit!" she said. She talked all the way through supper. "Dr. Sain likes having a polio working in his office. He said the children who come to his clinics need a role model—someone who knows what it feels like to have polio and has worked hard to overcome it. He wants me to inspire his patients. *Inspire*. That sure sounds high-minded, doesn't it?"

But of course Ellie loved high-minded things. "You inspire people already, Ann Fay," she said. "If you can do this, then I can go to college. Maybe even Yale." She gave Daddy a long look. He glanced at her and looked away.

I gave Ellie's foot a kick. Of course she couldn't go to Yale. She shouldn't be turning a perfectly good supper into a battlefield. And besides, it wasn't right for her to steal the attention from Ann Fay's accomplishments. "Ann Fay," I said, "did you find another ride to work?"

"Not exactly," she said. "But Mrs. Sain knows someone from Banoak who works at the bank in Newton. She arranged for me to ride with her. But I'll have to meet her at the crossroads."

"Oh, so that means Junior has to take you to the crossroads every day. That's perfect, Ann Fay. Everything is working out."

Ann Fay knew I was referring to her riding with Junior. But she ignored me. "Dr. Sain said I can have off the week of the Fourth to go to Tennessee."

Ellie rolled her eyes. "Maybe I'll work for Dr. Sain in your place that week," she said. "Since I won't be going to Tennessee."

She did go, though. Of course she wouldn't stay home in that house by herself while we went out of state. And for all her snobbishness about Rock City she couldn't help but like it. You could see seven states from Lover's Leap on Lookout Mountain. The view was the most gorgeous thing I'd ever seen.

There was beauty around every corner. And no wonder they called it Rock City. It was a huge rock formation with tunnels and caverns and bridges. It had cute little garden gnomes from Germany tucked into unexpected places. Ann Fay had brought her camera, and I made her take pictures of everything so I could draw it later.

Daddy held Momma's hand the whole way through and led her across the swinging bridge like he didn't have a fear in the world. Jackie loved the bridge and wanted to make it shake, and of course Ellie did too. I hung on to Ann Fay and tried not to look down.

That bridge reminded me too much of my life, the way it was suspended between two solid rock formations with a chasm below. For me the bridge was full of questions. Would the cables hold? Would Jackie and Ellie shake it too much and make it break loose?

By the time we reached the other side I felt shaky myself. Ready to sit on a big rock and feel how solid and dependable it was. I wanted everyone to go away and just let me sit there and take it in. To soak up how old and unmoving the rocks were. How they held you and made you feel safe even when life was constantly changing.

I knew communism was spreading through the world, and the Russians were racing us to build bigger atomic bombs, and if things didn't go just right my daddy could explode at any minute. But here, surrounded by rocks and flowers and quirky little garden gnomes, I could almost pretend the world was a peaceful place.

11

ELLIE
July 1952

"Of course," said Momma. "We'd love to come. I'm sure Bessie is making dessert, so I'll bring macaroni and cheese. And some garden vegetables."

Momma hung up the phone. "We're going to the Hinkle sisters' for supper," she said. "And to watch the Republican Convention. One of you girls, go tell your daddy."

"What if he doesn't want to go?" asked Ida. "Daddy's a Democrat."

"He's an American citizen," said Momma. "And he needs to know what the Republicans are saying."

"I'll tell him," I said. I was pretty sure I could talk Daddy into going. Ever since he robbed me of that trip to New England he'd been trying to please me one way or another. And I think he'd figured out that I wasn't going to keep tiptoeing around him for fear of a fight. Whatever was bothering him, I was ready to get it out in the open.

I filled a cup with cold well water because Daddy would be thirsty. He was down past the garden, fighting back the wisteria. Seemed like every year he got into a tangle with it. Otherwise that vine would be growing in our bedroom windows by now. Sometimes I wondered what he'd do without that stubborn wisteria to take his frustrations out on.

"Hey, Daddy. Want some water?"

Daddy set his pruning shears on the ground and pulled his big blue handkerchief from his pocket. He wiped sweat from his face and under his chin and all around the back of his neck before wadding it up and stuffing it in the pocket at the front of his overalls. He reached for the water.

"Momma made supper plans," I told him. "Looks like we're going to the Hinkle sisters'."

Daddy nodded. "Sounds good." He took a big swallow of that water and then he sat on the ground.

I searched around for some place to sit and decided on a rock about six feet away. "I guess it's kind of like a party. To watch the Republican Convention."

Daddy had the cup of water halfway to his mouth, but he stopped in midair when I said that. "Why would I want to watch the Republicans boo and hiss at each other? Just listening to them on the radio all week was bad enough. The people who want Senator Taft to be nominated actually broke into a fight with Eisenhower supporters."

"I know, Daddy. And we missed all that excitement because we don't have television. I want to *see* what's going on up there in Chicago."

Daddy shook his head and stared into the tangle of wisteria clippings at his feet. "Fighting is not entertainment, Ellie."

"Yeah, Daddy. I know. But now that they've nominated Eisenhower, don't you reckon the Republicans are done fighting?"

He stood and handed me the empty cup. "Thank you for the water, Ellie. And don't pay me any mind. It wouldn't be neighborly to refuse to go. Whether or not the Republicans are squabbling, it'll be a sight to behold, I'm sure."

Later, when it was time for the broadcast I realized that Daddy was right about that Republican Convention being a spectacle. General Eisenhower entered the big room while a band played the United States Army song, "And the Caissons Go Rolling Along." He stood in front of the microphones just sort of bobbing to the music, smiling and looking shy, waving at all those people cheering and holding up their signs.

And right then and there Daddy stood up, reached for a cigarette, and headed for the Hinkle sisters' kitchen. After all, that music was a battle song. But I guess Daddy was a little bit curious because he turned and leaned against the doorjamb.

It wasn't long until Eisenhower started talking about crusades. And how he'd led one—referring, of course, to World War II. The war that turned Daddy skittish. When Eisenhower talked about crusades, Daddy went through the kitchen and out the back door where he could light up that cigarette and get away from all the talk of war.

But honest, if you asked me, the convention was downright thrilling. The music, the clapping and shouting in the crowd. The flags waving. The things Eisenhower said sounded good to me—about sweeping out corruption. Uniting people where they were divided. Building a foundation for prosperity at home and peace throughout the world.

But Daddy didn't see it that way. I heard "peace" and he heard "war." Maybe it wouldn't be so bad if Eisenhower hadn't talked about fighting and battles. But he did. And with people getting weary of the Korean conflict it was hard to tell if General Eisenhower was planning to crank up that war or pull our troops out.

12

ELLIE
July 1952

On Saturday, our best friend Vivian called. "Hey, Ellie, want to go to the speedway? It's the first night race and my cousin Arnie is going. His daddy'll pick us up. Ida can come too if she wants."

"She won't want to," I said.

"Yeah, that's what I figured. But ask her anyhow. I'd hate for her to feel left out."

People always thought they had to treat us the same—to keep things fair.

"I gotta go now," said Vivian, "but we'll come by for you around six o'clock."

I hung up the phone and hollered, "Woo-hoo! I'm going to the races."

"Who with?" asked Ida.

"Vivian. And her cousin. And her uncle. I told her you wouldn't want to go."

"Thanks a lot, Ellie. What if I do want to go?"

"The races are miserable for you. Remember?"

"Yeah, and you know what else is miserable?" she said. "You, Ellie May Honeycutt—speaking for me. How about you let me decide what I want to do? And stop telling the world what I think."

I shrugged. "You can go if you want."

Ida wasn't interested in going to the speedway, but I knew she wouldn't mind getting out of the house with friends. She even put on her pedal pushers and pulled her hair back into a ponytail like she was thinking about changing her mind. Later, when they came to pick me up, she walked with me to the car—to say hey to Vivian. Or maybe she was actually thinking about hopping in and going along. After all, why else would she have tidied up?

Jackie was right there, chasing a hop toad in the yard, and by the time we reached the car he was talking to Vivian's cousin through the car window. And the cousin, I couldn't help but notice, was handsome as a shiny new Chevrolet. Where had Vivian been hiding *him* all this time?

He was also friendly—as friendly as the Watkins man who came around selling shoe polish and mop heads from the back seat of his car. "Howdy, buddy," he said to Jackie. "We're going to the speedway. Ever been there?"

"The speedway!" squealed Jackie. "Hot dog! Can I come too?"

"No, Jackie. You can't," I said. I turned and called for Daddy to come get him.

"I'll take him," said Ida. She reached for Jackie's hand, but he dodged her.

Vivian's cousin said, "It's fine by me if he wants to go."

I declare, when he said that, the light in Jackie's eyes could have lit up that speedway. With him at the night races they wouldn't even need electricity. "Don't get any bright ideas, Jackie," I said. "You're staying home." I climbed in the back seat with Vivian, hoping her uncle would drive off. But he just sat there.

"This is my friend Ellie," said Vivian. "Ellie, that's Uncle Bud driving. And you've heard me talk about Arnie. He's heard all about you, too."

Her uncle Bud gave me a nod and didn't say a word. But Arnie said he was pleased to meet me, and when he did, he flashed a smile that made my heart stop dead still, then rev up and take off real fast.

Jackie was trying to open the car door, and Ida was there tugging on Jackie's hand. "He can go with us," said Arnie. "Right, Dad?"

Vivian's uncle shrugged; it appeared he wasn't much of a talker.

"No," I said. "Jackie, go back to the house." The truth was, Jackie was so cute, the way he wriggled all over with excitement, that even *I* hated saying no to him. He broke loose from Ida's grip and ran to Daddy. And Daddy rarely says no to Jackie.

Ida said hey to Vivian, and then Arnie said, "You must be Ida. You coming?"

She shook her head.

"Ida hates the races," I said. The words weren't out of my mouth before she threw me a glance. I knew what it meant: I should keep my mouth shut. But if she didn't explain things herself, what was I supposed to do?

Jackie came running back to the car then—squealing that Daddy said he could go. Arnie opened the door and hopped out. "Sit in the middle," he said. "Up here with the men." He looked at Ida and pointed to the back seat. "There's room for one more."

Oh, for Pete's sake. Stop being such a nice guy. And let's get out of here before she changes her mind.

Ida shook her head, but she was chewing on her lip the way she did when she was trying to hide some disappointment. As if an invitation from Mr. Nice Guy up there might be turning all that dust and noise she hated into something as grand as Rock City.

But Vivian's Uncle Bud was putting the car in gear now and rolling forward. Ida threw her shoulders back and waved. "She's going to miss the excitement," said Arnie.

"Oh, don't worry," I told him. "Staying home and reading a book is plenty exciting for Ida."

"And drawing," said Jackie. "Ida's a good drawer."

"So that's why she had a pencil behind her ear," said Arnie.

"She did? I'm so used to it, I didn't even notice," I said. But *he* had noticed. I wondered if he thought she was prettier than me. Was he disappointed she hadn't come along? "You should've seen Ida at the first race," I said. "She didn't know whether to plug her ears or cover her eyes. And if that wasn't bad enough, she needed a third hand just for digging her fingernails into my arm."

Jackie bounced on the front seat and leaned forward like he thought that would get him to the speedway faster. He jabbered sixty miles a minute.

"Sorry, Arnie," I said. "My brother can talk the ears off a cornstalk. Jackie, sit still and be quiet."

Vivian grabbed my hand. "Let them talk," she said. "Sit back with me."

I didn't realize I was leaning forward. "Sorry," I said. "I'm just so excited about getting to the races."

She leaned over. "No," she whispered in my ear, "you're excited about Arnie Ledford."

I forced myself to pay attention to Vivian, but that didn't stop me from glancing at her cousin every so often. He and Jackie were hitting it off just fine.

At the speedway, while Vivian and I found seats on the bleachers Jackie dragged Arnie down to the fence to get a good look at the cars and their drivers in the infield—Ned Jarrett, Gwyn Staley, Junior Johnson, and all the others. Arnie's father sat a few rows ahead of us with another farmer.

When they finally came back to us, Jackie was arguing with Arnie about who would win the race. Arnie was pulling for Gwyn Staley.

"Hey—no!" I said. "Why aren't you rooting for one of our local boys? Ned Jarrett is from right there at Propst Crossroads. He's practically your neighbor."

"But Staley's my daddy's cousin," said Arnie. "I've got to be loyal to family."

"Well, we're loyal to Ned," I said. I started a little chant and Jackie joined in. "*No. 99 has the fastest time. No. 7 is coming in eleventh!*"

"Well," said Arnie, "I was thinking of buying some popcorn and maybe even sharing it. But never mind." He winked at me. At least I think he did. Maybe I imagined it.

Jackie stopped chanting when he heard "popcorn." Arnie took him by the hand, and off they went to the concession building. I couldn't help but notice how Arnie seemed to listen to every word coming out of Jackie's mouth—nodding, then boxing him on the shoulder in a teasing way. And Jackie danced along beside him, looking up into Arnie's face like *he* was a famous race car driver.

Vivian shook my arm. "Good grief!" she said. "I should've invited Ida. At least she'd talk to me."

I pulled my eyes away from Arnie. "I'll talk to you."

"No, you won't. Your mind is on my cousin."

"Well, he's hard not to notice. Why didn't you introduce us sooner?"

Vivian shrugged. "It never crossed my mind. He's just Arnie, after all."

"Oh, my word. He's so dreamy," I said. But I made myself not watch for him to come back.

It was thrilling to be there at night. As the sun went down, the trees beyond the speedway became silhouettes. Then they turned on the lights, changing how it felt to be at the racetrack. The smell of smoke and dust was still there, but the lights made everything more dramatic.

It was a crazy night. Junior Johnson rolled his car three times. Then two other cars crashed and went flying through the air right in front of the bleachers. I screamed so loud you'd think I was Ida.

Gwyn Staley won. And we found out at the end that Ned Jarrett hadn't even raced. Some Hefner fellow was driving No. 99. He finished in tenth place, just like Ned had the last time. "That's not fair," said Jackie. "Ned should've drove."

"I can't believe Junior Johnson rolled three times and his car kept on running," I said. "He sure knows how to put on a show."

"Know why he's such a good driver?" Arnie leaned in close and lowered his voice. "His family is into moonshine. So he's had lots of experience outrunning the cops with his car full of illegal whiskey."

"Does your *cousin* run moonshine too? Is that why he's so fast?"

Arnie shrugged. "You'd have to ask my dad about that."

Ahead of us, his dad stood and gave his head a little jerk, and we knew it was time to leave. Jackie was still latched on to Arnie's hand, asking what moonshine was.

"Illegal whiskey," said Arnie.

I followed along with Vivian, watching the way Arnie cocked his head slightly, and seemed to take in everything around him—like he was soaking up the atmosphere at the tracks.

How was I going to see him again? Too bad he lived in Banoak. But wait—the new school. It was consolidated. Banoak and Mountain View students would all be going to Fred T. Foard! I whispered to Vivian, "What grade is Arnie in?"

Vivian rolled her eyes. "Ninth this fall. And I can see you scheming already."

"Not scheming," I said. "Just dreaming."

13

IDA
July 1952

I pulled out my sketchpad and tried to capture the puffy clouds hovering over Bakers Mountain. There was just a hint of gold and pink in those clouds. It wouldn't be long until the sun went down and the sky would light up and show off.

I imagined Ellie and Vivian at the races and half wished I'd gone too. But why? Because of the cousin with the flashing brown eyes? It would still be too noisy for me.

I decided to tell the story of this evening. I moved to the end of the porch, sat on the floor, and began—making a quick sketch of the road leading away from the house. Of course that car taking Ellie to the races was halfway to Hickory by now, but I put it in there anyway. I drew the cornfield by the road, and then I started a new drawing. Up close. I sketched the porch with Daddy and Momma rocking side by side. Ann Fay reading the *Hickory Daily Record* with Mr. Shoes stretched out at her feet, pouting because Jackie and Ellie had left him behind.

I even added words from the front page of the paper. Presidential race. Russia. North Korea. Car wreck.

Later, I was brushing my teeth when Ellie came home. "Let me in," she said, knocking on the bathroom door. "I need a bath."

I opened the door. Her brown hair had a layer of red dust, and her face looked grimy too. "You can say that again. Did Ned Jarrett win?"

"Would you believe some other guy drove No. 99 for him? The race was great, though. A car even burst into flames."

"Ellie! That's not great!" I couldn't believe she was bragging on something so terrible.

"Don't worry, Ida. The driver got out first. And oh, my goodness—Vivian's cousin." Ellie leaned against the bathroom door and closed her eyes. "Ida, he's such a dreamboat. And friendly, too. But of course Jackie stole him away from me."

I snorted. "Stole him from you? When did he become yours?"

"You know what I mean. Jackie grabbed Arnie's attention and talked his ears off." Ellie giggled. "He has big ears—so cute. Anyway, he was sure fun to flirt with, and I think he even winked at me." Ellie put the stopper in the tub and while it filled with water she washed her face at the sink.

"You *think* he winked at you? Why wouldn't you *know* something like that?"

"Well, I thought maybe I imagined it."

"Yeah, Ellie. You probably did. I mean, what do you think? That he fell in love at first sight?"

"Mmm." There she was, making dreamy sounds again. "Why not?" she asked. "I think *I* did. Oh, and guess what, Ida—he's a freshman. Did you hear that? A freshman! So I'll see him again in just a few weeks. Oh, my stars, I cannot wait for the first day of school. I'm going to start sewing our back-to-school dresses tomorrow."

"Tomorrow is Sunday," I reminded her.

Ellie stepped into the tub and reached for the soap.

"Whoa. Look at your bathwater," I said. "It's disgusting! Why would that dreamboat even look at you twice?"

"Ha!" said Ellie. "By the time we left, Arnie was dusty as No. 99 itself. And it didn't hurt his looks one bit."

Yeah, I had noticed Arnie's good looks. And the second I did, I knew Ellie would fall for him. He hadn't winked at me. But he did invite me to go along to the speedway. And when I told him I wasn't going, I thought I saw disappointment in his eyes.

But then again. I probably imagined it. He'd surely fallen for Ellie the minute he caught sight of her.

I left the bathroom and discovered Daddy scrubbing Jackie in a washtub on the kitchen floor. "Why did you let him go?" I asked. "If you want my two cents, racing is just noise and dirt going in circles."

Daddy laughed. "You and me don't have to like it. But that don't mean other people can't have a good time with it."

Maybe he was right. Why should I care if Ellie wanted to go off and have fun and flirt with boys without me? I had my art. It wasn't flashy and it sure wasn't noisy, but it could make me happy for a whole evening. And when that was over I still had a lifetime of drawing left over.

Ellie mooned over Arnie all weekend. After church on Sunday she pulled out dress patterns and started dreaming. "Ida," she said, "which collar do you want? Round or pointed? And which sleeve? Puffy or flat?"

"I don't know, Ellie. You decide and make mine like yours."

"I'm not making them exactly the same," she said. "We're going into ninth grade, for heaven's sake. Isn't it time we stop dressing alike?"

Ellie was changing, setting herself apart from me, and I had a feeling it had something to do with that cousin of Vivian's. But it was more than that. Ever since Daddy changed his mind about going to Connecticut she'd been different. More determined than ever to outgrow her family. She'd picked a fine time to do it—just when we were going off to high school and I wanted her moral support more than ever.

But I was not expecting the announcement she made on Monday after being at the Hinkle sisters'. I was frying chicken when she walked in the back door, and without so much as a howdy doody she said, "Miss Pauline is signing me up for Latin this year."

"What?"

"Latin. I'm dropping home economics."

"Dropping home economics?"

Ellie picked up a fork and poked at the chicken in the skillet. "Home economics is sewing and cooking. I already know how to do both. And Miss Pauline says taking Latin my freshman year will help me get ahead." She turned a drumstick over in the frying pan. The grease spattered and she jumped back.

"Leave my chicken alone," I said. "*Who*, exactly, are you trying to get ahead of? Me?" I knew the answer to that, even if she wouldn't admit it.

"No," argued Ellie. "Not ahead of you. Just further along for me. You know I want to go to college and I need to be ready. Miss Pauline thinks I can handle it."

"And I can't. Is that what she said?"

"Of course not. She'll call the school and get *you* in, too—if you want."

"What's the point of studying Latin? Nobody even speaks it anymore."

"It lives on in all the Romance languages—Italian. Spanish. French. Not to mention, hundreds of words in the English language are influenced by Latin. Like premier, prime, primary. Miss Pauline says they all come from *primus*, the Latin word for first."

She sounded like a smart-aleck already. I wasn't interested in hearing about how studying Latin would make Ellie smarter than me. "Why are you doing this?" I asked.

"Doing what?"

"Making decisions without me?"

"Good grief, Ida! This doesn't even affect you."

"What about our schedules? We won't have all our classes together."

"Don't be silly, Ida. You can go to home economics by yourself. It'll be all girls and not the least bit scary. You won't even miss me. We'll both be making new friends this year. Maybe you'll meet a boy even."

Sure. I'd meet a boy. Lots of them. But that didn't mean a thing, because even if I liked one, he'd probably fall for Ellie.

14

IDA
July 1952

Two weeks after the Republicans held their convention, the Democrats had theirs. Of course the Hinkle sisters invited us to come watch it on their television.

The Democrats had nominated someone I'd never even heard of. Adlai Stevenson. But he had a good personality. In his acceptance speech Stevenson poked fun at the Republicans, and Daddy got good laughs out of that.

"I don't like him," said Ellie on the way home. "He's too intellectual."

"Too intellectual?" I asked. "Aren't you the one who decided to take Latin? Besides," I whispered, "Adlai Stevenson makes Daddy laugh. And that's good enough for me."

"Maybe so," said Ellie. And she wasn't whispering. "But you're not voting. Americans want someone down to earth—like us. Like General Eisenhower. *I like Ike. I like Ike*," she chanted. You'd think she was purposely agitating Daddy.

Daddy shifted into high gear and stepped on the gas. Never mind we were practically home and he should be slowing down.

I jabbed her in the ribs and hung on to Ann Fay.

Thank goodness Ann Fay threw in her two cents' worth. "We've always been Democrats in this family," she said. "And Stevenson made a good speech. I like him just fine."

"Honestly!" said Ellie. "This family is so predictable. Don't you realize people are ready for change? The Democrats have been in office for almost twenty years. Most Americans will vote for Ike."

"Be quiet, Ellie," I said. "Why do you always have to stir up trouble?" In the light from the dashboard I could see Daddy chewing on the inside of his cheek, and I could tell he was doing his best not to let Ellie get under his skin. He downshifted and turned into our lane. And he didn't say a word to Ellie about General Eisenhower.

The truth was I liked Ike too. He seemed friendly. But he was a Republican and he used war language and that upset Daddy. Ellie didn't seem to worry about that. Ever since Daddy canceled that trip on her, she no longer bothered with keeping the peace. Sometimes it felt like she wanted a fight. As if life wasn't enough for her unless there was some excitement going on.

That's why she liked the races so much. She could escape to a thrilling little oval world with speed and crashes and cars bursting into flames.

The next Saturday night she talked Junior into taking her there. She even asked Ann Fay to go along. "I've got plans," said Ann Fay. "Peggy Sue and I are going to the movies. Maybe Ida wants to go."

"No, Ida doesn't want to go to the races," Ellie said. "She hates the speedway and you know it."

The truth was neither one of them wanted me tagging along. And I didn't blame them. Peggy Sue and Ann Fay probably wanted to talk privately. And Ellie sure wasn't interested in sharing that Arnie fellow with me. I could tell from how she prettied herself up she was hoping to bump into him.

She walked up to Junior's to catch a ride so Jackie didn't figure out where she was going and tag along. But afterward she came home disappointed. "Boo-hoo," she said. "Dreamboat wasn't there. And on top of that, Ned Jarrett won't be racing anymore."

"Ned Jarrett's not racing? What happened?"

"According to Junior, Ned's father is afraid people will think he's a moonshiner like those other drivers."

"Are all the drivers into moonshining?"

"No, but lots of them are. And since Homer Jarrett is a respected member of the community he doesn't want anyone getting the wrong idea. If you ask me, it doesn't matter what people think. One look at Ned and you know he's not breaking the law. And anyway, why should his father be controlling his life? For Pete's sake, he's a married man."

"Maybe because he works for him," I said. "At least *Ned* respects his father."

"Hey," she said. "If you're talking about me, I respect my daddy."

"Yeah, when you get your own way. But when he canceled that vacation you started butting heads with him. You don't even try to stay out of his way."

"Well, I was disappointed, Ida. But you know what else? Those war wounds Otis was talking about are leaking pus a little bit at a time, and it's keeping us all on edge. Maybe it would be better if he just exploded like an atom bomb."

I hated it when Ellie talked like that. But she'd never been frightened by Daddy like I had. Maybe she thought it was nothing for him to grab me up the way he had all those years ago. But she hadn't seen the look in his eye when he did it.

"What about Momma?" I asked. "Remember that black eye he gave her? You'd feel real bad if he did that again."

"But he wouldn't," argued Ellie. "When he almost hurt you, Momma sent him away until he got straightened out. He knows she'd do it again. And besides, Daddy's not mean. He's just scared."

I was scared too. Scared of what could happen to our family. I didn't want Momma sending Daddy away. And I didn't want Ellie setting off an explosion.

That night when I went to bed I dreamed about war,

and the people fighting were our family. Momma had two black eyes, and I knew in my dream it had to be Daddy that hit her.

Daddy and Ellie had guns pointed at each other and I was hiding with Mr. Shoes under the kitchen table. But every so often Ellie would swing around and point that gun at me.

I woke up and Ellie was pushing on me. "You're on my side of the bed," she said. "Move over."

I wanted to snuggle into her the way I used to when we were little. But that wouldn't make her happy. So I pulled over to my side of the bed and tried to put myself back to sleep by tracing the outlines of the room in my head. Doorway. Window. Bureau. Mirror. In my mind I sketched Ann Fay's bed and her black hair on the white pillow. Our bed.

And Ellie with her back to me.

15

ELLIE
August 1952

On Saturday, Vivian called to see if Ida and I wanted to go to the movies.

"This afternoon?" I asked.

"Tonight. I don't have a ride this afternoon."

"Um, Vivian, I'd love to but I told Ann Fay I'd go to the races with her and Junior."

"Uh-huh. And I know you just hate going," teased Vivian. "But you'll do it for Ann Fay. With a little luck my cousin will be there and you'll have yourself a double date."

"Yeah, except Jackie's tagging along."

Later, at the speedway, Jackie dragged Junior to the front row of the concrete bleachers so he could get a good look at the cars in the infield.

"Is your Arnie friend here?" asked Ann Fay.

I looked around and there, about four rows up, I saw him sitting with his father. Both wore overalls and straw hats. "That's him," I said. "Up there with the straw hat. I've never seen him in overalls before."

"Kind of reminds me of Junior," she said.

"Does that mean you think he's cute?"

"It means he's wearing overalls," said Ann Fay.

"Arnie," I called. He waved. And that smile—it made me want to run up those bleachers. "Follow me, Ann Fay." We climbed up to where he was, and Arnie shook Ann Fay's hand like a proper gentleman.

"This is my father," he said. "James Ledford."

His father glanced at Ann Fay and then me. "How d'ya do?" He gave a quiet nod. I noticed he was wearing a pin on his overalls that said I LIKE IKE.

He saw me looking and reached up to move it. When he did that, Eisenhower's face appeared. "Wow! Ann Fay, look at that."

Mr. Ledford smiled real slow and flashed the pin for Ann Fay to see.

"She's pulling for Stevenson," I said. "But me, I like Ike."

"Sit," said Arnie. "You didn't bring your twin?"

"She went to the movies," I said. "I told you Ida hates racing. I like that hat. And your farmer outfit."

"Sorry," said Arnie. "Been haying all day. Didn't have time for a proper bath even. But I did try to clean up. And I put on cologne so I don't smell like cows. Hope I don't have hay in my ears."

I pretended to look him over real good. "Nope." I said. "You're just perfect. All you need is a little racetrack dirt to finish you off."

Junior and Jackie came to sit with us. "Move over, Ellie." Jackie tried to squeeze between me and Arnie and wouldn't you know Arnie scooted over to make room for him.

"I thought you were sitting with Junior," I said. "You're gonna hurt his feelings."

"No. Junior's gonna sit with Ann Fay."

"Well, that'll sure make Junior happy," I said, pretending not to care one way or the other about not sitting beside Arnie. But the truth was I wanted to drag my little brother down to the first row and tell him to stay there.

Ned's racing partner John Lentz was heading to the car. At least I thought it was him because Ned wasn't racing anymore. They looked a lot alike—both tall and kind of skinny. But they didn't walk the same and if you asked me the guy wearing the helmet walked like Ned—there was something almost shy about the way he moved.

"Junior," I said. "Is Ned driving tonight?"

He shook his head. "Nah, I doubt it."

"But look. Isn't that him climbing into No. 99?"

Junior squinted and shaded his eyes with his hands. "Maybe. I don't know how you could tell. No. That's John's plaid shirt. I saw him earlier."

"Oh, okay. But I thought for sure it looked like Ned."

Soon the race started and dust and dirt clods went flying. In the first heat a car hit the wall and went spinning across the track. First one car slammed into him and then another. No. 99 zigzagged around them and Staley did too. I don't know who yelled louder—me or Arnie.

But a bunch of drivers weren't so lucky. There was a huge pileup and about four cars had to leave the race. They put out the caution flag and it got quiet enough to actually talk. "It's good Ida didn't come," I told Arnie. "She'd be hiding her eyes and wanting to go home." I wasn't exactly trying to make her sound boring. But I wanted Arnie to know that I was the twin who liked having a good time.

The announcer said how Gwyn Staley was the champion of the short track coming into the season. "But he faces a tough competitor in Junior Johnson," he said. "Johnson has nerves of steel. Even on that slippery third turn he never holds back."

When the first heat was over, Junior took it. Gwyn came in second.

"Sorry," I told Arnie.

He shrugged. "We'll get him in the main race. I'm going to the concession stand." He left and came back about ten minutes later with two bags of popcorn. He handed one to Ann Fay. "Y'all can share that," he said. "Ellie and Jackie can help me with this one." He held it out to me. "Have some?"

"Sure. Thanks."

Just that quick, Arnie was yelling for No. 7, which was coming around the turn just before the grandstand. Staley rode up onto the banked turn and his car wobbled. "Ooooh!" It looked like he would flip. But he held on to the dirt and kept going.

"Way to hang on!" Arnie threw his hands in the air and his popcorn went flying all around us.

"Hey!" I hollered. "You're wasting good popcorn."

But Arnie didn't hear me or notice what he'd done. His mind was on the race. I glanced at his father still sitting on the bleachers. His eyes followed the cars around the track but he sat there the whole time quiet as a dead engine. As far as I could tell he was completely opposite of our daddy—when it came to loud noises anyway.

Gwyn Staley didn't win because his car overheated and he couldn't finish the race. "He *would* have won though," I told Arnie.

There were multiple races that night. In one of them No. 99 led the whole way and I think I yelled through every second of it. Ned's car would win first place. I just knew it. But then, all of sudden No. 10 roared right past him. One more lap and the race was over. No. 99 came in second. I was heartbroken for Ned even if that wasn't him driving the car.

Jackie was so disappointed I thought he was going to cry.

But the driver wasn't crying. I couldn't miss the grin on his face when he climbed out the window. "Look, Junior," I said. "That *was* Ned Jarrett driving tonight."

"Hmmm," said Junior. "I might have to do a little investigating."

As the crowd was leaving, Junior waited by the driver's entrance until No. 99 came through. Jackie tagged along. While we waited on them I watched the taillights of all those cars. Dust swirled beneath the street lights. The warm night smelled of cherry cigars, hotdogs, and car exhaust—a strange combination.

It was one of those moments when I felt sorry for the rest of the world—all those other people who weren't there to experience this. Except for Ida. Having her there would just complicate things. Sharing Arnie with Jackie was bad enough.

Arnie waited around with us while Junior talked to Ned.

After a while Junior and Jackie headed our way. Jackie yelled right out. "Ellie, you were right. That was . . ." Junior clapped his hand over Jackie's mouth.

"He doesn't exactly want everybody to know," he said. "But yeah, Ned drove tonight. Lentz is sick so they switched shirts. And nobody knew the difference."

"Except Ellie," said Arnie. "She's a smart one." He looked at me. "How'd you know?"

I shrugged. "I could just tell. I've seen how he walks. And how he drives—like a champion."

Arnie shrugged. "If you say so. I keep *my* eyes on Staley. Well, I've gotta go. That's my daddy out there honking his horn. But I'll see you at school in a few weeks."

I waited until his father's car drove out of the dusty parking lot and then I exploded. "School!" I shouted. "I cannot wait two more weeks for school to start!"

16

IDA
August 1952

Our bus dropped the elementary students off at Mountain View School. Jackie ran to the building, stopped and waved to us and hurried through the door. I almost wished he weren't so excited. If he'd been the least bit nervous I could have gone inside and helped him find the first-grade teacher. Mountain View was like an old family friend. Familiar. Safe. And I was leaving it behind.

According to Ellie, going to Fred T. Foard High on the first day was like riding in a fast car—scary, but something you'd never want to miss. At the crossroads the buses came from every direction—four different school districts.

"Think of all the new friends we'll make," Ellie said.

"Yeah. Like Vivian's cousin." That's what my twin was really thinking about. I was just hoping to have classes with Vivian. Or anyone from Mountain View.

"So nifty," said Ellie, when she saw the new school. It was long and low and modern and didn't look much like a school to me. Red construction dirt covered the yard, and yellow machines sat off to the side—as if they'd barely finished the parking lots before the buses pulled in.

Students streamed toward the building. Most of them I'd never seen before. It was a warm August morning, but I felt shivery.

"See that cute boy in the blue shirt?" Ellie whispered. She nodded toward a tall guy with a crew cut who was horsing around with his friend. The redheaded fellow with him caught us looking their way.

"You're twins," he said—as if we needed his help to figure that out.

For Ellie it was the perfect opportunity to introduce herself. "I'm Ellie."

The fellow looked at me. "Let me guess. If she's Ellie, you've got to be Nellie."

I'd heard that one before. Ellie had too, but she giggled anyway. "Actually, she's Ida."

"I'm Duncan. And this is Reggie. We'll see y'all around."

There was a clump of students at the door, a regular traffic jam, and now we were in the middle of it, surrounded by perfumes and hair tonic, by plaid-shirted fellows and girls in princess waistlines and flared skirts. All of us in our back-to-school clothes, trying to impress each other. Ellie and I had debated whether to dress the same. In the end we wore matching dresses with different collars. The truth was, as much as Ellie wanted to separate herself from me, she liked the attention people gave her for being a twin.

After we squeezed through the double doors, posterboard signs aimed us in the right direction. Arrows for freshmen pointed ahead, so we kept going. Outside the classroom doors were signs showing where you belonged if your last name started with A–G or H–Q or R–Z.

"Q?" asked Ellie. "Is there anyone in the wide world whose last name starts with Q?"

I shrugged. "I don't think so. Not around here."

We followed the freshmen signs and found the H–Q room. A bald man with dark-rimmed glasses stood by the door. "Good morning," he said. "I'm Mr. Van Horn, your homeroom teacher."

Ellie led the way, of course. She headed for the back of the room. And no wonder. Vivian's cousin was there—almost like he'd been waiting for her. "Hey, Arnie," she called. "Oh, my stars! I can't believe we're in the same homeroom. Been to any races lately?"

If Arnie couldn't see how crazy she was about him, then he was just plain blind. But I had a feeling he knew it.

I saw him glance at me. Maybe he wanted her to introduce us. No, I'd imagined that. But he gave me a little wave while Ellie jabbered. And he smiled at me, too. The guy seemed every bit as nice as Ellie had claimed. And just as good-looking—even if he did have ears that stuck out noticeably. And a cowlick of hair that would not lie down. But those things made him interesting. Just the kind of person Ellie would fall for.

To help calm my nerves, I doodled on a sheet of paper, doing quick sketches of other students. Drawing helped me to see them better—whether they were bold and chatty, dressed to the nines, or especially shy.

Maxine and Betty from Mountain View School arrived, caught my eye, and waved. "Hey, twins!" Maxine glanced at Ellie and Arnie, wiggled her eyebrows, and made kissy lips.

Good grief!

"Hey, Maxine. Hi, Betty," called Ellie. "Hip, hip, hooray, we're high schoolers now. This is Arnie. He's from Banoak. And, oh, he's Vivian's cousin."

"But don't hold that against me," joked Arnie.

"Oh, don't worry, Arnie," said Ellie. "We love Vivian, so of course we'll love you too."

Of course.

Betty and Maxine found seats on the far side of the room, right next to a blue bulletin board that said WHO WILL BE OUR NEXT PRESIDENT? in large white letters with pictures of Dwight Eisenhower and Adlai Stevenson staring at each other.

But the board that grabbed me had a black background with a Russian map and a picture of Joseph Stalin on the left side and one of the United States and President

Truman on the right. Between them was Korea divided into North and South. A mushroom-shaped cloud hung low overhead.

I knew that bulletin board was meant to make me feel safe. President Truman claimed that nuclear weapons would prevent a third world war from breaking out. Just the threat of nuclear war was supposed to keep communism from spreading.

But how could Truman predict what the communists would do?

I hugged myself and rubbed at the chill bumps on my arms.

Except for that bulletin board, the room felt bright and airy. The walls were pale green at the top and darker at the bottom. The big windows had slatted metal blinds and wide black windowsills. The floors were covered in green tiles with white swirly designs.

A bell rang and Mr. Van Horn went to his desk. "Welcome. You will start and finish your day right here since I am also your world history teacher." He opened his attendance book. "When you hear your name, please come forward for your class schedule."

One by one, Mr. Van Horn called our names. The quiet, classy-looking girl across from me was Laura Quincy. Ellie snickered a little when she realized there actually *was* a student whose name started with Q. "What's so funny?" asked Laura. She stood and looked down her nose at Ellie.

"Nothing," said Ellie. "I was just saying earlier I didn't know anyone whose last name started with a Q. But now there's you! Isn't that nifty? I'm Ellie, by the way."

Mr. Van Horn called Laura's name again. And he glared at Ellie, who was still jabbering. "Shh . . ." I said.

I tried to capture Laura with my pencil. She was perfect—hair, face, and that polished cotton dress with the white bodice and deep blue flared skirt. Everything about Laura Quincy seemed a little extra shiny, including her name.

Mr. Van Horn explained that our schedules had the room numbers beside each class and he described the layout of the school. There were lockers in the hallway for storing our books and our locker numbers were on our individual schedules.

The principal, Mr. Lynn, came on the loudspeaker. He welcomed us to Fred T. Foard, home of the Tigers, and he led us in saying the Lord's Prayer and the Pledge of Allegiance.

The bell rang. According to my schedule I had home economics first period. Ellie had dropped that to take Latin. For the first period of the day I had to face total strangers without her.

17

IDA
August 1952

We didn't have books yet, but Ellie opened her locker anyway. "Phooey," she said. "They could have left us candy or something! Wish me luck, y'all. I'm off to Latin class. Anybody want to go along?"

That redheaded guy, Duncan, was at a locker across the hall. "Hey, good-looking," he said to Ellie. "Latin class? I'll walk you to the door. But don't ask me to step inside."

Ellie giggled. Couldn't she see he was just a flirt?

Laura Quincy stepped up. "I'm going to Latin. Room 14. Mind if I tag along?" Laura was from somewhere else. You could hear it in the way she talked.

"Sure," said Ellie. "Let's go." She leaned in and whispered in my ear, "No flirting with Arnie Ledford while I'm gone, twin sister." Then she grabbed Laura's elbow and off they went. Duncan pushed his way between them and offered an arm to each like he was a proper escort.

Ellie took it. But Laura slipped around behind him and put herself on the *other* side of Ellie. That girl knew how to look out for herself. And she had more common sense than my sister did.

Ellie didn't have to worry about me flirting with Arnie. I wouldn't know how. But he stopped by my locker. "I've got shop and agriculture next," he said. "What about you?" He was broad and tanned, and there were white lines at the side of his eyes from squinting against the sun. He smelled like Old Spice cologne.

I felt my breath catch. "Ho-home economics," I stuttered.

He pointed to a posterboard that directed us down the hall. "This way."

As we followed signs pointing us to our classes, Arnie made conversation. I learned that he'd been up since four thirty—milking cows before school. "Glad I have agriculture first. That'll keep me awake. Oh, here you are," he said at the door to my home economics class. "See you later. In history, if not before. Hey, cousin."

Vivian was just inside the door. "Boy, am I glad to see you!" I said. "Thank God I have at least one class with you."

"Same here," said Vivian. "Can't wait to see the rest of your schedule. Wow! Look at this place."

The home economics room was bright and sunny, with rows of sewing machines and even a real kitchen. Our teacher, Mrs. Curtis, instructed us to find seats at tables. There were two other girls at our table, dressed alike in pink shirtwaist dresses with pink kerchiefs tied in their hair. I didn't think they were twins, though. Probably not even sisters. One was tall and blond, and the other was shorter with brown curls that looked like they refused to behave. She wore glasses and had obviously painted the frames with nail polish. Pink, of course.

"Hey, y'all," said the blond one. "I'm Stella from Startown. And this is Patsy. She's from Startown too." The way she said Startown, you'd have thought the place was Hollywood and she was a movie star. She kind of looked like one with her bright pink lipstick, or even just by the way she held her head so high.

"We're from Mountain View," said Vivian. "And I'm Vivian."

Stella looked at me—waiting for me to introduce myself.

"Ida," I said.

"Hey, Vivian. Hey, Ida." Stella whispered something in Patsy's ear while glancing at me from the corner of her eye. I reached for my collar. Was it straight? Why did just being close to Stella from Startown make me feel as if I had egg on my dress?

Mrs. Curtis called the class to order. "We'll begin our year with a unit on social behavior." She talked for the whole period about learning to be ladies and what that meant for how we dressed, how we behaved in class, and how we acted on dates.

"Dates," whispered Stella to Patsy. "With Reggie." She fluttered her eyelids and smiled flirtatiously. She glanced my way, and for some reason she seemed to be looking down her nose at me.

I wasn't ready for high school and all these strangers. I didn't care about brand-new classrooms with fancy equipment. At Mountain View the old wood floors would be freshly waxed and the desks and blackboards would be scrubbed. It was all so familiar in my mind that I could almost smell it. Except for Stella's Tabu perfume getting in the way.

Before the bell finished ringing at the end of that class, I was in the hall. Vivian and I agreed to meet again at lunchtime.

At noon there was a line going into the lunchroom, so I parked myself at a window and waited. Ellie came before Vivian did. She was still with Laura Quincy, and from the sound of it the two of them were practicing Latin.

Was this going to be my future at Fred T. Foard— listening to those two babbling away? Thank goodness, I saw Vivian coming toward the lunch line just then.

The cafeteria had painted block walls with shiny tiles—nothing like the lunchroom in the basement of Mountain View School. Through the windows on one side I saw a scraggly field and a big white farmhouse. For some reason this low, modern school building sitting in the middle of farmland reminded me of myself. Like it was trying to be something it wasn't quite ready for.

The four of us found a table. In no time, along came Stella from Startown, with Patsy right behind her. Stella glanced at me and Vivian and looked for another table. But then she stopped in her tracks, turned back, and headed for ours. "Oh, my stars and garters!" she said. "There are two of you! Twins! I love twins. This is so nifty." She plopped her tray on the table and sat across from me. "Which one of you is Ida from home ec? Why didn't you tell us you had a twin?"

Now all of a sudden I was nifty.

"Why didn't she ask?" muttered Vivian.

Ellie pointed to me. "She's Ida. I'm Ellie. And your food is getting cold." I knew she was enjoying this attention, even though she liked to pretend that being a twin was boring.

Stella took the cardboard cap off her milk bottle and took a drink. I felt her studying me, but I kept my eyes on my green beans. If she thought I was going to sit there and endure her comparisons, she was wrong. "I think Ida's face is rounder," said Stella. "And she has a mole above her mouth. Just like Marilyn Monroe. Aren't you jealous, Ellie?"

"Yeah," said Ellie. "Green as a dollar bill. Aren't you going to eat?"

Stella took a bite of potatoes. "I know you can't be exactly alike. Which one of you makes better grades? Who's the nice one? Do you have boyfriends? How do they tell you apart?"

Ellie opened her mouth to speak, but Vivian jumped in first. She'd heard all these comparisons before, and she knew one of us always got our feelings hurt. "Obviously you and Patsy are twins," she said, "since you're dressed the same. So, which one of you is the nice one? And who's smarter? Wait—don't tell me. Patsy is smarter. And nicer. And she has more boyfriends. Am I right?"

At the other end of the table, Laura Quincy, so pretty and proper, started to laugh just when she'd taken a swallow of milk. She grabbed her napkin, covered her mouth, and tried not to choke.

Stella's nose twitched and her eyes narrowed. She stabbed at a green bean with her fork and held it in front of her face. While she stared at Vivian she nibbled away at that bean. "Now I know who's *not* nice," she said. "And I'm *not* talking about the twins either."

18

ELLIE
August 1952

At sixth period, when Ida came into Mr. Van Horn's room for history, Arnie was with her—grinning down at her in a way that made my heart stop dead in its tracks. Was that a pure accident, or had they walked to class together?

I gave Ida a hard, squinty look. She knew exactly what I was thinking because she caught my eye, shrugged, and shook her head, letting me know she hadn't planned it.

She sat in front of me and Arnie took the desk across from her. I didn't like how this was shaping up. If I sat back here and talked to Laura, then the two of them might get chummy. Oh, well—at least this way I could keep my eye on them.

Right now Arnie looked tired. He folded his arms across his desk and rested his head on them. "Arnie, was your day that bad?" I asked. "Tell us all about it. Who were your best and worst teachers?"

"Miss Honeycutt! It's Ida, I believe?" That was Mr. Van Horn fussing. I hadn't realized he'd just called the class to order.

Ida sat there shaking her head. "Uh. Not me."

"I'm sorry, Mr. Van Horn. I'm Ellie. I didn't hear you. And don't blame my sister. Ida never talks out of turn. I'm the blabbermouth in the family."

Mr. Van Horn nodded, and I could tell he was trying not to smile. "I see," he said. "So now I know *you* will always have something to say. And if I want to hear from your sister, I'll have to call on her."

Oh, brother. Ida is going to give me down the road for this.

Mr. Van Horn turned to the rest of the class. He took off his dark-rimmed glasses and waved them as he spoke. "World history. Why should we bother with it?" He paused and waited for some guy in the front row to stop mumbling. A girl in the middle of the room was tapping her toes until she realized Mr. Van Horn was watching her. When the room was completely silent he began again. "After all, who cares about what's going on across the ocean? How does anything over there affect you and me—especially if it happened fifty, a hundred, or even two thousand years ago?"

He put his glasses back on and stared up and down the rows, like he was waiting for someone to speak up. So, of course I did. "What about communism?" I said. "Wasn't Russia the first communist country? Wasn't that about fifty years ago? And now look. It's spreading across the world."

"1917," said Mr. Van Horn. "That's an excellent point. Some of you have family members defending South Korea, right now. What are they fighting for?"

"Freedom." I blurted it out.

Mr. Van Horn stopped, looked at me like maybe he thought I was talking too much, and went on. "Yes. Democracy. Freedom from a communist takeover by Mao Tse-tung of China and Joseph Stalin of the Soviet Union. What do I mean when I say the Soviet Union?"

"Russia." This time it wasn't me blurting it out. Half the class said it.

"Yes," said Mr. Van Horn. "But more than Russia." He started walking around the room, circling our desks like he was trying to intimidate us. "The Soviet Union is that conglomerate of nations under Russian control. All forced to become communist. But what, exactly, *is* communism?"

He stopped right behind my desk.

"Ida?"

Does he mean Ida? Or me? I started to speak, but Mr. Van Horn interrupted. "Ida?"

I heard her gulp. "Um. It's a form of government."

Ida could explain more but I knew she wasn't about to make a speech in front of strangers on the first day of school. Not if she didn't have to.

"Yes? What sort of government? Arnie Ledford?"

"Hmm?" Arnie jerked his head up. His elbow was propped on his desk and he was leaning into his hand.

Evidently he'd fallen asleep that way. He probably had no idea what Mr. Van Horn had asked him. Poor Arnie.

I raised my hand but didn't wait for Mr. Van Horn to call on me. "Communists believe everyone should be on the same level," I said. "They don't allow people to choose what jobs they want. So they'll take away your farm or business and make it a government-run farm or business. And you just have to let them do it."

"Thank you, Arnie," said Mr. Van Horn. He sounded a little sarcastic. "Make no mistake," he said. "We're fighting in South Korea because Soviet-backed communists in North Korea invaded the South. The United States will not tolerate such aggression. Because next, communists will seek to take Vietnam, and then they will move on until they've dominated all of Asia, and they won't stop there. Their goal is world domination. And that includes us."

Buster, a tall, skinny fellow in the front row, said communists were already in this country. He declared that lots of Yankees were communists—Jews and Catholics and people who believed in unions. People who wanted whites and coloreds to be equal. "Everybody's not equal," he said. "And they might as well just give up and admit it."

You can believe Laura Quincy from Massachusetts did not take that sitting down. Her hand was only half in the air when she started talking. "Have you been sleeping for the last ten years?" she asked. "Didn't you notice that millions of people died in Europe because of your ideas?"

Buster mumbled something and Mr. Van Horn told him to keep those opinions to himself. But if you ask me, that creep was itching for trouble.

Sure enough, after class he was waiting for Laura at her locker—leaning against it with his arms folded across his checkered shirt. "No wonder you were so fired up in there. You're a dad-burn Yankee, aren't you?" he sneered. "Nobody around here talks like that. Bet you're a commie too."

Laura gave a tiny gasp and I could just feel her shrink up a little. I grabbed her elbow, but when I tried to pull her back from him she stood her ground and stared Buster down. He lowered his eyelids and the sneer just sort of slid off his face.

"Step aside, Buster," I told him. "Laura's my friend and it's none of your business where she's from. And she sure isn't a communist."

"Really? You figured that out in one day, I reckon. Or you been chums for a while now? Maybe you're *both* commies." Buster pulled a cigarette from his pocket and waved it between two fingers. Maybe he thought that would make him look tougher.

A few people had gathered, including Arnie. "Move it, Buster," he said. "And leave my friends alone."

Buster and Arnie stared at each other until finally Buster looked away. "Ledford," he said, "I never took *you* for a commie sympathizer." He edged away from Laura's locker. Then he put that cigarette between his lips and swaggered down the hall toward the exit.

"Good riddance," said Arnie. "You girls okay?"

Personally I was mad as a stepped-on yellow jacket. I wasn't sure if Laura was mad or just scared. Maybe both. But her face was flushed. She let out a loud breath. "I'm fine," she said. "But thank you, Arnie. You're my new hero."

Arnie shook his head. "It's okay," he said. "I've known Buster all my life. He can be ignorant, but he won't actually hurt you. Just don't let him get under your skin. And let me know if he bothers you again."

Arnie didn't have to raise a fist or flex his farmer muscles. There was something about the look in his eye and the set of his jaw that had let Buster know he wasn't fooling around. It made me proud to know him. And glad to be seeing him five days a week for the whole school year. But of course I was already excited about that.

19

ELLIE
August 1952

The next morning Buster was in his desk at the front of the room with his legs stretched into the walkway like he intended to trip someone. Laura noticed and pulled me down the first aisle so we could avoid him. We circled the desks and settled behind Arnie.

I wanted to talk to Arnie, but I was nervous about my Latin conjugations, so I gave him my book and asked him to call them out to me. He took one look at it and handed it to Laura. "You help her," he said. "That right there makes me want to go back to bed." He rested his head on his desk.

"Oh, Arnie, why are you being such a sleepyhead? A little bit of Latin will wake you up. I promise. Help me out."

Ida sat down in front of me. "Leave him alone, Ellie," she said. "You'd be sleepy too if you had to milk cows at four thirty in the morning."

Wait a minute. How does she know that about him?

Laura started calling out conjugations to help me study. *Do, das, dat.* But my mind was on Arnie and how my sister had gotten so chummy with him in one day of school.

Ida answered for me. "I give, you give, he/she/it gives."

"Yippee for you, Ida," said Laura. "What about *voco, vocas, vocat?*"

"I call, you call, he/she/it calls."

Arnie sure wasn't asleep now. He was watching Ida and looking impressed. "Stop being a smart-aleck, Ida," I said. "I'm the one who needs to study."

"Believe me," said Ida, "you know it already. I learned it from you saying it over and over like a stuck phonograph record."

"*Amo, amas, amat,*" said Laura.

I held my hand over Ida's mouth and answered for myself. "I love, you love, he/she/it loves." Ida was probably right. I didn't need to worry about Latin.

In class I managed to recite all my conjugations and even repeat the Latin phrase Mrs. Reitzel threw at me. But she didn't like my pronunciation. Laura's Latin was practically perfect. "How do you know so much already?" I asked her between classes. "Have you been studying Latin for a long time?"

"I'm Catholic. We celebrate the mass in Latin."

"Catholic?" I stopped in the middle of the hall.

Laura stopped too and looked me in the eye. "Yes, Catholic. You *do* know what that is?"

Of course I did. But I'd never actually met a Catholic, much less imagined being friends with one.

I guess I stepped back from her a little, because Laura laughed and said, "Are you afraid it'll rub off on you? It's a religion, Ellie. Not polio."

"I know what Catholics are. And I know about their church services being in Latin. It's just that we don't have Catholics around here."

"Of course you do. There's a church in town. My family has been going there."

"Oh. Of course. I don't get to that part of town very often." I stood there in the middle of the hall with people passing us by and looked her over. Laura Quincy from Massachusetts. Pretty as a Christmas ornament in her fine clothes that made me downright jealous. Now, to top it off, she was Catholic. I thought about what Buster said during history class the day before. About Jews and Catholics and Yankees being communists. "We can't let Buster know," I said.

"And why not?" asked Laura. "Are you ashamed of me now? It's not too late to find a new friend."

"No. That's not what I meant. But Buster—he's mean. And he hates Catholics. I don't want you to get hurt."

Laura shrugged her shoulders. "What can he do? He sits three whole rows away from me."

"That's just one hour of the school day, Laura. Ignorant people can do all kinds of things that a nice person like you would never think of."

Some guy bumped into me and kept on going. "Hey, you two," he hollered back at us. "This is a hallway. Not a parking lot."

"Yes, sir!" I called after him. I looked at Laura. "See what I mean? Let's go."

"Speaking of people who aren't that nice," said Laura. "Whatever we do, let's eat with someone else at lunch today. We can do better than Stella for sure."

"Fine with me."

But at lunchtime Stella caught us looking for a table, and she waved. "Yoo-hoo! Ellie, Laura—over here."

I looked at Laura. She shrugged. "I guess we'll have to wait for another day to do better," she said.

Stella and Patsy were dressed the same again. Dark blue skirts. White blouses. And silky red scarves tied around their necks. "We saved you seats," said Patsy.

"We *could* have our own little group of six," said Stella. "I was willing to forgive your friend Vivian for being rude yesterday. But your twin and Vivian acted like they didn't see us. They avoided us in home ec too, didn't they, Patsy? So now we won't have any problem telling you apart. The stuck-up twin is Ida. And you're the friendly one."

"Maybe Ida's not stuck up," said Laura. "What if she's just shy?"

Stella rolled her eyes. "When someone invites you to sit with them and you act like they don't exist, that's not shy."

"Ida's a loner," I said. "Ignore her and talk to me. Then we'll all be happy."

Laura cleared her throat a little—reminding me not to get too friendly, I guess.

"What clubs are y'all joining?" asked Patsy.

We were in the middle of discussing clubs when Stella caught sight of Reggie and his friend Duncan taking their trays to the dishwashing window. "Oops!" she said. "I believe it's time for me to go." She stood, took a last bite of mashed potatoes, and grabbed her tray. "Gotta snag Reggie. I've been sweet on him since seventh grade. He loves chocolate cake. You know what they say—'The way to a man's heart is to give him your dessert.' Patsy, you can catch up with me."

Patsy shook her head. "That girl is crazy," she said. "I wouldn't give up my cake for any boy." She watched Stella go. Sure enough. Reggie was thrilled with the cake. But he blew Stella a kiss and left her standing there.

She made a pouty face and scraped her leftover food and napkin into the garbage can while Reggie sauntered through the cafeteria with that cake in hand and came straight to our table. He sat beside Patsy where Stella had been. "Hey, Patsy," he said. "How about you introduce me to your friends?"

Patsy pointed to us one at a time. "Ellie Honeycutt. Laura Quincy."

Reggie glanced at me and nodded. "We met," he said. It was Laura he really wanted to know. "Laura Quincy from somewhere else. Right?"

Laura nodded.

"Massachusetts," I said.

Under the table, Laura whacked her knee against mine. Evidently she didn't want Reggie to know where she was from. Or didn't want me speaking for her. I put a forkful of cake into my mouth.

Reggie had Stella's cake half-eaten. He took a bite. Chocolate icing smeared across his upper lip. He turned to Duncan, who was leaning against the cafeteria wall, waiting—watching me.

"Duncan," Reggie said. "Pull up a chair from that table over there."

"No need to grab another chair," said Laura. "I was just leaving. Duncan can have my seat." She gathered her plate and utensils. "It was good to meet you," she said. "But I really have to go now. Are you coming, Ellie?"

"Yeah," I said. "Sorry, fellas. I've gotta go."

"Aw, man," said Duncan. "I miss you already."

We took our trays to the dishwashing window. "Obviously, Duncan is a flirt," I said. "And I have a feeling Reggie likes you."

"Just another good reason to avoid Stella. I wouldn't want her to think I'm interested in her precious Reggie."

20

IDA
September 1952

Ellie and I were sitting on the front porch doing algebra homework, competing to see who could finish the fastest. Also to make the best grade. Or at least to both make A's when report cards came out. That's just the way it had always been with us.

I didn't realize, until we were in separate classes, how free I could feel without her there to compare myself to. Now, I never really relaxed until we said goodbye at the Latin class door. Once she was in that room, the air in the hall just felt lighter. I could actually carry on a conversation with Arnie.

Junior's car came down the lane—bringing Ann Fay home.

After work, Ann Fay almost always had a smile or a cute story. But today she was downright droopy. She plopped herself on the steps and didn't bother to wave to Junior when he backed out of the driveway. I could tell from the way he drove real slow and kept looking after her that he was concerned.

"What?" said Ellie. "You look like you lost your last friend."

Ann Fay fiddled with the clasp on her pocketbook, snapping it open and shut.

Ellie closed her algebra book and put it on the table between our rocking chairs. "Don't peek at my answers," she warned me. "Ann Fay, did you and Junior fight?"

I was sick of algebra myself and more interested in Ann Fay and Junior. "He won't quit giving you a ride every day, will he?" I asked. As far as I could tell, riding together wasn't actually making them any closer. But I kept hoping.

"Would y'all be quiet and stop jumping to conclusions? I just had a hard day at work." Ann Fay took a deep breath and blew it out real loud. "One of Dr. Sain's patients came in screaming from cramps in his legs. He was the cutest little baby, just two years old, and I couldn't do a thing to make him feel better." Ann Fay bit her lip and rubbed at her thigh like she was remembering what polio felt like.

"Oh, no!" said Ellie. "He had polio, didn't he?"

Ann Fay nodded. She let go of her pocketbook and pressed her fingertips to the side of her forehead. "Whatever you do," she said, "don't tell Daddy. He's got enough worries already without imagining that Jackie will get sick."

But the next morning while Daddy was shaving in the bathroom, Ann Fay pulled Jackie aside. "Jackie," she said, "don't be drinking out of the water fountain at school. Not today and not until I tell you it's safe."

Jackie frowned. "Why not? I like the water fountain. We have one in a little white sink at the back of our room."

"Because. You don't want to catch polio." She gave him a little shake. "Believe me. You don't."

"But I get thirsty at school," he wailed.

"Jackie, I mean it. Would you rather be thirsty all day or stuck in a wheelchair for the rest of your life? Or worse, even?"

"Ann Fay!" said Momma. "What are you doing? Trying to scare him?"

"Yes. I sure am. Polio isn't something to mess around with." She turned back to Jackie. "And don't breathe a word of this to Daddy. You hear me? Because he'll start worrying about you for no reason."

It sounded to me like Ann Fay was the one doing the worrying. She pulled Jackie close and held on to him until he started squirming. "You're smothering me, Ann Fay."

She let go and I saw that she had tears in those clear blue eyes. Ellie and I swapped glances, and she mouthed our other brother's name. *Bobby.*

I nodded. Ann Fay always did feel that Bobby dying was her fault.

Momma wiped her dishwater hands on her apron and reached for Ann Fay. She took my sister's head in her hands and looked into her eyes. "Listen to me. It was my job to take care of you and your little brother. I couldn't stop you from getting polio, and you didn't make Bobby have it worse just because you made him work in the garden. So let go of that guilt."

She pulled her into a hug then. Ann Fay closed her eyes and I could see her soaking up Momma's comfort. It seemed like whenever Momma held her she became a little girl again. But I also knew she always wished it was Daddy—holding her the way he used to. They were so close before the war.

Daddy still loved Ann Fay. We all knew that. But he stayed to himself more. Even with Jackie he went back and forth between keeping his distance and not letting him out of his sight.

"Is there an epidemic?" I asked. I reached for the newspaper on the kitchen table. But it had the usual headlines about North Korea and the presidential campaign. And a story about the Rosenberg spies giving our atomic bomb secrets to the Russians. Nothing on the front page about polio.

"There's epidemics all over the country," said Ann Fay. "But not here. And we're going to do our part to keep it that way. So don't you and Ellie be drinking from water fountains, either."

"Yes, ma'am," I said.

We drank out of water fountains all the time at Fred T. Foard, and I never thought twice about it. But that fountain was the first thing that caught my eye the next morning when Vivian and I were on our way to homeroom. Buster was there, putting his finger over the spout and aiming it at whoever he could. Ellie and Laura were so busy practicing Latin that they didn't notice. When Buster caught sight of them he directed the water right at Laura.

"Laura!" Vivian tried to warn her but it was too late. She squealed and whirled around.

Ellie dropped her books and threw her arms around Laura. "Buster Poovey," she screamed. "You won't get by with this." But Buster was gone, running into the boys' bathroom and laughing like a stupid little sixth grader.

"Laura, are you all right?" I asked.

Laura wiped at her face with the back of her hand. "He hit me right in the eye." Water dripped off her nose, and the lashes of one eye were plastered to her skin. She blinked, trying to open her eyelid.

Ellie pulled out a handkerchief and dabbed at Laura's wet face. "We're going to the principal's office," she said. "I hope Mr. Lynn expels him. Thugs like that shouldn't even be in school."

She started picking up her books, but Duncan Riley was there and had most of them stacked already. "I'll carry them for you," he said.

Reggie was right beside him, threatening to get revenge for Laura. "Give me ten minutes alone with that goon," he said, "and I swear I'll splatter his face with something besides water. Laura, are you okay?"

But Laura waved Reggie off. "I'm fine," she said. "Ellie, let's just go to homeroom."

"Are you kidding me?" Ellie reached for her books and took them right out of Duncan's hands. "Thanks, Duncan. We're okay now. Just gotta talk to Mr. Lynn. That's all." She grabbed Laura's elbow and dragged her off toward the principal's office.

As usual, Arnie was in homeroom ahead of me. He had his head on his desk, but he opened one eye. "Is it morning yet?" he asked. He opened the other eye and grinned. "Where's the rest of your gang?"

"In the principal's office."

Arnie sat up. "Don't tell me Ellie got herself in trouble."

"She's tattling on Buster. He squirted Laura at the water fountain."

Arnie rolled his eyes. "Ellie should let that go."

"Ha! You don't know Ellie. She loves fighting other people's battles."

Ellie and Laura never did make it to homeroom. It wasn't until Arnie and I passed that water fountain on the way to my home ec class that I remembered Ann Fay's warning about polio. I didn't actually think our fountain had polio germs. Still, it did worry me a little.

21

IDA
October 1952

Buster had taken to glaring at me and muttering stuff like "commie lover" and "traitor" under his breath whenever he walked by. I could have told him I wasn't the twin who tattled on him, but instead I avoided him as much as possible. Ellie did too.

In homeroom she'd study with Laura and in the middle of that she'd switch gears to talking race car drivers with Arnie. Or dairy farming. Not that she was interested in cows. But Arnie claimed they had personalities. And his father's cows all had names too. "How are your cows doing?" she'd ask. "Are they in a good mood today? When are you going to name one after me?"

I usually studied or worked on art. And I almost always kept my mouth shut. Lately I felt more and more like a turtle around Ellie—like I had to pull my head in and not be noticed or she'd send me looks. Letting me know that she claimed Arnie for herself.

I knew that. I'd known it since the night she first met him. In fact, it was clear as glass before they even drove away. He'd invited me to go along, and as much as I didn't like racing, part of me had wanted to. But I could feel Ellie giving me a hard stare. She'd fallen for his good looks and charm the minute she caught sight of him.

Maybe I had too, because for some reason I was crazy enough to imagine that he had actually wanted me to go. But why would he, when fun-loving Ellie was around?

One morning on the way to first period Arnie said, "You're always drawing. Do you ever stop?"

I shrugged. "It helps me think."

"Drawing helps you think?"

"Yeah, you know. Sort things out. Some people write in diaries. I draw instead."

"Do you ever let people look through your book?"

"Uh. If they want to."

"I want to."

"You do? Oh, well, here it is." I pulled the sketchbook from inside my binder and handed it to Arnie. He stopped and leaned against the wall, nearly dropping his books, trying to juggle everything.

"Here," I said. "Let me hold those."

I felt shaky inside. I knew my art was good, but still, sharing it always made me feel like someone was staring into my eyes. Searching me. What if they didn't like what they saw?

Someone stopped just behind me. I turned and there was Buster, not three feet away. Patsy was with him. "Are you the rat that squealed on me?" he asked.

I shook my head.

"I think this is Ida," said Patsy. "Come on, Buster. Leave her alone."

"See ya later, pal," said Arnie.

Buster walked away with Patsy. Arnie watched until they disappeared down the steps and then he opened my sketchbook. He gasped a little at almost every drawing. I knew he was impressed, and the admiration in his eyes sent a warm flush over me. Every so often he'd glance up and look me in the eye, like he was trying to see more than the picture was telling him.

Something in there tickled his funny bone. "What?" I said. "Why are you laughing?"

He turned the sketchbook so I could see the picture of Ellie sewing that dress for Ann Fay's new job—chewing her lip and staring at the seam she was working on. "She looks so determined," said Arnie. "Like she's driving a race car and she plans on winning. You're good, Ida."

"Thanks. Do you draw?"

"Yeah," he said. "I draw water from the well behind our house." He laughed. "And I draw attention to myself when I fall asleep in class. Does that count?" The bell rang then, and he glanced up the hall. "Uh-oh, Mr. Lynn is watching." He closed the sketchbook and called out, "We're sorry, Mr. Lynn. We lost track of time." He lowered his voice. "Better move fast. But don't run."

As we hurried down the hall he handed my sketchbook back. "Do you ever draw cows?" he asked.

"Cows?" I laughed.

He nodded and his eyes brightened. "I like cows. You should draw cows."

I hurried through the door to home economics class. Mrs. Curtis was calling the roll. "Ida," she said. "I'm afraid I already marked you absent."

"I'm sorry," I said. "I got tied up. It won't happen again."

I slipped into the chair by Vivian, and when I did I heard Stella at the next table. "Tied up, huh? With Arnie Ledford. I wonder what her sister will say about that."

My sister? You better not say a word to Ellie.

Mrs. Curtis gave us a pop quiz on table manners. After I answered questions about which direction to pass the food and how to cut meat and the proper way to spoon the last bit of soup from a bowl, I turned in my paper and began drawing—doodling the way I always did.

I thought about Arnie's question. No, I never drew cows. But I could try. I worked from memory—drawing the head shape, trying to remember exactly where the horns should be in relation to the ears.

Patsy walked past, returning her test paper to Mrs. Curtis. On her way back she slowed down. "Look," she said. "It's a cow. Are you one of those Future Farmers of America? Isn't that an all-boys club?" I stopped shading and waited for her to pass. "Sorry," she said. "Didn't mean to bother you."

Vivian was reading a book, but she hadn't missed Patsy's interruption. She scribbled something in her notebook and slid it into my view.

Somebody wants to start trouble. And by the way, do you have a crush on my cousin, too?

I shook my head and pushed back the warmth I'd felt when he admired my art, the feeling that he admired *me* too. I wrote in her notebook, *Are you kidding? Ellie would kill me.*

22

ELLIE
October 1952

Stella tapped my tray with her fork. "Ellie," she said. "I'm talking to you, Ellie."

"Oh. Sorry." I pulled my eyes away from Arnie. "What did you want?"

"I see you staring at Arnie Ledford over there. Do you and Ida always fall for the same boys? Is that part of being twins?"

"What do you mean?"

"Ida was late to home ec class today. And from the look of things, Arnie was going to be even later to his class. If you ask me, she was downright dreamy when she came into the room."

Stella might as well have stabbed her fork into my chest. Was she *trying* to hurt me? Was Ida actually hiding something from me? How could she?

"And when did Ida start drawing cows?" Patsy asked. "Does that have anything to do with Arnie?"

Cows? She better not be drawing cows. At least not because of Arnie Ledford.

"Ida draws everything," I said, trying to sound casual. "Look at her over there." I pointed to the table where Ida was sitting. "You think she's listening to her friends. But she's probably drawing them in her mind, figuring out how to capture Vivian's dimples. Or maybe the pimples on somebody's nose."

But how did I know she wasn't drawing cows in her mind? She could be sketching Arnie himself. Maybe that's why she was so quiet in homeroom every morning. While the rest of us talked she was probably memorizing the tilt of his head and the shape of his mouth.

Truth be told, when it came to Ida and Arnie walking to class each day, I was green as the peas on my tray. Sometimes, after they were gone, I'd watch them from the doorway, hoping to convince myself they weren't enjoying it too much. But what could I do? I was the one who'd signed up for Latin, which I just had to take if I wanted to go to college. I was the one who messed up our schedule.

At Mountain View we'd been in the same classes for eight years, and now that we weren't, I had a feeling she liked it that way. Ida didn't need me so much anymore. Maybe she didn't even want me around.

Stella and Patsy finished their dessert. "Gotta go," said Stella. "Reggie's out there walking the halls. It's still ten minutes to class time and I want to accidentally on purpose bump into him."

Laura waved goodbye as they left. "If you ask me," she said, "Stella is stirring up trouble. Why do you even want to sit with her? And Patsy—she's just there to prop Stella up."

"I know you don't like them," I said. "But think about it. If Ida is after my man, shouldn't I be told?"

"But what if she isn't?" said Laura. "Ida almost never talks to Arnie unless we're all talking to each other. And then she mostly listens. Can't they be friends? You want your twin to get along with your boyfriend, don't you?"

Boyfriend. I liked the sound of that. But sadly, I knew it wasn't true. When he joked around about his cows or bragged on Gwyn Staley winning at the racetrack, I imagined he was flirting with me. But he was friendly with everybody, and as far as I could tell, everybody liked him. It would be hard not to like Arnie Ledford.

"I just need to go to the races again," I told Laura. "Can you believe I haven't been since school started? They got rained out for three weeks in a row, and besides that I don't think Junior likes taking me unless I can drag Ann Fay along. But I'm going this weekend—you watch me. Why don't you come too? Think your father would drive us there?"

23

ELLIE
October 1952

Laura's father dropped us off at the speedway. "Thank you for the ride, Mr. Quincy," I said. "Are you sure you don't want to stay? Racing is loads of fun. I bet you never saw anything like it in Massachusetts."

"Young lady, you're right," said Mr. Quincy. "Massachusetts does have NASCAR, but I personally have never attended. I prefer golf." He looked at Laura. "I'll be back for you two at ten o'clock."

Laura and I watched him drive away, steering his shiny gray car carefully around the muddy spots. Then we headed for the ticket booth.

It had rained earlier, and the soles of Laura's saddle oxfords were caking with red mud already. Her blue jeans looked brand-new, and the blouse and sweater she was wearing would be church clothes for me. "Didn't I tell you to wear old clothes?" I said.

She shrugged. "These *are* old. And you didn't tell me to wear mud boots."

We bought our tickets and went inside. As usual there was a crowd. "Look," I said. "There's Junior and my big sister. Even Ann Fay's friend Peggy Sue is here. I sure didn't expect to see her at the races."

"Want to sit with them?" asked Laura.

"Are you kidding? I want to sit with Arnie Ledford, but where is he? Oh, there he is. Near the top bleacher. Beside the man in the straw hat. That's his father."

"Uh, no," said Laura. "I'm not sitting up there."

"Why not? His father won't bother us. I'll be surprised if he says one word the whole evening." I waved to Arnie, but he didn't see me.

Laura tugged at my elbow. "Look who's right behind him."

I squinted. "What's Buster Poovey doing here?" I muttered.

"Let's go sit with your family."

Now I was really mad at Buster. He'd just ruined my chances of sitting with Arnie.

We found seats with Ann Fay and the others. "Hey, y'all. Got room for two more? This is my friend, Laura."

I introduced the others. As always, Peggy Sue looked like she'd just stepped out of a magazine. If you asked me, she and Laura were two of a kind. Pretty and perfect without being prissy.

"Peggy Sue, what are you doing here?" I asked.

"You know me," said Peggy Sue. "I heard there'd be some big names at the races tonight."

The truth was, Peggy Sue had probably tagged along because Ann Fay didn't want to give Junior any ideas about this being an actual date.

It was getting noisy and Laura was rolling her eyes at me. "You promised this would be fun! Where's the famous Ned Jarrett?"

"Watch for No. 99. He's not exactly famous yet. But he will be."

"There's some stars here tonight for sure," said Junior. "Fonty Flock, for one. And Fireball Roberts. We'll see how those famous boys handle our short track. This speedway is a tough one."

The first heat started and Laura grabbed my hand. "Heaven help! Do you actually *like* this?"

"It's fun! Pick a driver and pull for him. No. 99 isn't in this heat, but you can cheer for him in the next one."

I honestly didn't think Laura was going to relax and enjoy the race, but she did. Every time the cars came along the straightaway in front of us they'd sling mud out to the sides, and the people down front would turn away and squeal because they were getting splattered. Laura would jerk away too and squeal along with the rest. In no time she was laughing and having herself a ball.

But right in the middle of the second heat, when we were on our feet screaming for Ned Jarrett to show the others how to drive, I heard a voice pushing its way between us. "So, how's the Yankee enjoying the race?

Bet you don't have good times like this where you come from, do ya? Mind if I join you?"

Buster. Right there behind us. Just like that, I forgot about the races and turned to face him. "Go away!" I hollered. "Get out of here."

But Buster wasn't planning to go anywhere. He stood there with his arms folded across his chest. "I bought my ticket same as you did," he yelled. "So I'll sit wherever I want. It's a free country—at least until the commies take over." He jerked his head toward Laura.

She stood there facing him, glaring through squinty eyes.

"Laura," I said, "go sit next to Junior. He won't let Buster bother you."

Laura shook her head and waited for the cars to pass us and move on around to the other side of the track. "Are you kidding? I heard this is a free country, so I'll sit here if I please." She tossed her head and turned away. The cars came roaring past the bleachers again, and she went right back to yelling for No. 99.

I cheered too, but this time I was hollering for Laura. "Woo-hoo, Laura!" I gave Buster the evil eye and saw Arnie squeezing into his row.

"Move over, Buster," he said. And when the crowd sat back down Arnie Ledford was right there behind us.

I wanted to cut up and have a good time with Arnie, but that was impossible with Buster back there. I kept my eyes on the race.

No. 99's radiator boiled over and Ned had to go to the pits for water. A car spun out and another one rammed into it. Gas spilled all over the track and the race had to stop while it burned off.

Buster hollered about everything so loud I knew he was just trying to intimidate Laura. But she yelled too and yee-hawed like she was born for dirt track racing. Maybe she was having a good time, but more than anything I think she was showing Buster Poovey that he wasn't going to get her goat.

He did, though. Because after the race, while we were picking our way through the muddy parking lot, a pickup truck went by, and instead of avoiding the ruts and potholes like everyone else did, it zoomed past and splashed mud all over us. We both screamed and jumped back, nearly knocking each other down. I never did see the people in that truck, but I heard Buster's voice: "Now go back where you came from, you filthy commie."

24

IDA
October 1952

On Monday morning while Ellie ate breakfast she fretted over her Latin test.

"Don't worry," I said. "Even *I* could pass your test. You were quoting Latin in your sleep. '*Illis quos amo deserviam*. For those I love I will sacrifice.' What else do you want to know?"

Ann Fay dropped sandwiches and a yellow apple into Daddy's lunch pail. She did the same for her and Momma.

I heard a little toot. That was Junior letting Ann Fay know he was there to pick her up. "Oh, gotta go. Junior's here," she said. "See ya, Momma. Bye, Daddy." Ann Fay grabbed her lunch and half ran toward the front door, steadying herself as she went—grabbing hold of the stove, then the cabinet and a chair on her way to the living room.

"Slow down, girl," said Daddy. "That boy'll wait for you."

"I know, Daddy. But he's doing me a favor. I don't want to aggravate him."

Just then I heard a squeal and a crash and a thud. "Ann Fay!" yelled Daddy.

Every last one of us ran to the living room. "What happened?" asked Momma.

Ann Fay was sprawled across the living room floor and Jackie was too, half underneath her. Daddy helped Ann Fay to her feet and she leaned against him. "Are you okay, girl? I told you to slow down."

"Jackie tripped me."

"Did not. You ran overtop of me." Jackie's voice sounded mushy, and he had blood streaming from his mouth.

When Daddy saw blood, just that quick he dropped Ann Fay onto the couch and fell to his knees beside Jackie. "Myrtle, come! Jackie's hurt."

"I'm here." Momma reached for Jackie.

"Don't move him," said Daddy.

I kept glancing from my brother to Ann Fay, not sure who I should be worried about. "Did you get hurt, Ann Fay?"

But Ann Fay wasn't thinking about herself. She was watching Daddy hang on to Jackie as if his life depended on it.

Momma tried to look in Jackie's mouth, but he was squalling and gurgling blood.

"He's hurt, Myrtle. Don't force his mouth open." Daddy's voice sounded wobbly and high pitched. Scared. I could tell he was seeing more than what was right in front of him. He was seeing something from the battle-field again.

Jackie started gagging and spitting out blood. "Ellie, grab a washrag," said Momma. She had her hand under Jackie's chin, catching blood and drool.

"I'll get it," I said. Anything to get out of that room—away from Daddy. Who knew what he'd do next? But Ellie was closer to the kitchen, and she ran for the rag before I could start. I reached for Ann Fay's hand and hung on.

Momma grabbed the wet cloth and shoved it under Jackie's chin. She turned his head sideways, and out came more drool. And a tooth.

"A tooth! Leroy, he lost his first baby tooth!" Momma started laughing, and I let out a long breath. Everything would be okay.

But Daddy didn't laugh. He just sat there staring. Hanging on to Jackie. "I'm sorry, Jackie. I'm sorry," he said. "It's all my fault."

"He just lost a tooth," said Momma. "It'll stop bleeding in a few minutes. This is good. Jackie, you're growing up!"

Jackie giggled. But a sob slipped out too. He wiped at his tears with the back of his hand.

"I'll stay home with him," said Daddy.

"Leroy, no! He needs to go to school. And you have to work." Now Momma was agitated. She hoisted her-self to her feet. "Get up, Leroy."

Daddy shook his head and pulled Jackie onto his lap. "He's hurting."

"Let me take him to Momma." That was Junior. I never even heard the door open, but he was right there beside me, hovering over Ann Fay. "My mother can watch him today."

But why did anybody need to watch him? His tooth was out. Everything would be fine.

"Hey!" Ellie fussed. "*I* never stayed home from school when I lost *my* teeth."

"I'll stay with him," said Daddy, his voice still wobbly. "I need to keep an eye on my boy."

"Leroy," said Junior, making his voice real deep so Daddy would know he was taking charge. "Your family's counting on you. Momma'll treat your boy real good. You know that."

Now Daddy was hugging Jackie up against his chest as if letting go of him just then was the hardest thing in the world. But Jackie wiped at his tears and said, "I wanna go to Junior's house. Bessie makes bread pudding. And sometimes Ned Jarrett comes by."

"That's right, little buddy," said Junior. He sat on the sofa beside Ann Fay. "What about you?" he asked, his voice getting real soft. "I was watching through the window and I saw you go down. I thought sure you'd be hurt. Look. You got a scrape." He ran a finger over her arm. Sure enough, she had a brush burn just above her wrist.

That was Junior, always worrying about Ann Fay. "I'm fine," she said. "It didn't even break the skin." And *that* was Ann Fay, always acting tough. But I noticed she teared up when Junior asked how she was doing. Maybe she was tired of being tough. I knew one thing— if she'd just give in to him, Junior would spend his life protecting her.

Daddy followed Momma and Jackie out to the kitchen sink, hovering over them like an army helicopter. I followed after them on my way to the bathroom to brush my teeth.

It was a relief to be outside. Sometimes, especially in freezing cold weather, I wished our bathroom was in the house instead of being added on to the back porch. But mostly I was glad for the freedom I felt when I stepped out there. I stood on the porch and shivered. It was chilly, but the shiver was from something else. Daddy. Some days, sure, a bump on your head could seem bigger than Bakers Mountain, but why get this upset about a tooth?

Had the sight of blood brought back all his war memories?

Junior insisted on driving us to the bus stop, and he waited while Daddy half carried Jackie like he was rescuing a wounded soldier off of the battlefield. "Junior, you go on so these girls get to the bus stop on time. Myrtle and I will drop him off at your momma's."

Junior shook his head. "Leroy, really, I don't mind taking him."

"Go on," said Daddy.

So Junior backed out the driveway and headed up the road. "Your daddy is behaving real strange," he said. "You'd think by now he'd be used to children losing their teeth."

"It's been a long time since the twins were that age," said Ann Fay. "And you know how Daddy is with Jackie. He's going to make sure nothing happens to his only little boy."

"But Lordy, Ann Fay. You fell too. Are you sure you're not hurt?"

"Really, Junior. Quit worrying. I told you I'm fine." Ann Fay was doing her best to sound annoyed—letting Junior know he was about to smother her.

While we waited for the bus Ellie paced back and forth, conjugating Latin verbs.

I stared at the field across the road. The barbed-wire fence. The cows grazing. I wanted to draw that peaceful scene. To focus on weeds and twists in the wire instead of the mess at home.

Ellie shook my arm.

"What?" I said.

"What are you thinking about? Cows?"

"What do you think I'm thinking about? Daddy just went crazy over Jackie losing a tooth. There's something wrong with that, Ellie."

"Of course there's something wrong with it. But does he want to face it? No. Why do you think he canceled that trip last summer? And the whole family except me seemed to think going to Rock City, Tennessee, was a perfectly good substitute. Evidently no one else in the family can face it either." Ellie was pacing faster now, her voice going up like someone was turning the volume knob on Daddy's radio.

"What if every last one of us had stood up to him then? But no. We were afraid he'd go off like a bomb. Well, guess what, Ida. One of these days he will. And it won't be the worst thing in the world. In fact, it might be just exactly what this family needs."

25

IDA
October 1952

Ellie scared the living daylights out of me, the way she talked about Daddy exploding. Almost like she wanted him to. The races and Arnie and school had helped her not to stew so much over that trip. But deep down inside, she was still mad. Sometimes it felt to me like she might explode too.

She went to school looking for a fight. Usually she avoided Buster Poovey. But today she went right up to his locker and just stood there and stared. He pulled back and squinted at her. "What do *you* want?"

Ellie put her hand up against his locker door and banged it shut. "Who do you think you are, slinging mud on Laura and me at the races on Saturday night?"

Buster smirked. "Wasn't me. I don't even drive."

"Yeah. I know. Somebody else was driving. Was that your ignorant daddy? Because if you want to get family involved, I can have my daddy meet yours and they can fight it out. Just so you know—my father came home

153

from the war with some anger that spills out every once in a while. So I know who would win."

"Shut up!" Buster flung his locker door open so hard that it nearly hit Ellie in the face.

Ellie jerked back. "You're asking for it, Buster."

I grabbed her elbow and pulled her back to her locker. "Be quiet, Ellie. You're gonna get yourself in trouble. And you can't win with the likes of him anyway. Come on."

Ellie followed me into homeroom, but she didn't stay quiet. She filled Arnie and Laura in on everything that had just happened, including the fact that she threatened to send Daddy to fight his father. "Our daddy's got war in his head," she said. "So Buster Poovey better watch himself."

"Oh, Ellie," I said. "Daddy's not a fighter and you know it."

"Buster's father won't be fighting anybody," said Arnie. "He's dead."

"Huh?" said Ellie.

"He was killed in the war. His body is over there somewhere. In Europe."

Ellie was on the edge of her seat, her hand clenched around a pencil like it was a weapon. But now she sagged back into her desk. She rolled the pencil into its groove. "Why didn't you tell me?"

Arnie shrugged. "I guess it never came up. Sorry."

"Maybe that explains why he's always looking for a fight," said Laura. "We should just ignore him. Not fight back."

For once Ellie didn't have anything to say. She opened her Latin book, and I could tell she was trying to forget about that scene with Buster. At least our daddy came back alive. We were lucky, whether we felt like it or not.

I pulled my pencil from behind my ear and started drawing on my desk. I wasn't thinking about what I was doing until Arnie reached over and took the pencil out of my hand. "People get in trouble for things like that," he said. He pulled the extra eraser off the top of my pencil and handed it to me. I erased the design. It was nothing in particular. Just a series of circles in different sizes.

Later, on the way down the hall, my mind was on Buster's father being dead and on mine being unpredictable.

"I'm sorry," said Arnie. "About your father. I didn't realize." When he put his hand on my arm I felt wobbly inside. I tried to steady myself because the last thing I needed was to go crying into home ec class.

Some boy zoomed past, bumping into me. "Hey!" yelled Arnie. "Where do you think you're going—to the races?" But the fellow, whoever he was, just kept running, dodging groups of girls chattering at their lockers and a couple whispering to each other at the corner by the library.

"If you want to talk about it," said Arnie. "I've got big ears."

That made me laugh. And for some reason it made me want to talk to him. "Some mornings just go wrong from the minute you wake up," I told him.

"Yeah," he said.

"Daddy is just unpredictable. Sometimes he's himself —the way he was before the war. But sometimes he just flies off the handle. This morning he was scared. And there was no reason to be."

We turned the corner and passed the principal's office. Arnie stopped me just before we came to the home ec room. I leaned with my back to the wall and he stood in front of me with one hand against the wall by my head. Almost like he was creating a shelter—his arm blocking my face so others couldn't stare at me. I wanted to hang on to this moment in the shelter of Arnie's arm because for now I felt less frightened by Daddy's outburst. "Things just set him off," I said.

"What do you mean? Set him off?"

"He goes crazy over things that normal people would think is nothing. When my brother lost a tooth this morning, Daddy saw blood and the way he hollered you'd have thought Jackie was dying. Jackie is six years old. He's *supposed* to lose teeth. But Daddy kept him home from school."

Arnie's brown eyes squinted slightly—like he was listening hard. Like he cared. He leaned in and I let my head fall against his shoulder. I felt his chin on my hair—his hand patting my back. I wanted to stay in that space he'd made for me. But the bell rang.

There was no time for crying. No time for talking. That walk between homeroom and home ec—it was always too short.

26

ELLIE
October 1952

"I think I did okay on the Latin test," said Laura. "What about you?" She looked in the bathroom mirror and straightened her collar, which, as far as I could see, was perfectly straight already.

"My mind was on Buster. And Daddy."

"Oh, Ellie. I bet you made an A. You always do. But I'm sorry about your father."

"What?" That was Stella coming into the girls' room. "Did something happen to your father? Because Ida was practically in tears when she came into home ec this morning. Arnie tried to comfort her, but the bell rang so he couldn't just stand there and hug her all day." Stella pulled out her lipstick and put it on. She pressed her lips together and offered it to me. "Want some? This color would look great on you. It's Stormy Pink."

I felt stormy pink already—angry with Daddy for not being himself. Mad at that stupid war that killed Buster's father and at me for saying what I did. And now a hot rush of jealousy flooded me. Was Arnie actually hugging my sister for all the school to see? Or had Stella exaggerated?

"Everything's fine," I told Stella. "Just hunky-dory. Let's go, Laura—I've got an apple in my locker, and if I don't fetch it now, break will be over before I have my first bite."

It felt powerful to walk off and leave Stella standing there, wondering. But another part of me wanted to grab her by the shoulders and drag more information out of her. "What did Stella mean?" I asked Laura. "Do you think Arnie was actually hugging my sister?"

"He was probably just trying to cheer her up," Laura said. "You know she was upset."

Arnie and his pals were just ahead—outside a classroom door. He stood there with his fingertips in his jeans pockets, laughing about something. I caught his eye, and he nodded in a quiet way that reminded me of his father. As I went by I caught a whiff of his cologne, and it almost stopped me dead in my tracks. But I kept going. "Maybe he's falling for her," I said.

"Maybe," said Laura. "Or maybe Stella is making things up."

I doubted that. Laura didn't trust Stella and I had my doubts too, but I needed Stella to keep me informed. The way I figured it, there was some truth to the story.

History class was like every other day as far as Arnie and my sister were concerned. She doodled in her notebook, and he put his head on his desk for a snooze until

Mr. Van Horn called the class to order. As usual, Mr. Van Horn managed to go from the lesson in our book to current events. He held up a newspaper. "The Rosenbergs," he said. "There's been a new development in the case. Who knows what I'm talking about?"

Laura raised her hand. "Julius and Ethel Rosenberg lost their appeal for a stay of execution. If you ask me, that's terrible."

"But they gave atomic secrets to the Russians," said Mr. Van Horn. "That's terrible too."

"Right," said Buster. "Which means millions of us could die because of what they did. I say give 'em the electric chair. The sooner the better."

I knew I was supposed to feel sorry for Buster because of his father. But why did he have to be so mean? I raised my hand. "Weren't there other spies involved? Why aren't they executing them?"

Laura raised her hand. "The other spies testified against the Rosenbergs to save their own necks."

"What do you care?" asked Buster. "Oh, that's right. You're a commie just like them."

"I care because the Rosenbergs have children," said Laura. "Two young boys are about to lose both parents. Losing one is bad enough. Don't you think so, Buster?"

Well, that shut him up, which meant we could actually have a discussion. Some people in the class thought it was right to execute the Rosenbergs so other spies and communists in America would know they couldn't get by with anything.

And others said if you were going to kill one spy you should kill them all. I kept my mouth shut for a change. The whole thing felt complicated to me. Why did life have to be full of so many hard things?

Later, when we came home from school, Daddy and Jackie were both at the house—outside, wearing their jackets and looking downright chilled. Jackie had built Hickory Speedway into the sandbox and was racing his little wooden cars around. Daddy sat on the steps whittling another one for him.

I sat beside Daddy and leaned my head against his arm. "So you didn't go to work after all."

"Nope." He didn't bother to explain, and I guessed I didn't have the fire in me to push him on it. I watched Jackie making his cars fly through the dirt.

Last summer seemed like so long ago—that night at the speedway when I met Arnie for the first time. I closed my eyes and remembered that feeling. The sky turning deep blue. The lights coming on. Exhaust and dust hanging in the air.

We could've had a good time last Saturday night. Maybe if I went again, without Laura this time, Buster would mind his own business. I could sit with Arnie and it would be like that first night.

While I sat there imagining this, the telephone rang. I jumped up and ran inside to answer. "Hello."

"Hey."

Oh, my stars. It was him—Arnie. I'd given him my number weeks ago, and he'd never called.

"Arnie!" I told myself to calm down. Act normal. Just like I was bumping into him in the hall at school. What if he was calling about the race on Saturday night?

But he wasn't saying much. Or maybe he'd said something and I'd missed it. "I thought you'd lost my number," I said.

"Uh, no. I've been carrying it in my wallet."

His wallet. So sweet. Like he'd been protecting it there. Maybe working up his courage to call.

"Think I could talk to Ida?"

Did he just ask to talk to Ida? Did he? Have mercy, I give him my number and he calls my twin? I think I gasped a little.

"She was upset today. But there wasn't much time for talking at school. Is she okay?"

Is Ida okay? Maybe. At least until I get my hands on her neck.

"She's fine," I said. "She's probably doing homework or drawing. I'm not sure where she is right now."

"Maybe you can look?"

Yeah. Maybe I can look. And maybe I just can't find her.

"I'll look," I said. "It was nice talking to you, Arnie." I could hear the bitter edge in my voice. I didn't want it to be there. Or maybe I did, but I didn't want him to actually hear it.

I went to the bedroom. There she was, sitting on the bed, drawing something. "What're you working on now?" I asked. "Cows?"

Ida looked up, squinting at me like she didn't know what I was talking about. But I was sure she knew exactly what I meant. And she'd probably figured out who called. The walls in our house didn't shut out much sound.

"The telephone is for you," I said.

"Who is it?"

"Who do you *think* it is?" I stood there, waiting for her to say his name. To admit that she was expecting his call.

She gave me a look. Like she was confused. Like she didn't have a clue that Arnie Ledford was on the phone, asking for her instead of me. When she left the room, I picked up her sketchpad and pencil. She'd been lettering. Practicing the alphabet in a fancy script. I wanted to take her pencil to the page and scribble all over it like a toddler getting my hands on a crayon for the first time. I wanted to poke the lead through the paper and ruin the drawings underneath.

I threw the sketchbook on the floor and tiptoed to the door to listen to Ida's conversation. "Vivian?" she said.

27

IDA
October 1952

"Uh, no. Not Vivian."

"Oh." It took me a few seconds to figure it out. This was Arnie. Calling me? "Arnie?"

"Yeah. We didn't get to talk much this morning. There's never enough time at school. Anyway, I wanted to see how you're doing."

"Um . . . okay, I guess." I talked as quietly as I could without whispering. "Daddy's here so I can't say much. I'm just staying out of his way."

"So it's still not a good time to talk?"

"There's not much privacy here." I wasn't just thinking about Daddy overhearing me. Ellie could be eavesdropping through the bedroom walls. How could I talk to Arnie about anything with her listening in?

"Maybe we can sit together at lunch sometime."

"Maybe," I said. But I was thinking, *No. We can't do that. Ellie would have my hide.* "I better go, Arnie. Thanks for calling."

I hung up the phone and stared at the dial. He must have gotten our number from Vivian. No wonder Ellie was mad when she said the phone was for me. Then again, what did she have to be mad about? Arnie could call me if he wanted to.

It didn't take her two minutes to come out of the bedroom. She'd probably heard the whole thing. "So I guess it's true," she said. "Stella wasn't lying to me, was she?"

"Stella? What did she say?"

"That Arnie was hugging you this morning. I guess you get real close when you walk to class together. You've been hiding something from me. Haven't you?"

"No," I said. But I could still feel the warmth of his shoulder when I leaned my head against it. I'd memorized the feel of his hand patting my back. Stella must have walked past us. What had she done? Rushed back to Ellie's Latin class to tattle? "It wasn't hugging, exactly," I told Ellie. "You know I was upset this morning."

"Yeah." Ellie's voice oozed with sarcasm. "I do know. Looks like one of us is bound to be upset. And right now, it's me." She turned and headed to the back door and I could see from the toss of her head and the set of her shoulders that she was fixing to start something.

She probably wanted me to hear what happened next, because she left the kitchen door wide open.

I watched her through the door, but I kept my distance just in case Daddy exploded like a hand grenade left over from the war. "Daddy," Ellie said. "I don't see why you stayed home from work. You were supposed to take Jackie to Bessie's."

Daddy barely nodded. And kept on whittling.

"Leave him be, Ellie," I said.

Ellie pushed in. "Bessie had other plans, I guess? Or maybe she didn't want Jackie?"

I stood there in the kitchen, shaking. It was chilly outside, and I really should've shut the door and kept myself snug and warm. But the shaking was mostly on the inside, and I hoped to stop Ellie from getting Daddy worked up.

Jackie maneuvered Ned Jarrett's car around the oval in the sandbox. "He's going through the slippery third turn," said Jackie. "But he made it. He's out ahead of Junior Johnson and Gwyn Staley. I bet he's going to win this race."

I would've thought that Jackie was too caught up with racing to hear what Ellie said. But apparently not.

"Daddy was worried," Jackie said. "He came home and got me."

"You went to work with Momma?" Ellie asked. "And then came home? Where's the car?"

Daddy started hacking at the wood he was whittling. If he wasn't careful he was going to ruin it or maybe cut off his finger.

"He *walked*," said Jackie.

I could hardly believe it. The mill was all the way in town. Still, I wished Ellie would leave Daddy alone. But no. She was mad at me and taking it out on him.

166

"You walked home from the mill?" she asked. "That's a far piece." I backed even further from the door.

"I had to check on Jackie."

"Shh . . ." I hissed, hoping Ellie could hear me. "Just leave him be."

But she was in high gear now. "Daddy, you should have known Jackie was okay."

"Stop it, Ellie," I said.

"He lost a *tooth*. That's all. It's perfectly normal."

That's when Daddy exploded. He dropped the wood and jumped to his feet. He raked his fingers through his hair with one hand and waved that knife with the other. "There was blood pouring out of his mouth," he hollered. "You think that's normal? How could I know there wasn't internal bleeding? How do *you* know that?" He waved that knife right in her face.

I screamed, "Ellie!"

She leaned away from him, but she stood her ground. Sometimes when I watched her I wondered if we really were identical. She should be pulling back right now, running into the house. Not picking a fight with him. How could she not be melting into a puddle of fear?

"He looks just fine, doesn't he?" said Daddy. Then his voice went up. Higher. Louder. "But you don't see what's going on inside. I have to keep a watch on him. I've lost one boy and I'm not losing this one." He stared down to the mimosa tree where our Bobby was buried.

Maybe Ellie finally realized she'd done enough damage. She turned and marched into the house and slammed the door. I watched from the kitchen window now. Daddy took that little wooden car he'd been whittling and threw it hard and fast up against the garden shed.

Jackie was watching Daddy, and the look on his face reminded me of that feeling I had years ago when Daddy grabbed me up like I was his enemy and shoved me into the wall. I reckon that as far as Jackie was concerned, seeing Daddy fling his beloved race car up against the wall was like being slapped in the face.

28

ELLIE
October 1952

According to Ida, who was watching through the window, Daddy stomped off into the woods. I figured he'd come back after a while and go to bed without eating. And then he'd lay out of work again tomorrow.

When Ann Fay came home, she knew right away something was wrong. "What's going on?" she asked. "Daddy's here, isn't he?"

"Yep," I said. I didn't offer an explanation, but Ida did.

"Ellie couldn't just let him be. She had to go fussing at him, and she drove him off into the woods."

"I did not drive him there. He went of his own accord."

"Oh, Ellie, you know good and well he was sitting on the back porch doing just fine until you had to cause a ruckus."

"No, Ida. You're the one causing the ruckus."

"Would you two hush?" said Ann Fay. "See if you can agree on something to fix for supper. I'll go fetch Daddy."

Momma brought Otis home with her, sat him down to the table, and put a plate with chocolate cake and a cup of milk in front of him. She fretted the whole time. "Why does he get like this, Otis? He does just fine for long periods and I think it's finally over. But then it comes back on him."

Otis shoveled a big bite of cake into his mouth. "Might never go away. It's like dreaming, only you're awake. You see things, and not what the people around you see. It's a bad picture show inside your head."

"What do *you* do, Otis?" asked Momma. "When it happens to you?"

Otis shrugged. "Having a junkyard comes in real handy. Those rusty cars out back of my house know all my war stories."

"You talk to the cars?"

"Some people think I'm loony, if you know what I mean."

I snickered and Momma threw me a scowly look. But she was half smiling too. Sometimes I did think Otis was loony, but he knew how to settle Daddy, and Momma liked that. Lately though I'd wondered if settling Daddy down was like covering a dirty sore with a bandage. If you asked me, it wasn't making him better.

"Take that old green Studebaker. I've tore that thing apart a dozen times and put it back together again. That's when the pictures go away. When I put it back together."

Otis saying that reminded me of Ida. Whenever things went haywire she started rearranging or cleaning. Bringing order out of the mess in her life.

But Ida was in the middle of a tangle now. Me and her and Arnie. And she sure couldn't make me go away.

I heard Junior Bledsoe's voice out back. "Let me see that snaggle-toothed smile of yours." I went out onto the porch and there was Junior, playing in the sandbox and teasing Jackie. "*I'm* Ned Jarrett," he said.

"Nuh-uh! You gotta be Junior Johnson on account of you're Junior. *I'm* Ned Jarrett."

"Oh, all right." Junior pretended to be aggravated. "I'll be Johnson, but that means I'm gonna whup your hind end."

"Nuh-uh! Gentlemen, start your engines." Jackie held his hand in the air and then he dropped a pretend flag.

Just like that, he and Junior started kicking up some dirt with those cars flying around that speedway. And of course Junior Johnson crashed into the wall and Ned Jarrett won the race.

"You're dead," said Jackie.

"Nuh-uh. I'm Junior Johnson and I'm used to crashes. Nothing kills me. I'm going inside now." Junior headed for the porch. "Hey, Ellie," he said.

"Junior, if you're going to the race tomorrow night, can I tag along?"

"Whoa," said Junior. "Don't you think you could say

hello before you start begging? Maybe I'm going to the races. And maybe you can go along."

Good. That meant I could go. Maybe, just maybe, Arnie would be there. The two of us could have a good time, and I'd leave Ida in my dust. If she thought I was going to sit back and watch her snatch Arnie away from me, she could think again.

I followed Junior inside. "Evening, everybody," he said. "I came to check if everything's all right. I heard Leroy came for Jackie about ten o'clock this morning."

"He was worthless at work," said Momma. "Mr. Rhinehart finally told him to take the day off. Want some cake?"

"Don't mind if I do." Junior sat to the table.

Momma cut him a slice. "Sometimes," she said, "I wish we'd named that child something else. But Leroy picked the name. And at that time I didn't know about the other Jackie."

"Who's the other Jackie?" asked Junior.

"Leroy named Jackie after his war buddy. The one who was killed. It seemed like he was finally ready to face that family, but then he canceled that trip last summer."

The trip. Daddy might be better by now if we'd gone to see those people. I'd missed my chance to see New England—to visit Yale and dream about a bigger life. How could I ever get that back? "We should have just taken that trip and got it over with," I said.

172

The back door opened then and Ann Fay came in with Daddy right behind her. Jackie too. Daddy stood just inside the door and stared from one to the other of us. He looked at Otis, and I think I saw relief go across his face. "Well," he said. "It looks like they brought the psychiatrist in. Otis, you going to fix me up?"

29

ELLIE
november 1952

Saturday's race was the last one of the season, so we went to the speedway early. It was just me, Junior, and Jackie. Junior was a little growly because Ann Fay was planning to go but changed her mind at the last minute and stayed home with Ida.

I imagined them lying across their beds having a heart-to-heart about Arnie. Just thinking about it made me feel left out. Ganged up on. Like I was the bad guy.

Cars were warming up when we arrived, gunning their engines and taking laps around the track. I shaded my eyes against the lights and peered around the stadium, but I didn't see Arnie.

"Looking for someone?" asked Junior.

I tried to sound casual. "My friend Arnie might be coming."

"James Ledford's boy. I guess he's your sweetheart?"

"Just a friend."

We stood by the fence and watched the warm-ups, but I also kept my eyes on the entrance and recognized the top of Arnie's head as he came up the ramp into the stadium. As usual, his father had brought him. "Jackie," I said. "Arnie's here."

Jackie took off to meet him.

"Nope, not your boyfriend," said Junior. "And you're not the least bit interested, are you?" He gave me a friendly jab with his elbow. "Kind of like I don't think twice about Ann Fay Honeycutt. Come on. We'll sit with them."

Junior plopped himself down by Mr. Ledford in the row ahead of us. I couldn't help but notice that Mr. Ledford was wearing his I LIKE IKE button on his jacket.

At least this time Jackie didn't have to squeeze between me and Arnie. I claimed one side of Arnie and he took the other. But of course Jackie hogged most of his attention. "Are you Ellie's sweetheart?" he asked.

"Jackie!" I said. "You hush!"

"Uh," said Arnie.

"Never mind him," I said. "*Somebody's* been putting ideas in his head. And it wasn't me." I noticed Junior just ahead of me, snickering. I gave his backside a little kick. "See what you did, Junior."

I guess Arnie decided to change the subject. "Ellie?"

I loved the sound of his voice saying my name like that. "Yeah?"

"How's your daddy doing?"

I looked into his brown eyes. They weren't flashing and fun-loving right now. They were serious. Caring. But was he really thinking about Ida?

"Daddy's been on edge. I'm sure the election coming up on Tuesday has him worried about nuclear war." I leaned over and whispered, "What about your father? Didn't he serve in the war too?"

Arnie shook his head. "No. Farm deferment. Someone had to keep the cows milked during the war. Stocking the grocery stores. Feeding the soldiers."

"I guess so. Arnie, I didn't know about Buster's daddy dying or I never would've said what I did." I looked around on the bleachers but didn't see Buster anywhere. "Is he here tonight?"

"Haven't seen him."

The race started, but honestly, compared to last week with all the mud flying, cars flipping, and fire on the track, this race wasn't nearly as exciting. Some driver I'd never heard of smashed into the bank, but other than that, nothing happened. Ned never came close to Junior Johnson and Gwyn Staley fighting for first place. So I pulled for Staley.

I still loved the look of Arnie jumping up to watch when things got exciting and cheering for all he was worth when Staley and Johnson almost crossed the finish line together. But Staley came in second.

After all that screaming and hoping and barely breathing at the end, I think I felt as sad as Arnie that Gwyn didn't win it.

"*Ladies and gentlemen,*" said the announcer. "*In points, Junior Johnson and Gwyn Staley are tied for the season. So the race next Sunday afternoon will determine the season champion. Join us in North Wilkesboro for the exciting finale of this racing season."*

North Wilkesboro. I'd never been there. "I've got to go," I said. "Junior, you'll take me, won't you?" But Junior was busy talking to Arnie's dad.

"Arnie," I said, "will you be going to the race?"

"Depends," said Arnie. "On what Dad decides to do. But he hates missing a race, so I have a feeling he'll want to go."

It was hard to believe James Ledford cared that much about racing. It seemed like he could sit all the way through a race and not change his expression. Right now he stared at his feet while Junior talked about the election coming up on Tuesday. Junior was a Democrat all the way to his bones. But Arnie's father shook his head and fingered that Eisenhower pin on his lapel.

"Is he always this quiet?" I whispered. "Doesn't he ever talk?"

"To the cows," said Arnie. "He complains to them plenty. Believe me, they know exactly who he's voting for. Not just for president but for Congress too."

I decided to be like him and not show Arnie what I was feeling. Which was scared. Afraid he'd say no to the question I was working up my nerve to ask.

"If you do go next Sunday, I don't suppose you'd let me tag along?" I tried to sound casual. To not let on that my heart was sputtering like an old jalopy. I just needed him to say yes. Because if there was one thing I knew, racing was something the two of us had in common. And Ida? There was no way she'd be at the racetrack next Sunday.

"If we decide to go," said Arnie, "I'll ask Dad if you can ride along."

30

IDA
November 1952

On election night Daddy roamed the house, turning the knob on the radio up and then down. Jackie marched through the living room singing a campaign jingle about everybody liking Ike.

"Be quiet!" said Daddy. "I don't wanna hear you singing that!"

Election results wouldn't be final until the wee hours of the morning, but the commentators seemed to think Ike would win.

Ellie went to bed singing "I Like Ike" even though I kept telling her to be quiet. "Would you quit? You do not need to be upsetting Daddy."

"It's just one of those songs," she said. "It gets in your head and it won't get out."

"Yeah," I said. "But you *do* like Ike and you're hoping he'll win, and the rest of us don't want to hear it."

The next morning, before I was out of bed, I heard Daddy talking to the radio. I went to the kitchen and General Eisenhower was on, making a victory speech about the weight of responsibilities that we'd placed on him.

"Yes," said Daddy. "And God help us if you don't get our boys out of that conflict."

Ann Fay sat at the table with him, patting his hand. "It'll be okay, Daddy," she said. "Eisenhower is going to visit Korea. Maybe he knows how to get us out of the war without dropping a bomb." She was trying to keep Daddy from going downhill, but the truth was we'd won the last war by bombing Japan. And now that we had that awful weapon it seemed like using it would be just too easy.

On the bus I thought about how lots of people were bound to be upset today. Losing always hurts. But this wasn't like Ned Jarrett losing a stock car race. The election was personal because real people were sending their sons off to Korea to a war they didn't think we could win. And everybody thought their candidate could fix things. Now we'd just have to wait and see.

In the hall at school, on top of all the talking and the slamming of locker doors, people were chanting. It moved down the hall in waves. "*I like Ike. I like Ike. I like Ike.*"

I shoved my history book into my locker and banged it shut. "Some people have no respect," I muttered. "Whatever happened to being a good sport?"

Arnie was in his seat and I could see the words on his lips too. He bobbed his head to the beat of it. But he stopped when he saw me come through the door.

Buster, who was almost always making a racket in the hall or sitting there in homeroom looking to trip somebody, did not seem to be around. At least I didn't have to listen to him being obnoxious.

Ellie ran to greet Arnie and for a minute I thought she was going to hug his neck. "Arnie, our man won. Woohoo! Are we celebrating by going to the big showdown between Staley and Johnson on Sunday? Please say yes. I've never ever been to North Wilkesboro."

It amazed me how she could just invite herself like that with no shame at all. I tried to push back the jealousy, but it wasn't staying where I put it.

Arnie shrugged. "Dad says he's going. So yeah, you can ride along." Did he glance at me when he said that? I thought so. Or maybe I imagined it.

"I can go? Did you hear that, Ida? Yippee! I'm going to the races. Laura, you should go too," she said. "We'd have us a grand time, rooting for Arnie's cousin."

Arnie reached over and tapped my desk with his pencil. "I know your father wanted Stevenson to win. How did he take the news?"

"Well, he didn't blow up, if that's what you mean," said Ellie. "But he's sure that Ike'll drop the atom bomb on North Korea."

Good grief, Ellie! Aren't you in the middle of a conversation with Laura? Arnie isn't even talking to you.

Later, when Ellie and Laura disappeared into their Latin class, I let out a deep breath.

"Good riddance?" said Arnie. "Is that what that means?" He laughed. Until he asked that question I didn't even realize I'd sighed.

"Sometimes it's hard," I said. "Being the quiet one. Having all that chatter around. Staying out of her way."

"But why do you have to stay out of her way? I asked *you* about your father, and she answered. Why do you let her talk over you like that?"

"Maybe it's just a habit. She's been there my whole life. I don't even know what it's like to be just me—without Ellie always competing for whatever I'm after. But we can't fight all the time, so sometimes I don't try. I just stay out of her way."

"I shouldn't have asked about your father with her there."

"There's no telling about Daddy," I said. "If Eisenhower gets us out of this war, maybe he'll be fine. But if he steps it up, things could be scary at our house."

Arnie put his arm across my shoulder and pulled me close for just a second. "Maybe you just need to get away from things at home. Why don't you come along to North Wilkesboro on Sunday?"

"Me?" I stopped and stared at him. "You want me to go to the races? Ellie's told you how much I hate them."

"I'll bring cotton to plug your ears. And ear muffs for overtop of that."

I declare, the way he pulled me aside and leaned against a locker looking down at me so sweet, he made me want to go. I almost agreed. But I couldn't do that to Ellie. I shook my head.

He pretended to be hurt. "Are the races that miserable?"

How was I going to tell him about Ellie? I stood there trying to figure that out. "If I went, Ellie . . ." I stopped. I couldn't make myself say that she had a crush on him and would be furious with me. That would seem like I thought he was asking me for a date. And what if he was just being nice?

"Hey," said Arnie. "I'm no dummy. I know Ellie likes me." He put his hand under my chin and tilted my head. Now I had to look him in those eyes that were brown as chocolate drops and made me feel all melty inside. "But you know what?" he said. "I like Ida."

Me? Arnie liked me? Really? Not Ellie? She was the fun twin who was easy to talk to. Other students passed by, but I barely heard them. There was just this sweetness tucked into a corner by a locker painted gray as a battleship. Had I just heard Arnie Ledford say he liked me?

"You do?" I asked.

Now someone went past singing that song so loudly I couldn't miss it: "I Like Ike."

Arnie took my arm then and we started walking toward the home ec room. He sang along with the others except he put my name in where Ike's should be. "*I like Ida.*"

I knew not everybody liked me. But apparently Arnie Ledford did. And that was all that mattered. I didn't even care that he was singing a little off-key.

31

ELLIE
november 1952

Laura and I left study hall and headed for history class. We passed Stella, talking to Reggie, who was leaning against the trophy case. He caught sight of us, and I saw how his eyes lit up when they landed on Laura.

Every once in a while he still tried to get her attention. But Laura never, ever gave him the time of day. Duncan flirted with me too, but he was that way with lots of girls. We rounded the corner, and then I heard Stella behind us.

"Ellie! Laura! Wait up!"

"Ugh," said Laura. "It's Stella."

We slowed down and Stella grabbed my elbow. "I'm having a pajama party," she said. "On Friday night. I hope the two of you will come." She looked at me. "Is it okay if I don't invite Ida? Because then I'd have to ask her friend Vivian too. And honestly, I just don't have the space. But we'll have a swell time, I promise. I've got a record player and a stack of records. We'll listen to Perry Como and Slim Willet and eat pizza pie. And gossip."

Music and pizza pie? It sounded great to me. I sure wouldn't mind seeing how Stella lived. I imagined her in a fine brick house with matching furniture. "It's really okay about not inviting Ida," I said. "She's not very social, you know." Truth was, Ida didn't like Stella, and the feeling was probably mutual. And Stella for sure did not like Vivian. She hadn't since Vivian insulted her on the first day of school.

"What about you, Laura? Will you be allowed to come?" asked Stella.

I knew the answer to that already. Even if Laura's parents said yes, she'd say no.

"Probably not," said Laura.

"Oh, too bad," said Stella although she didn't sound the least bit disappointed. "Ellie, we'll make arrangements later. See ya. Gotta go before Reggie disappears."

"Wonder why she invited you," I said. "She doesn't even like you."

"Because she knows I won't come," said Laura.

To be honest, I didn't know why Stella had invited me. It's not like we were actually friends. But I didn't much care. A pajama party sounded like fun.

We were almost to our lockers now. I could see Arnie there swapping books out. Mostly I saw the silhouette of him. His lean shape, his muscled shoulders, that perfect head, and those big ears.

How was I going to wait until Sunday afternoon when I'd have Arnie all to myself without Ida anywhere close?

He was a few feet away now. He'd closed his locker, and all I could see of him was his back. I walked up behind him just in time to hear my sister's voice. "I like you too, Arnie. I really do. But I can't go to the race on Sunday. I just can't hurt Ellie that way."

I stopped in my tracks. Apparently neither one of them realized I was nearby. "But Ida," said Arnie, "you're the one I like."

Laura grabbed my elbow and steered me around them. I saw my sister's face when I passed her—the color draining away from her cheeks. The guilt in her eyes. I heard her shocked little gasp.

She was so surprised? What did she think? That I was miles away? Couldn't they have figured out that I'd be coming by on my way to history?

I didn't hear much of Mr. Van Horn's explanation about the Electoral College votes. Eisenhower had won, but who cared anymore? Not me. It appeared that Ida had won too. Without even trying.

32

ELLIE
November 1952

I sat at the back of the bus so Ida couldn't sit behind me. I didn't want her staring at me and putting it all down in that sketchbook of hers. A portrait of defeat and betrayal. Only she was the betrayer.

I saw her come out of the school with Arnie close behind. He pulled up beside her and said something. Then they stopped in the middle of the parking lot like a couple of stalled cars while others had to go around them.

Arnie was sweet on Ida. And I was probably the last one to figure it out. I didn't want to go home today. I wished like crazy I could get on Laura's bus and ride along to her house in Blackburn. I needed to cry on her shoulder.

Ida stepped up onto the bus, glanced my way, and took a seat in the second row. On the way home, she mostly stared out the window at the shabby countryside. Dried corn stubble and leftover cotton plants waited for someone to plow them under. We passed old farmhouses that had never seen an actual coat of paint. Just like ours.

When the bus stopped by Mountain View School Ida slid over so Jackie could sit with her. Good. I couldn't handle it if he jabbered in *my* ear the whole way home. At the bus stop he took a shortcut through the field toward our house. But Ida waited for me, guilt all over her face. "I'm sorry," she said.

I walked past her. "Oh, sure you are."

I heard her hurrying to catch up with me. "I never intended for this to happen. I'll stay home on Sunday. You go to North Wilkesboro and have a good time." Her voice broke when she said it, and I could see she didn't want me to go any more than I wanted *her* to.

"You think I'm that selfish, don't you, Ida? That I could try to take your precious boyfriend away when it's obvious who he really likes. Well, I do have some decency, just in case you never noticed."

I kept walking. Fast. For a while she tried to keep up, and then I guess she got tired of chasing my anger. When I turned the corner that led to our driveway, I could see that Daddy's car was at home. At three fifteen in the afternoon.

"Something's wrong," I said. And we both took off running.

I was out of breath by the time we reached the driveway. I slowed to a walk and Ida did too. If something bad had happened maybe we didn't want to know about it after all.

Daddy and Momma were in the living room. He was slumped on the sofa with his eyes shut. Momma sat on a chair between the woodstove and the kitchen door with Jackie shaking her arm, asking questions. "What's wrong, Momma? Is Daddy sick?"

Momma just shook her head. "Hush, Jackie."

"What happened?" asked Ida.

"We're just sitting here until Ann Fay comes home," said Momma. "Then we're having a family meeting. Do your homework if you want. Or cook supper. But I'm sitting right here. And your daddy is too."

The way she said it, I knew not to ask any more questions. Daddy was in trouble—like a naughty schoolboy in the principal's office. I'd never heard of a woman principal, but from the look of things, Momma would've made a good one.

Ida tiptoed past me into our bedroom. She shut the door as if *that* would keep the bad feelings out. But it seemed like this day, which started out with Eisenhower winning the election, was going to end on a bad note all around.

I needed something to do, so I peeled potatoes and cut them into a pot of water. By the time Junior and Ann Fay pulled into the driveway I had potato soup ready to eat. "It'll have to wait," said Momma. "We're having a meeting first."

By now Daddy was sitting with his elbows on his knees, rubbing the sides of his head, his fingertips buried in black hair mixed with gray. Through the living room window I saw Ann Fay getting out of Junior's car.

She stopped in the doorway. "What's wrong?"

"Shut the door," said Momma. "It's cold in here."

Ann Fay dropped her pocketbook on the floor and hurried to the woodstove. She laid her hand on top of it. "Of course it's cold," she said. "The fire's out."

Momma motioned for Ann Fay to sit. "We need to talk."

"In a minute, Momma." Ann Fay yanked open the stove door and pulled kindling from the box in the corner. She stacked the wood strips into a little teepee shape and stuffed crumbled newspaper in there before lighting it with a match and blowing on the flame. I noticed Daddy watching her, and in spite of whatever else was going on his mind, I could see he was proud. He puckered his lips and blew right along with her.

Momma shivered and hugged herself. Was she just now noticing the room had turned cold? She tapped her foot impatiently while Ann Fay got that fire going and added wood.

Finally we were all sitting there looking sideways at each other and listening to the fire starting to crackle. Waiting for the chill to leave the room. And then Momma got down to business. "Your daddy lost his job today," she said.

Ann Fay jumped to her feet. "Daddy!" The way she said it—so judgmental—it sounded like a whole hellfire sermon delivered in one single word.

Daddy flinched and lowered his eyes. But he tried to defend himself. "Myrtle, that's not what happened." But he said it so low it was like he was talking to himself.

"Mr. Rhinehart gave you an ultimatum," said Momma. "And until you follow through on it, you're out of work."

Good for Mr. Rhinehart. Maybe he was like me. Fed up to high heaven and done with second chances and being patient.

"Come on, Momma," said Ann Fay. "If you're gonna call a meeting it can't be just the two of you knowing what's going on."

Momma looked at Daddy. He pulled out a cigarette and put it between his lips. He didn't light up because he knew Momma wouldn't want him smoking in the house. "Oh, go ahead and smoke it," she said. But he didn't.

"I got into an altercation at work today," said Daddy.

"What's that?" asked Jackie.

Thanks to Latin class, I knew what it was. But I didn't think Daddy even knew such a word. "A squabble," I told Jackie.

"No. It was more than an argument," said Momma. "It was a fistfight."

Really? Daddy got into a fight at the mill?

"What in high heaven?" said Ann Fay. "Daddy, you don't let us fight, and you're not a fighter either."

Daddy just sat there shaking his head like he was trying to rattle the answer out but couldn't jar it loose. "It was about the election," said Momma. "One of the stock boys was singing 'I Like Ike' and going on about how this country was going to turn around now that the Republicans were in office. Your daddy took issue with that. They got into a heated discussion, and next thing I knew they were slinging their fists."

"You weren't even there," said Daddy.

"I heard about it," said Momma. "You have publicly humiliated this family, Leroy. And I think Mr. Rhinehart was right to fire you."

"He didn't fire me."

"You're right," she said. She looked at us then. "Mr. Rhinehart told your daddy he can come back to work as long as he has proof he's seeing a doctor for whatever ails him. So the two of us are going to see Dr. Johnson first thing in the morning."

Dr. Johnson. He was the one who suggested Daddy take that trip to Connecticut last summer. I figured he'd offer the same advice all over again. And I knew one thing. I, Ellie May Honeycutt, was in a mood to drag Daddy all the way to New England. I couldn't wait to get out of this town.

33

ELLIE
November 1952

I grabbed Laura at her locker. "I dread this day. Talk to me in homeroom. Talk constantly because I do not want to make conversation with Arnie or Ida, either one."

"Me, talk constantly? That's you, Ellie. But we can practice Latin vocabulary."

"Sure. That would be good. But I probably won't remember a single word. I didn't sleep much last night. Ida and I have barely spoken since we got off the bus yesterday. And on top of this whole horrible mess with Arnie, Daddy's about to lose his job for getting into a fistfight at work yesterday. Over the election. Laura, that's just stupid."

"Holy moly. You've been through the wringer, haven't you?" Laura shoved her books into her locker and gave me a big hug. "Uh-oh. Don't look back. Arnie is coming. Let's go." She grabbed her books and we headed toward homeroom.

But Patsy came rushing through the hall and stopped right in front of us. She grabbed my arm. "Did you hear about Buster?"

"Buster? What about him?"

"He's got polio."

"Polio?" I couldn't have been more surprised if she told me he was elected president. "Are you sure?"

"Positive," said Patsy. "My mom works with his. Didn't you notice he was out of school the last few days?"

Well, of course I'd noticed. School was just easier without Buster there.

But now I find out he has polio?

Homeroom was buzzing with the news, and Mr. Lynn announced it on the P.A. system. "I regret to inform you that we have a case of polio in our school," he said. "Buster Poovey was diagnosed yesterday morning, and he's been taken to Charlotte Memorial. His doctor's office called me to recommend precautions."

He went on to explain what he meant by precautions—something about people who had close contact with Buster. That wasn't me except for that day at his locker. Surely I couldn't get polio from that. But what about Laura getting water squirted in her eye? What about Arnie? They rode the same school bus. I glanced at Arnie. He was more awake than usual and he didn't seem the least bit sick.

I just couldn't believe it. Polio? Here at Fred T. Foard, just when polio season should be winding down?

Focusing was hard. There was so much to think about besides my schoolwork—polio, Daddy going to the doctor, and of course Arnie. But I kept my chin up and tried to smile, pretending everything in the world was hunky-dory.

After history Arnie walked Ida to the bus, carrying her books. Obviously she'd decided to quit worrying about my feelings and just go ahead and be his girl.

We didn't speak two words to each other on the walk home from the bus stop. I opened my literature book and tried to read our short-story assignment. But I didn't feel like reading about someone else's conflicts. I had plenty of my own.

Ida was ahead of me, and I could tell from how she was dawdling that she'd rather be going the other direction—toward school and Arnie Ledford. Away from home. Away from me. I finally closed my literature book and passed her up.

I half expected Daddy to be home in bed, but no one was there when I arrived. I sat on the sofa and forced myself to study.

Ida tried to do homework too, but that didn't last long. She picked up the broom and started sweeping— looking for cobwebs in the corners and moving furniture even. "Do you think Momma has him out looking for another job?" she asked.

"I think she took him to Dr. Johnson and he told Daddy to make this trip. And this time I won't let him back out of it."

Junior brought Ann Fay home and he came inside with her. "Any word on your Daddy?" he asked.

"If he's not here," said Ann Fay, "then it probably means he's back at work already."

Turned out she was right. Momma and Daddy came home at their usual time. Evidently they only missed a half day of work by going to Dr. Johnson's office. Momma put a new bottle of pills on the shelf by the kitchen window.

"What is it?" asked Ann Fay.

"Something to calm his nerves," said Momma.

"Is that all Dr. Johnson did?" I asked. "Send him home with a bottle of pills? What did he say about that trip he recommended?"

"He still thinks Leroy should go," said Momma. She sighed. "Too bad we missed our chance."

"What makes you think we missed it?" I asked. "Connecticut is right where it always was. And there's still a train track running between here and there."

"Ellie, don't be a smart-aleck," said Momma. "Your daddy doesn't have a week of vacation coming up. None of us do. There's no way we could take a trip this time of year."

"Some of us could," I argued. "Thanksgiving is just around the corner, and I'll be out of school. I could go with Daddy then. I'll make sure he doesn't chicken out."

Momma frowned, but I could tell the idea was starting to sink in and maybe she even thought it was a good one. "Ann Fay could go," she said. "She knows how to manage your father. And she's more mature."

"No," I argued. "Ann Fay doesn't want to go to Connecticut."

"Who said so?" asked Ann Fay.

"Look. I'm the one who got my heart broke when he canceled the trip. The rest of you were perfectly content to see little old Rock City, including you, Ann Fay."

"Maybe Otis, then," said Momma.

"Otis? Doesn't he have to stay here and look after his mother? We don't need Otis. Why don't you trust me? I'll ask Daddy myself."

Daddy was just outside the door—sitting on the top step, cigarette glowing in one hand, coffee in the other. It was chilly and damp out, and I couldn't help but notice he was shivering. "You're freezing, Daddy," I said. "Why don't you come inside?"

"I'm thinking."

I went inside and grabbed a quilt from the chest behind his and Momma's bed. But the smell of their room stopped me. It was the faint smell of cigarettes, Momma's talcum powder, and Daddy's aftershave.

As much as I wanted to rush that blanket out to Daddy, I hated to leave their room. I stared at the bed and soaked up those odors, remembering mornings when Ida and I were little—younger than Jackie. We'd run in and pounce on Momma and Daddy's bed and they'd play a guessing game about which one of us was Ida and which one was Ellie. Daddy would try to confuse us so that even we wouldn't know. Mostly we giggled.

Before he went to war Daddy laughed a lot. Momma did too. None of us had figured how to get that back. Sure, things were better for a while. But the war in Korea and the nuclear arms race just seemed to bring it all back up.

We couldn't keep living like this. But we *could* take that trip Dr. Johnson recommended. Daddy needed it and I wanted it. And this time I intended to get it.

I took the quilt outside. "Here, Daddy," I said. I sat on the step beside him and pulled the blanket around us both. It wasn't like being four years old and giggling under the covers with him and Momma, and it wasn't exactly warm, but I looped my arm through his and leaned onto his shoulder. "Whatcha thinking?" I asked.

He dropped his cigarette butt on the stone step and ground out the glow with his foot without looking at it. I didn't know for sure what he was staring at, but the garden shed was straight ahead, and off to the side was the woodpile and chopping block. Maybe Daddy was thinking about how much work he had around here. About how much trouble we were to take care of. It seemed like some days he just wanted to forget about being responsible.

"Remember how we used to be?" I said. "Back before the war." I reached for his hand, and we sat there with our fingers locked together. "It was so peaceful here."

Daddy didn't say a word one way or another. But I heard him breathing, and that gave me courage to keep going. "I guess it was peaceful inside your head too, huh?

I heard Dr. Johnson wants you to take that trip. I'll go with you, Daddy. We can go over Thanksgiving."

Daddy surprised me then. "I'm not making any promises," he said.

I'd expected him to argue. But he didn't sound dead set against it. I kept quiet because if he was actually considering it, I wasn't about to break the spell.

"Would you really want to go?" he asked.

"Are you kidding me, Daddy? I've never been anywhere. Except to Georgia to see Mamaw and Papaw."

"What about Rock City?"

"Yeah. Rock City. But Daddy, that's not like visiting Yale University. And besides, those people you need to see are in Connecticut. You're scaring us. Especially Ida. You don't want your kids to be scared of you. Do you?"

His fingers twitched and he tightened them around mine.

"If I go, I'm taking Jackie," he said.

"Jackie! He won't be nothing but trouble."

"Those people," said Daddy. "I want them to meet Jackie."

I wanted in the worst way to take that trip with Daddy, and I sure didn't want my little brother tagging along. But if taking Jackie was the only way I could go to Connecticut, then I figured I could put up with him. "Jackie can go," I said. "As long as you take me, too."

"If I knew that trip would make a difference..." Daddy's voice trailed off.

"It will, Daddy. I know it will. Everything we do makes a difference. Maybe it'll be good and maybe it'll be bad. But you gotta take a chance. We can't keep on like this."

He let the blanket drop from around his shoulder and reached for the pack of cigarettes in his pocket. I let go of his other hand so he could light up.

"You wanna know what I think?" he said.

"What, Daddy?"

"I think it's too bad you aren't a boy. Because you would make one heck of a lawyer."

And *that* right there was when I knew my daddy was going on that trip. And I knew something else, too. He was going to take me with him.

I stood up. "Who says girls can't be lawyers?"

34

IDA
November 1952

"Ann Fay?"

"Yes, Ida?"

From the sound of her voice I could tell she was almost asleep and not thrilled about me waking her up. But *I* couldn't sleep—not without Ellie. "Know what I think?"

"What do you think?"

"I should've never let Ellie go to Stella's."

"Don't be silly. You couldn't have stopped her. She wanted to go."

"She went away mad. But Ann Fay, I never meant to take Arnie from her."

"Ellie knows that. And she'll get over this. Before long you'll go back to being close again."

"It feels like a long time since we were close." I plumped up my pillow and tried to get comfortable. "I want her back, Ann Fay. I don't know if I can sleep without her."

"Oh, poor baby!" Ann Fay put on her pitiful voice. I heard her turn over in bed, and I figured that was my cue to toughen up and let her go to sleep. Except then I heard her feet crossing the floor and next thing I knew she was yanking my covers off. "Move over."

"Oh. Yes, ma'am." I scooted to Ellie's side of the bed and Ann Fay settled in on my side.

"There. Is that better? Sorry I'm not Ellie. But I'll try to be the next best thing."

I reached for her hand. "You're Ann Fay. My older, stronger sister. And what would I do without you?"

Ann Fay squeezed my fingers. "You're strong too," she said. "I guess we all are, considering what we go through."

"Not me. I could never do the things you've done. Remember when Daddy was gone and Momma was out of heart from Bobby dying—how you looked after us? Then *you* got polio but you came through it, and look at you now: You're working in a doctor's office. And helping with polio clinics."

"But I didn't feel strong back then. After life clobbers you over the head, that's when you find out how much strength is inside of you. You can handle more than you think you can, Ida."

I let go of her fingers and turned over. "I don't want to find out how much I can handle. I hate hurting Ellie. You know that carving on the bureau? That's how I want us to be. Holding hands. Being friends through thick and thin."

"Don't worry, Ida. She'll always come back to you. Y'all are lucky, you know. Because you've always had each other. Before you were born I begged God for a little sister, and He gave me two. At first I thought that was the best thing ever. But you know what? You and Ellie were a pair, and I was still . . . just me. By myself."

"Really?" I'd never thought that Ann Fay might be jealous of me and Ellie. But I knew I couldn't imagine life without a twin to share it with. "You need someone too," I said. "You could always get married."

"Hmm," said Ann Fay. She yawned.

"I guess it's not working, is it?"

"What?"

"You riding with Junior to the crossroads every day."

"What do you mean?"

"I was hoping you'd fall in love."

Ann Fay was quiet for a long time—as still as the mirror hanging on the wall, reflecting the moonlight so that I could see everything in the room. Her bed with the quilt fallen halfway to the floor. Pictures on the wall. And the clutter Ellie left in a pile in the corner. Finally Ann Fay spoke up. "You know what my friend Imogene said, back when I was in the polio hospital?"

"Yeah. *It mostly hurts at first.*"

"Well, yes, but not that. She said I was true blue like Daddy's overalls. Faithful as the sky above."

"Imogene was right."

"Maybe. But Ida, you know who really *is* faithful as the sky above?"

"Momma."

"Yeah, her too. But I was thinking about Junior."

Now I was the quiet one. I stayed real still. Afraid if I breathed, it would change something. Ann Fay might, all of a sudden, say, "But don't be getting any ideas about me and Junior getting married."

I closed my eyes and remembered the first time I heard Arnie saying, "But I like Ida."

"You're real lucky," I said. "Having Junior love you the way he does."

"Yeah. I've been thinking about that."

"And I'm lucky too. Because Arnie likes me. Can you believe it? Arnie likes me!"

But saying that, or even just thinking it, made me feel like Judas in the Bible. Like I was betraying my twin. Because we couldn't both have Arnie. And that meant we couldn't both be happy.

35

ELLIE
November 1952

I stared at Stella's bed with the fringed bedspread and tufted headboard. It suited her just perfectly. Pink and prissy and princess-like. It was big enough for two, and she had it all to herself. What would that be like? She also had a nightstand with an alarm clock, lamp, and a record player. Just as I imagined, all the furniture matched—even the dressing table with its round mirror and padded stool.

"You can put your things right there," said Stella. I tucked my brown suitcase into the corner as far as possible. But it was too late. She'd already seen how shabby it was.

"It's a shame no one else could come," said Stella.

"Not even Patsy?"

"No. Can you believe it? She planned to ride home on the bus with me, but this afternoon she felt sick. So I uninvited her. I hated to do it, but I didn't want you to catch anything. You don't think she has polio, do you? Her mother works with Buster's mom. Maybe it got passed around somehow."

"I doubt it," I said. "Because wouldn't their mothers have to have polio first?"

"I guess so," said Stella. "Anyway, I'm kind of glad it's just you and me. We can never really talk at school with Laura always hanging on. And Patsy." She kicked off her shoes and sat on her bed with her legs crossed beneath her. "Sit," she said. "Tell me everything about you. Where do you live exactly? And what's your family like?"

"My family?" Oh, dear. She wanted to know about my family? I had to think of something to tell Stella. Something that was true, but not the whole truth. "My dad and I are going to New England," I said. "Over Thanksgiving."

"New England?" Stella's eyes widened. Good. She was impressed.

"He has friends in New Haven, Connecticut. And we'll visit Yale University. Maybe they'll open it to girls and I can go there someday. Daddy thinks I should be a lawyer."

"Oh, my stars!" said Stella. "I didn't know you were planning to be a lawyer. No wonder you're taking Latin. Ellie, you're such a brain. You'll have to help me with my homework while you're here. But not now. Let's go make pizza pie. Mom says we can eat it in here. Away from my pesky brother."

Stella's kitchen was every bit as sleek as her bedroom. While we made the pizza pie I tried to picture her at my house. But I couldn't.

We laughed and talked and licked tomato sauce off our fingers, and Stella went on and on about Reggie and how she'd been running after him since seventh grade. "But I have a feeling," she said, "that my fate is about to change. Of course Reggie doesn't know it yet. But he'll find out soon enough."

"What are you talking about?"

Stella slid the pizza pie into the oven. She put her finger to her lips and whispered, "Shh, can't talk about it right now. Mom and Dad are in the living room." She put the cheese back into the refrigerator. "You should go for Duncan," she said. "I know he likes you. I watch his eyes follow you around the cafeteria." She leaned in and bumped against me playfully with her elbow. "But your eyes are always on Arnie Ledford. Oh, my goodness, I see that Arnie and your sister are together now. Do you just hate her?"

I could feel myself tearing up. Then I decided maybe this was what pajama parties were for. Crying on each other's shoulders. So I started talking. "I met him first," I said. "One night last summer when I went to the races with Vivian. And oh, my goodness, it was love at first sight. I even adored those big ears of his. But from that first morning in homeroom he'd be listening to me but watching her. We do have good times together, honest we do—arguing about race car drivers and sometimes studying for tests. But obviously he likes the quiet type."

"Quiet," said Stella. "Well, that's not us. Not you and me. We like fun times, and when it gets too quiet we make things happen. Like tonight. I have a feeling we're going to have a really good time. But we can talk about that later."

Talk about what later? Why was Stella being so mysterious?

When the pizza pie was ready we carried it and other food into her room—Moon Pies, potato chips, and RC Colas. We sat on her bed and listened to "Tennessee Waltz," which made me cry because Patti Page was singing about her best friend stealing her man.

"Oh, honey," said Stella. "We've got to find something more cheerful to listen to." She lifted the phonograph needle and removed the record. "How about 'Dear Hearts and Gentle People' by Dinah Shore? That's a sweet one."

And it *was* sweet, but honestly that one made me think of Arnie too. Apparently I'd come to Stella's house to cry.

"Listen," said Stella, "I know it hurts. But you'll get over this. If you can't have Arnie Ledford that means there's someone else out there for you. Believe me, there's more fish in the sea. Lots of fellows at Fred T. Foard."

"Is that what you tell yourself?" I asked. "If you can't have Reggie Sigmon you'll just have someone else?"

"Uh. Maybe. But I'm not giving up yet. I have a feeling my luck is about to change. And yours is too, Ellie. Because you and me are going to have ourselves a double date tonight."

36

ELLIE
November 1952

"Double date?"

"Yes. You know. Two girls and two boys in the same car."

"Car? Two boys? What are you talking about? And who?"

"Who am I in love with? And who's sweet on you?"

"Reggie?"

Stella danced a little jig. "And Duncan. Yay!"

"They're coming here?"

"Shh . . . No, not here. Well, yes, but we're going for a short drive. I can count on you, right, Ellie? I hope you're up for an adventure."

"Uh. Um. Your parents won't know?"

"Are you kidding me? They'll go to bed soon." Stella was changing clothes, pulling on blue jeans and a long-sleeved shirt. "How do I look?" She sat on the stool in front of her dressing table and watched me in her mirror. "You seem nervous about this. Come on, Ellie. Don't back out on me."

"Back out? When was I ever in?"

But Stella was charging ahead whether I was in or not. "Can you believe it? I'm going for a drive with Reggie. I've been waiting for this for years. Please don't be a party pooper, Ellie. Duncan's counting on you."

Me, a party pooper? I didn't see myself that way. But I'd never sneaked out of the house at night either. At least not to go driving with boys. For one thing, Ida would never let me get by with it. She was probably sleeping soundly right now. Dreaming about Arnie.

Ida. Arnie. Jealousy and anger washed over me.

They were going off to that stupid race on Sunday. Without me, because there was no way I'd show my face there now. And if Gwyn Staley lost that stupid championship it would be just fine with me.

But I sure didn't want to sit at home feeling sorry for myself. Like Stella said, Arnie wasn't the only boy at Fred T. Foard. Duncan Riley liked me and all I'd ever given him was a cold shoulder. Maybe he deserved a chance. After all, this was just one night. I might as well enjoy it.

A shiver of excitement ran through me and I rubbed at my arms. "I've got goose bumps," I said.

"That's the spirit," said Stella. "Goose bumps. Aren't they delicious?"

They were. And now that I'd made up my mind to do this, I didn't want to wait around. But her parents were just going to bed.

Stella sat me down and put mascara on my eyelashes. "There!" she said. "That'll set you apart from your twin." She shared her foundation and blush too. "And lip color," she said. "The boys love it. But of course Duncan likes you already."

Now that I saw myself in the mirror, I had to agree with Stella. There was a definite difference between me and Ida.

We put on our coats and slipped out the back door. Stella led me to the end of the driveway. "They'll be coming from that direction," she said. "When they pull up, get in the back. Quick. We don't want Reggie's car sticking around our driveway for long."

I saw headlights then, and a car slowed down and pulled up beside us. "Reggie!" squealed Stella. "You're right on time." She opened the door and pulled the seat forward so I could climb in the back.

Sure enough, Duncan was in there. "Ellie! There's my girl."

His girl? Maybe so. At least for tonight. "Hi, Duncan."

I noticed that Stella slid across the front seat—close to Reggie. I stayed by the window. But Duncan slid closer to me.

"Don't be shy," he said.

The goose bumps were back. Even with my coat on, I could feel them.

"Where's Laura?" asked Reggie. "I thought she was going to be with you."

"Ellie, where are we picking up Laura?" asked Stella. "Doesn't she live in Blackburn? Head that way, Reggie."

I was confused. Stella wanted me to show them where Laura lived? I wasn't about to lead Reggie to her house. "I've never actually been to Laura's house," I said. "And, um, she's not coming."

"Not coming?" asked Reggie. "Stella. You promised."

"I know," said Stella. "And I tried. Didn't I, Ellie? I thought it was all planned. What happened, Ellie?"

Something was wrong. Evidently Stella had tricked Reggie into taking this drive by telling him Laura would be along. But she'd known from the beginning that Laura wasn't coming. And now she was making it my fault? I wasn't going to sit still for that. "Laura said that her parents would never let her," I said.

"Oh, goodness," said Stella. "What do you expect? They're Yankees. And get this—communist too, from all I've heard."

"Communist? No," I argued. "Laura is not a communist."

"Maybe not Laura herself," said Stella. "Although you know what they say. Like father, like daughter. I heard her father works at one of the mills. He's a union organizer or something. And you know those union people are communist."

I couldn't believe what I was hearing. I mean, I'd heard Buster make stupid comments about Laura and communism. But Stella wasn't in our history class, so how would she have heard that nonsense?

"But let's just forget about Laura," she said, snuggling up to Reggie. "Show me how fast this car will go."

We were sitting at a stop sign. Reggie could have turned around and taken us back to Stella's driveway. But apparently Duncan wasn't ready for the night to end. "Reggie, since we're out here, give us a ride," he said.

Reggie nodded. "Wanna see me pop the clutch?" He pulled the gearshift down, and the car jerked and jolted and took off with the tires squealing against the pavement. I didn't know if Reggie was mad or just decided to show off, but he stepped on the gas and didn't let up.

Duncan reached across me and rolled down my window. "We need to feel the wind in our hair," he said. "But don't worry, Ellie. I'll keep you warm."

There was something about that drive that made me feel more alive than I'd ever been—the open window with cool air pushing against my face, the night sounds rushing by, the feel of the car zipping around the curves. Suddenly I didn't care about Arnie Ledford, who was probably too sensible to do anything as fun or as scary as this.

I reached for Duncan's hand and leaned back to enjoy the night air. And when I did I saw the moon—big and round, traveling the sky. I felt Duncan's arm go around my shoulder. He pulled me close.

The car swerved, and Reggie jerked it back onto

his side of the road. He laughed. I closed my eyes and squeezed Duncan's hand.

"We're going almost sixty miles an hour!" said Stella.

"Maybe you should slow down," I called out. My voice was squeaky.

But Duncan hollered, "Gun it, Reggie! Outrun the moon up there. Give us a ride to remember."

Reggie gunned the engine, skidding around a curve and turning almost sideways as he tried to regain control. I screamed, and Duncan put both arms around me. "Don't worry," he said. "I've got you."

"Want a repeat?" asked Reggie.

No. I did not want a repeat. Maybe if Ned Jarrett was driving. Or Gwyn Staley. But this was Reggie, a sophomore without a driver's license.

He kept going—barely slowing down around one curve and then another, skidding and sliding until I thought for sure he'd roll that car.

"Stop it, Reggie!" I yelled. "Slow down! Slow down!"

Then just as we came around a curve I saw a car coming toward us. Stella screamed, "Reggie!"

We all screamed. Even Reggie hollered out, "Oh, my God!" He jerked the steering wheel to the right, and this time he couldn't control the car.

I felt us going, hitting the shoulder of the road, lurching. I heard screaming and crunching and thuds. And then I felt a big jolt and heard glass breaking.

37

ELLIE

November 1952

38

IDA
November 1952

I reach for Ellie. But she pushes me away. I can see her in a fog, her hands out like two stop signs telling me to keep back. And her voice. "You stole Arnie from me. But you'll regret it, Ida." And then—clear as day— I hear her yell, "Slow down! Slow down!" I hear a crash. And Ellie screaming.

The screaming. It jolted me awake.

I was there in my own bed seeing the shimmer of the mirror from moonlight coming in the window. I could see Ann Fay's bed across the room. The blankets thrown back and hanging to the floor. The dream was over. But something was wrong. I could feel it all the way to my bones. "Ann Fay, wake up! It's Ellie. She's hurt!"

Ann Fay moaned sleepily and rolled to the other side of the bed. I scooted closer and grabbed her shoulder. "Ellie's hurt, Ann Fay."

She sat up. "You were dreaming, Ida."

"But I heard her. She's in trouble."

I'd had bad dreams before. Dreams of Daddy being angry. Of him beating our momma or me. I'd even dreamed of losing Ellie. But something was different this time. Something that made my bones ache. I started crying.

"Shh . . . It's okay." Ann Fay turned and snuggled me into her. "You're awake now. It was just a dream." She stroked my arm and sang to me, *"Hush little baby, don't say a word."* Her holding me like that and the singing—they almost convinced me. I focused on the feel of her hand on my arm. The sound of her voice. Comforting. Soothing. But her stroking slowed down. Her voice went softer. She put herself back to sleep.

But I didn't sleep. I couldn't. I tried to tell myself it was only a dream. But I knew better. My bones hurt. *I should be with Ellie. I should be with her.*

There was a lump under her pillow. I felt around and realized it was a flashlight. And paper that smelled of mimeograph ink. I turned on the flashlight. Ten Latin Quotes. Her study sheet for extra credit. I searched the list for familiar quotes. *Pax vobis.* "Peace to you." I understood that one.

I started reviewing her Latin. *Illis quos amo deserviam,* "For those I love I will sacrifice." Did that mean I should give up Arnie so Ellie could be happy?

While I studied those quotes, the telephone rang. I sat up. "Ellie!"

Ann Fay woke up fast this time. "Ida, you're dreaming again."

"No! The telephone. I heard it." I jumped out of bed and felt my way through the living room. A light came on in the kitchen. Momma was there before me, shading her eyes. Squinting. Reaching for the telephone.

Daddy was right behind her. "I'll get it, Leroy," said Momma. She picked up the receiver. "Hello. Yes, this is the Honeycutts."

Momma sat down on the chair by the telephone. "Accident?"

"Ellie!" I screamed. I slumped to the floor. "I knew it! Ellie's been hurt." My legs ached.

Ann Fay sat on the floor too. She grabbed my arm. "Shh . . . Stay calm."

Calm? She wanted me to be calm. Momma didn't seem calm. She shook her head like she was trying to come out of a bad dream. "What kind of accident?" she said. "But she's at a friend's house. Isn't she?"

I heard the voice coming through the receiver.

"Richard Baker Hospital."

39

IDA
November 1952

"Is—is—is she dead?" My teeth were chattering. My legs. They felt weak.

Momma shook her head. "No. Just hurt. I don't know how bad. But I've got to go. Ida, come." She pulled me to my feet.

"I'm coming too," said Daddy.

"No, Leroy. I won't let you see her. Not tonight." She was afraid of what Daddy would see—worried about how he'd handle it. But then she changed her argument. "Jackie needs you here. Ann Fay needs you."

"Not me!" said Ann Fay. "I can't stay home. Not with Ellie hurt."

"Ann Fay, it doesn't matter what you want. We have to do what's right for Ellie." Momma nodded her head slightly in Daddy's direction, letting Ann Fay know she needed her to look after him. Daddy caught her meaning and rushed to get his clothes on.

"He can't see her," said Momma. "Who knows what he'd do? And we're not dragging Jackie into the hospital

220

at this hour. Ann Fay, grab me a dress from the ironing
pile. Ida, get your clothes and go to the car." Momma
pulled her coat on over her nightgown. "We'll change at
the hospital."

Normally she wouldn't step onto the front porch
dressed like that. But Momma had a whole family to
protect, and when she needed to, she could turn into the
boss of the house. She backed out the driveway just as
Daddy came through the front door. He leaped off the
porch and ran after us, but Momma shifted into first gear
and took off without him. I lost sight of Daddy, but in
my mind I could see him standing in the yard. I tried not
to imagine how hurt he was. Or how angry. I tried not
to think about Ann Fay tugging at him to come inside,
wishing she were with us. Feeling all alone. Again.

Please, God, don't let Ellie be dead.

Momma leaned forward, staring into the beam cast
by the headlights and telling me what she knew. Ellie was
with her friends. Out on the road. A boy was driving.
Four people injured. She didn't know who.

"Stella," I said. "Patsy. But who else?"

"Did you know?" asked Momma. "Did she tell you
she was going to do this? Is that why you didn't go?"

"No, Momma. It was a pajama party. That's what I
knew. I wasn't invited. I have other friends."

*Vivian. Arnie. I could use them right now. But they'd
both be sleeping.*

"What time is it, Momma?"

"After midnight." Momma gripped the wheel and drove faster.

At the hospital we hurried past families huddled in the hallway, and we almost outran the nurse who was leading us to Ellie. At the door to her room the nurse stepped aside so we could enter. We stopped—not ready for the sight of Ellie so still and covered in bandages. Her eyes swollen shut. Her face bruised. Was she breathing?

The sheet that was pulled up to her shoulders—it fluttered. Momma must've seen the breathing at the same time. We ran to her, one on each side of the bed. "Ellie, what happened? Ellie?"

But Ellie didn't respond. Her breathing was ragged. Uneven.

"I'm here, Ellie. And Momma is too." I stroked her hand. Brushed her bruised knuckles with my fingertips. Her arm was bandaged. Her head wrapped. Blood oozed along the bottom edge of the gauze. Thank God our daddy wasn't seeing her like this.

Dr. Johnson came in with a clipboard. "She has bruises. Two broken legs. We'll set those and put her in casts. Our immediate concern is swelling on her brain. Myrtle, it could be days before she's conscious. Or weeks. I recommend you go home and rest."

But of course we didn't go home. We stayed in the waiting room and held our breath and prayed. Other families were there. Stella's. And Reggie Sigmon's and Duncan Riley's. Stella and the boys were all conscious.

But they were hurt. Lacerations. Broken ribs. Broken nose. Concussions. I wasn't sure who had what.

Reggie and Duncan? I just couldn't imagine it. *Ellie, how did you end up in a car with them? I thought you didn't like Duncan. It was always Arnie you wanted.*

Arnie. She wanted Arnie. She did it because she was mad. Not thinking. Not caring. Probably just out to have a good time with whoever she could. This was all my fault. *Oh, Ellie, I'm so sorry.* My throat ached. Fear squeezed at my insides.

The nurses brought pillows and blankets and we tried to sleep in chairs. But poor Momma. Between praying for Ellie and fretting over Daddy, she couldn't settle. She paced the halls or talked to the others—the moms who were crying, the fathers staring at the elevator door.

Stella's mother reached for me. "You must be Ida. You look just like your sister. I am so very sorry." She couldn't stop apologizing to Momma. "I don't know why I didn't hear the girls leave the house."

"It wasn't your fault," said Momma.

Of course not. It's my fault. Mine and Arnie's. I needed to be alone. Away from the people who wanted to make me feel better but couldn't. I curled into a chair and hugged the pillow a nurse had given me. The murmur of voices moved farther away.

I heard another voice. "I think she's sleeping. Should we wake her up?"

Was that Vivian? I opened my eyes and realized it was daylight. It took me a minute to remember why I was curled into this chair. My back ached. My neck hurt. I looked up and sure enough—Vivian was there. She held out her arms and I stood and fell into them.

"Is Ellie okay?" she asked, sobbing.

I shook my head. Finally I managed to speak. "She's unconscious. Her brain is swollen. We just don't know."

Vivian pulled away and I saw him standing there. Arnie. Looking awkward. Worried. He reached for me and I let him hold me. *I shouldn't be letting him hold me. It's my fault. Mine and his.*

But I didn't say that to him. I couldn't. And I couldn't let go either.

40

IDA
November 1952

Vivian's mother had made breakfast biscuits filled with eggs and ham. And other people brought food too. Laura's parents came with coffee in a large thermos bottle. Cups. Cream and sugar. Pastries, napkins. All packed neatly in a large basket. The Quincys seemed just like their name—classy.

Laura had been crying, and when she saw me she started up again. "I should have gone to the party," she said. "I could have stopped her from getting in that car."

"No. It's not your fault. It's mine."

"Would you both stop blaming yourselves?" said Vivian. "Ellie Honeycutt is too strong-minded to let either one of you tell her what to do. And she's strong enough to come out of this too. We just gotta pray and believe."

I'd been sending up prayers off and on all night. But believing? That was harder.

They told us we'd be allowed ten-minute visits twice a day. In the late morning a nurse took me and Momma back to see Ellie. She was the same still, white form under a sheet, but her right eye and cheek had turned more purple. "Don't worry," said the nurse. "That's normal."

It was impossible for me not to worry. I had a hard time believing this was my twin—so broken and bandaged. So banged up and still.

When friends came I tried to describe to them what visiting Ellie was like. "You wouldn't recognize her," I said. "She's too still for Ellie. We talk to her, but I can't tell if she hears us."

Arnie held my hand for hours. But he couldn't stay the whole day. Vivian's parents had to go, and he was riding with them.

People came and went. Pastors. Friends of the other families.

Patsy came. She wouldn't stop crying. "It could have been me," she said. "I was almost at the party. But Stella uninvited me because—well, I guess because she was cooking up this joyride with Reggie." Patsy swiped her dripping nose on the back of her hand.

At suppertime Bessie and Junior came with enough meatloaf to feed half of Hickory. And they brought Momma and me clean clothes and toiletries from home.

"Leroy gave Ann Fay a fit after you left," said Junior. "I fussed at her for not calling me. But she didn't want to wake us. I fetched Otis, so don't worry; he'll help Leroy through this. They're in the woods now. Cutting up a log for firewood."

"What's Ann Fay doing?" I asked.

"Fussing, mostly. It's real hard on her not being here."

Junior and Bessie didn't stay long on account of wanting to be close to home in case Daddy and Ann Fay needed them. And honestly, although I hate to say it, I was glad to see them go. By the time that waiting room had cleared of visitors, I just wanted to hide in Ellie's room, where things were real quiet. But of course that would never be allowed.

That night, while trying to sleep in that waiting room chair, I dreamed I was at the North Wilkesboro Speedway with Arnie. Gwyn Staley and Junior Johnson and Ned Jarrett were all lining up their cars, only Ned wasn't driving No. 99. Ellie was. "No," I screamed, and I ran down the bleachers and tried to break through the fence and stop her, but the flagman dropped the green flag and the cars took off and Ellie went with them.

And some people were yelling for Gwyn and others were cheering for Junior Johnson and a lot were pulling for Ellie. I hollered for her to slow down, but Ellie was so determined that No. 99 was going to win that race. On the last lap, just when she was fixing to overtake Johnson and Staley both, she hit the wall with a horrible crash.

Thank goodness I woke up. But I wasn't on that chair anymore. I was on the waiting room floor, crying. Momma was on her knees beside me. "Ida, honey! You fell off the chair. Hush now. Don't cry." She had her arm around me, pulling me close and rocking me.

"I dreamed, Momma." I let her rock me for a while and then I reached for my pillow and pulled it off the chair. And Momma patted my back and hummed a little, and I guess I fell asleep asking God would he please, please wake Ellie up.

Momma shook me awake before daylight. "The hospital staff won't like you sleeping on the floor," she said. So I climbed back in the chair, but I couldn't sleep. I pulled apart the slats of the window blind and stared into the hospital parking lot. Cars were going and coming—the night shift leaving and the day people taking their place.

"We'll go home tonight," said Momma. "You need to sleep in your own bed." She whispered because Stella's mother was sleeping in a chair across the way. And Reggie and Duncan had family there too. One of the men was snoring.

"No," I said. "I need to sleep near Ellie."

"I have work tomorrow and you have school."

"You go, Momma. I can't think about school right now. Ellie needs me here." I just *had* to hold Ellie's hand whenever they'd let me. I could sing to her. And call her back to us. Surely she'd hear my voice and want to come.

Daylight slipped in through the blinds and the nurses started scurrying around.

Sunday was a lot like Saturday had been, with people bringing food and comforts. When Momma and I went back to see Ellie, she hadn't changed—unless maybe her bruises were darker. "Ellie," I whispered. "I dreamed you were racing and lots of people were cheering for you. I didn't want you to drive fast but I'm cheering for you now. Come back, Ellie. Please come back to us."

I watched for her eyelids to flutter or her lips to move. But she was still as a statue.

The others—Stella, Reggie, and Duncan—weren't hurt nearly so bad. On Sunday all of them were moved to regular wards. The crowd in the waiting room thinned out.

In the middle of the afternoon I sat in the waiting room half listening to people from church talking about the Reverend's sermon. Someone else was wondering how Dwight Eisenhower going to Korea would do us any good.

Everything outside this hospital seemed unimportant. I stared at the tile floor with the swirly designs, and my fingers itched for a pencil to draw what I was seeing.

And then I saw shoes. Arnie's shoes. I looked up. "Arnie. I thought you were in North Wilkesboro."

He sat in the chair beside me and leaned my way, and I leaned toward him until our heads touched. "I couldn't," he said. "For all I care, Junior Johnson can leave Gwyn Staley sitting there sputtering. I brought you something." He held out a magazine. *The Progressive Farmer*.

I reached for it and realized it wasn't just a magazine. Arnie had tucked a brand-new sketchpad underneath it. "Oh, Arnie. Thank you. How'd you know?"

"That's a silly question." He pulled a pencil from his pocket and then he took my chin and turned my head and slipped that pencil over my ear. "There," he said. "Now you look more like yourself."

I knew it wasn't true. At least I hoped I didn't look like this. My hair was a mess. My eyes were red from crying and I knew I had dark circles under my eyes.

"The magazine has cows in it," said Arnie. "In case you run out of things to draw. There are Holsteins in there. But look for the Jerseys. They're the best."

41

IDA
November 1952

On Sunday afternoon Dr. Johnson heard me talking to Ellie. "She can't hear you," he said. "Go on home. Get some sleep."

"Go, Momma," I said. "Check on the others. You can always come back. But bring Ann Fay. She feels left out."

Momma sighed. "Won't you come home with me?" she asked. "Take a bath and get some sleep. You need to change those clothes."

I shook my head. "I'm not coming. Ellie needs me."

I knew Momma would never forgive herself if she made me go. We could lose Ellie while I was gone. So she agreed to let me stay. "But Ida, you'll have to go to school eventually."

"Bring my books." I didn't see how I could study, but I didn't want to argue.

When the elevator door opened and I was hugging Momma goodbye, Laura and her mother were there with another basket. "Sandwiches," said Mrs. Quincy.

They didn't stay, but it was good to see Laura for even a few minutes. "Is she awake yet?" Laura asked. I shook my head and we hugged and I felt her shaking.

"Keep praying," I told her.

"I will. And tell Ellie, *pax vobis*. She'll know what it means."

I knew what it meant too. "Peace to you," I said.

"Yes," said Laura. "And peace to you, Ida."

Then the elevator door slid shut, and one by one Laura, Mrs. Quincy, and Momma disappeared.

That farm magazine kept me going for a long time. At first I just leafed through the pages. There was a lot more than cows in there. Other animals, but also advertisements for manure spreaders, a Hydra-Matic Oldsmobile, and Wrigley's Spearmint gum. A picture of a farmer milking a brown cow. It was a painting, not a photograph, and I studied it for a long time before I started drawing it. I smiled, just thinking about Arnie choosing that magazine for me.

Much later, after everyone else had left, I went to the toilet down the hall. When I came back to the waiting room, the lights were out and my pillow was gone. The hospital staff must've thought we'd all left for the night.

Maybe I should have asked for it back, but what if they didn't want me staying at the hospital without Momma? I pulled two chairs together and tried to sleep.

After a while my bones just ached. They hadn't really stopped aching since the night of the accident.

What does Ellie feel? Or doesn't she feel anything?

That thought scared me. What was she doing down in that room all alone? How was she supposed to get better like that? The doctors didn't know Ellie. They couldn't understand that she needed people around her. That she'd never make it in a room by herself with no one holding her hand.

Ten minutes of visiting twice a day was not enough for Ellie.

I couldn't just scrunch myself into this chair and hope to sleep while she was alone in that bed. I pushed myself up and paced the floor. How could I help her? Could I get to her without being seen?

I peeked out the door. At the nursing station, two heads with stiff white nursing caps were barely visible above the counter. One of them looked to be nodding off. The other nurse was busy typing. Good. I could duck down and scoot past the counter, and maybe, just maybe, she wouldn't hear me over the clatter of the typewriter keys.

I tucked my sketchpad and pencil into a corner under the telephone table and took off my shoes. After listening for that typewriter I ducked low and hurried down the hall, past the nurse's station.

The typing stopped. "Is someone there?" the nurse asked.

I froze. And waited for the typing to start up again. Then I moved on, but the typing stopped again and I heard the nurse push back her chair.

I'd been caught.

"Oh, my," the nurse said. "I thought all the visitors had gone for the day. Do your parents know you're here? Where are you going?"

"Can I use the toilet?" I asked. "I couldn't leave the hospital. My twin needs me nearby."

The woman crossed her arms across her chest, and she stood there biting her lip like she was thinking about what to do with me. "Twin? Ellie Honeycutt?"

"Well, I'm Ida. Ellie is hurt. Real bad."

The nurse nodded. "I guess we have to let you stay. Hurry and go to the toilet. Then get settled." She headed back to the nurses' station and then turned toward me. "Since your twin needs you."

"Thank you!" I hurried to the bathroom and stepped inside. I used the toilet and washed my hands and splashed water on my face. I needed to be alert if I was to make it to Ellie's room. I had to make it to Ellie.

When I was ready to leave I said a prayer even though I wasn't sure if God would help me break hospital rules. But surely He knew how important this was. I could still hear the typewriter down the hall. I peered in that direction and could see only the back of the nurse's head. I slipped into the hall, turned the knob slowly, slowly, and pulled the door shut before letting go of the knob. *Click!* Yikes. I ran down the hall to Ellie's room.

The door was open. I stepped inside and slipped around to the backside of the open door. I was by her bed—breathing hard.

But she seemed to be hardly breathing.

I listened. I couldn't hear a thing. Not from the nurse and not from Ellie's bed. I had to know if she was alive. I put my hand on her chest and waited.

Relief! I felt the slight movement. Slow, steady breathing. Different from how it was when we first saw her. I rested my head on the edge of her mattress. I felt for her fingers. "Squeeze my hand, Ellie," I whispered. "If you're in there somewhere, please squeeze my hand. I need to find you."

I felt nothing from her. Just the quiet sound of her breathing. I matched my breath to hers.

I remembered all those nights we'd breathed together. Snuggled into each other when we were little. I wanted to be that close to her now.

That nurse was still typing down the hall so I could stay for a little while. I slipped over to the bed and lifted Ellie's blankets. I'd have to be careful not to hurt her. I sat on the edge of the bed and slowly pulled my legs in. My foot bumped the cast on her leg. "Oh, I'm sorry. I hope I didn't hurt you, Ellie." I inched my way down onto the bed—scooting a little at a time until we lined up, shoulder to shoulder. She was on her back. I was on my side. It was crowded.

"Ellie," I said. "You're on my side of the bed." I let my head rest on the edge of her pillow. "But it's okay because I'm not supposed to be here. I hope you don't mind. I need you. I need to breathe with you." I reached for her hand. "I won't hurt you, I promise. Just squeeze my hand if you hear me. I'll breathe with you, Ellie."

For a long time I focused on breathing. I hoped it would put me to sleep, but my mind was moving. There was so much in my heart.

"I'm sorry, Ellie. I'm sorry about Arnie. I didn't mean for this to happen.

"Remember after the war, Ellie? When Daddy slammed me against the wall? It scared me so bad I couldn't breathe. I guess I was like one of those race cars that gets smashed and then it just limps around the track. But you stepped on the gas and kept going. Enjoying all the attention you could. You got ahead of me, Ellie. You liked being first. And you sure do hate losing. But it's not a race. It's just both of us driving the best way we know how.

"Here's my hand. Feel my fingers? You can squeeze them any time. I'm so sorry, Ellie."

I guess I fell asleep repeating nonsense to her like that. It must have been a deep sleep. A long one too, because when I awoke there was a nurse in the room. Right there by Ellie's bed. *Oh, no! I'm in trouble now.*

She probably heard my heart pounding. I didn't know whether to slide out of that bed real quick or stay where I was, but either way I'd been caught. She lifted her hand and swiped at her face. And then I thought I heard a sob. Was she crying?

"I'm sorry," I said. "I know I'm not supposed to be here."

The nurse gasped and stepped back. "Oh, honey, you scared me. I thought you were sleeping." She stepped up to the bed then and leaned in to whisper. "You can't let them find you here. The doctors won't approve because you might set her back. But what do the doctors know?" She laughed. "And don't you repeat that."

"No, ma'am. I won't say a word. You're not going to tell on me?"

"Sweetie, I have twins. Boys. Identical as two candy canes. I don't know how they'd've got to adulthood without each other. And I know one thing. If your sister pulls out of this it'll be your doing. She needs you. I'm the charge nurse for the night shift, so you're in luck. I'll come in every morning and wake you up. But when I'm not here, you're on your own. Those other nurses, they'll stick to the rules. Because they won't understand."

I let out a big breath. "Thank you, ma'am. I can't thank you enough."

"Jolene," she said. "Nurse Jolene." She reached over and patted my hand.

42

ELLIE
November 1952

Ida.

Her voice. Pleading. "Ellie, don't go. Please don't go."

Faraway. Sorrowful. Desperate.

"Ellie. I need you. Squeeze my hand."
Her hand.
What does she want?

"Squeeze my hand if you hear me, Ellie."

Where is her hand?
In the fog?
In the fog with her voice?

43

IDA
November 1952

Someone touched my arm. Nurse Jolene. "Shh. Move slowly. It's time to get back to the waiting room. I'll be leaving in thirty minutes."

"Okay." I turned to my sister and whispered, "Bye, Ellie. I'll be back. Don't leave us." I wanted to throw my arms around her and cling. But I had to cooperate with Nurse Jolene.

"I'll be back tonight," Nurse Jolene said. "Between now and then, you'd better mind your p's and q's."

"Yes, ma'am," I told her. "I'll be perfectly behaved. I promise."

She squeezed my hand. "You're a godsend, is what you are. And someday your sister will tell you so."

I sure hoped she was right.

Later in the morning I went down the elevator and sat outside on the hospital steps and shivered and prayed. I ate food that Mrs. Quincy brought in. And the rest of the time I drew just about every page in that magazine.

The advertisements, the artwork, and the photographs of cows.

Funny how some ordinary thing like cows—which I'd seen all my life and never thought much about—could suddenly seem so remarkable to me. Arnie loved them. According to him they had personalities. That intrigued me.

Just before it was time for the evening visit to Ellie's room, the elevator door opened and out stepped Ann Fay. "You came!" I said.

"Of course I did," said Ann Fay. "Momma is so wore out, I think she was glad to stay home and let me have a turn."

"Did Daddy come? I know *you* didn't drive here."

"Junior brought me. I couldn't wait to get inside, so he dropped me off out front while he parked the car."

"Good grief, Ann Fay. Sometimes you treat Junior like he's the hired man."

"No, I don't." She grinned. "He just treats me like royalty. Don't worry. He's a big boy. He'll find his way up."

She was right, too. We heard the elevator rattling its way from the first floor. Then the bell dinged, the door slid open, and there he was. "Hey, Ida. How's Ellie?"

"No different," I said. "She looks bad. Black and blue and swollen. And you've never seen her so still."

"Yeah—I dragged every detail out of Momma," said Ann Fay. "But I think she wanted to tell it so she could prepare Daddy. She knows she can't hold him back forever. But for now, he's listening to reason and staying home."

The nurse came then and said if we wanted to see Ellie this was a good time.

Junior stayed in the waiting room while Ann Fay and I went back. Ann Fay winced when she saw Ellie, but she walked right up to the bed. "Ellie Honeycutt," she said. "What in the wide world are you doing in that bed, looking so beat up? You've got too much spunk for this and you know it." Her voice faltered then. I guess even Ann Fay couldn't handle the sight of Ellie so busted up and quiet.

I linked my arm with hers, and the two of us stood there crying. After a few minutes I whispered, "Guess what? I slept in that bed with Ellie last night."

"You did what? Ida, you can't *do* that!"

"Shh . . . Yes, I can. It's a secret between you and me and the charge nurse. She has twins. She thinks I can help Ellie."

Ann Fay turned and wrapped both arms around me then, and now she was out and out sobbing. I guess I had most of my sobbing cried out of me, or maybe it was just time for me to be the strong one, because I held her and patted her back and told her we were going to pull Ellie through. "People everywhere are praying," I said.

When the visit was over, we found Junior sitting in the waiting room with my sketchbook. He held up my drawing of the Oldsmobile Rocket. "Now, that's a beauty," he said. "When did you start drawing cars?"

"When I started living at the hospital day and night. I'm copying pictures from that farm magazine Arnie brought me. It's from an advertisement."

Junior found the ad and sat there reading it out loud to us, but then he stopped and said, "Ann Fay, that's it. A Hydra-Matic. You could drive a car like that. No clutch to worry with."

"Junior Bledsoe, what are you talking about?" asked Ann Fay.

"I'm talking about you learning to drive. I'm gonna teach you. That's what."

Ann Fay was bad to argue with Junior about anything and everything, but this time she didn't. Instead she sat there, half smiling. And nodding slightly. Maybe she even liked the idea but hated to admit it.

Of course we didn't have a Hydra-Matic car for her to learn on, and Junior didn't either. But I figured that was their problem.

44

ELLIE
November 1952

Ann Fay's voice.
Telling me I shouldn't be here.
Where am I?

I hear her crying.

Ida's voice.

"I'll breathe with you, Ellie."

I feel it on my cheek.
Coming.
Going.
Coming.
Her fingers and mine weaving together.

"Squeeze my hand, Ellie, if you hear me."

I wiggle my fingers.

Her voice. Begging.

"Please, Ellie, please don't leave me. I need you.
Can't you please squeeze my fingers?"

I hear you.
I'm trying. I'm trying.

But she's crying.
She doesn't know that I'm trying.
Why am I so tired?

45

IDA
November 1952

By Wednesday afternoon I guess my daddy had enough of Momma keeping him away from Ellie. I was outside stretching my legs—pacing the sidewalk—when I looked up and there he was, two blocks away, crossing over the railroad tracks. I knew it was him by the way he walked.

And I knew what he was about to do. But it wasn't the right time of day for visits, and the staff would never let him see Ellie just then. I ran to him and he grabbed me in his arms and hung on tight. "Ellie?" he said. "Are you better?"

What? Why was he calling me Ellie? "Daddy. I'm Ida. It hasn't been that long, has it?" Daddy pulled away then but held on to my hands.

"Ida. Of course. My mind was somewhere else. How's my girl doing?"

"I'm okay," I said.

"Is she getting better? I need to know."

Oh, his girl. That was Ellie, of course. "The doctor hopes the brain swelling will go down and she'll be back with us," I told him. "She's going to be okay, Daddy. Where's Momma? How'd you get here?"

"Your mother's at work," he said. Then he chuckled, and his laugh had a bitter edge to it. "She don't have any idea I walked out of that plant."

"Daddy! What about Mr. Rhinehart?"

"What about him? Do you think if his Peggy Sue was laid up in a hospital he'd be at that hosiery mill right now? I don't own the place, but I have a right to see my baby girl when she's banged up." He took off then—running straight down that sidewalk toward the hospital.

"Daddy!" I chased after him, but he had a head start and his legs were longer than mine. He was in the door before I reached the edge of the hospital parking lot. And by the time I reached the elevator I could hear it clattering up and away from me on the other side of that door. I ran for the stairs, but I was so tired I thought I might not make it at all.

I heard the nurses yelling before I made it into the second-floor hallway. "Sir! Sir! Where are you going? What do you think you're doing? Someone call the police."

Every nurse on duty had come out of the woodwork and was chasing after Daddy. Except one of them was on the phone, saying there was an emergency on the second floor. "That's my daddy," I hollered. "I'll talk to him."

I don't know why I thought I could control him. I was the one who was always shying away when he was unpredictable. But it was only me there now, and I had to do what Ellie would do if she weren't in that bed.

Daddy was going in and out of rooms, calling for his Ellie. And he reached her door just as two nurses grabbed him by the elbows.

"Daddy!" I yelled. "Stop. We'll work something out."

But Daddy didn't stop. He yanked himself away from those women, and I got there in time to follow them all into Ellie's room. Daddy was at her bed then, on his knees on the floor, sobbing. The nurses stopped in their tracks and stared at him and then at each other and maybe they figured out that he wasn't going to do any more damage than he'd already done, which was probably to scare the living daylights out of them. Nurse Setzer's cap was knocked lopsided, and Nurse Pierce reached up to straighten it for her.

I walked up to Ellie's bed and reached for Daddy's hand, gripping the metal bed rail. "You can touch her, Daddy. She won't break. Stroke her hand. Hold it. Maybe she'll squeeze your fingers. Please, Ellie. Squeeze Daddy's finger for us."

But she didn't—even though he stared into her face and pleaded with her through tears.

The nurses left the room then, but I could hear them hovering in the hall. I heard other nurses asking questions. And Nurse Pierce telling them all to get back to work. That she'd handle this.

Finally she stepped inside and told us we'd have to leave. Daddy didn't argue. He'd seen his Ellie, and maybe that was enough. He walked down the hall with his arm around my shoulder.

A police officer met us in the waiting room. "Sir," he said, "I could arrest you for disturbing the peace and endangering the patients of this hospital. But instead I'm going to take you home."

Daddy nodded. Then he turned to Nurse Pierce, standing nearby with her arms folded across her chest like she wanted him to know she was in charge around there. "Thank you," he said. "For taking care of my girl." He turned and headed for the elevator.

Right before the officer pressed the button I realized I couldn't just let Daddy drive off with a policeman. What about Momma? She didn't know where he was. "Wait! I'm coming too." I didn't take time to grab the things I'd tucked under a chair in the corner. I slipped into the elevator. "Sir," I said, "my momma's at work, wondering where Daddy is. Can you take us there? She'll drive him home."

The policeman didn't argue. He just let me explain about Daddy and Momma working at the same place and about Daddy walking off the job. And he let Daddy show him the way to Rhinehart's Hosiery.

46

ELLIE
November 1952

Ida's breath on my cheek.
Coming.
Going.
Her voice in my ear.

"Pax vobis, Ellie. Pax vobis."
Peace to you, Ellie. Peace to you.

Her fingers.
I squeeze her fingers.
I'm trying, Ida. I'm trying.

Ann Fay's voice.
Bossy.
Upset with me.
I'm trying. I'm trying, Ann Fay.

Daddy. Crying.
He wants something.
I can't.
But I'm trying, Daddy. I'm trying.

47

IDA
November 1952

Maybe I was ready to get out of that hospital. Because when Momma drove away from the factory and said she was taking me home for a bath and to sleep in my own bed, I didn't argue. I slept through the night and half the next day. When I awoke, the house was filled with good smells.

I stared at the boards in the ceiling. So familiar. And comforting. I curled myself around Ellie's pillow, snuggled in, and went back to sleep. It was the middle of the afternoon when I awoke again.

Almost time for Jackie to come home from school. I slid out of bed and headed for the dresser to see what the mirror had to say about me. I needed to curl my hair. But the circles under my eyes weren't so dark anymore. And I thought I looked different in other ways too. Older, maybe. Stronger. I'd had to be the strong one for Daddy yesterday, and for some reason that made me feel closer to him.

I picked up that little wooden statue of me and Ellie that Daddy had carved so many years ago. There we were, holding hands like we could never be separated. But now we were. Maybe it was normal for twins to grow apart. But normal didn't mean it felt good.

On my way to the bathroom I passed Bessie reading the *Hickory Daily Record*. She reached for me, but I couldn't wait for hugs.

When I came back she had a plate full of food on the table. Ham and potatoes, creamed corn, and bread pudding. "Have mercy," she said. "How long has it been since you ate a decent meal?"

"Not that long," I said. "Since everybody and his neighbor have been bringing food to the hospital."

I spent the rest of the day wandering around the house trying to enjoy being there. But without Ellie, home felt hollow. Jackie came from school and I played Uncle Wiggly with him, but I kept watching the clock, waiting for Momma and Daddy. Eager for Momma to take me back to the hospital.

Ellie wasn't changed when we visited with her that night. But when Nurse Jolene came on duty I slipped past her station. And I climbed into bed with Ellie and felt more at home in that hospital with her than I had in our room curled into her pillow.

I whispered to her there in the darkness. "Ellie, the others are getting better. Stella and Duncan. Reggie went home from the hospital already. You can get well too. Everybody's pulling for you. Maybe in the morning you'll open your eyes and talk to me."

But when Nurse Jolene came and shook me awake, Ellie was just as still as ever.

I spent the morning in the waiting room. And once, while standing at the window and looking down into the parking lot, I saw Duncan getting into a car with his parents. I could see he was bruised and he wasn't exactly running, but he sure didn't have two broken legs and swelling on the brain the way Ellie did.

I knew Stella was out of danger too, probably down there socializing with other girls on her ward.

It's not fair. None of this is fair. I didn't want to wish bad on any of them, but after a whole week Ellie still wasn't awake. It didn't seem right that all of them were barely hurt except for my sister.

Arnie visited whenever he could. And Vivian and Laura, of course. They talked about people at school and rumors going around about the accident.

On Saturday morning Laura suggested we visit Stella. "I don't know about that," I said. "She never liked me. Only Ellie."

"She thought you were stuck up," said Laura. "This is a chance to show her you're not."

"But maybe I am, where she's concerned. This whole thing is her fault."

"You'll have to face her eventually," said Vivian. "Don't worry. We'll do the talking."

So I went along with them. Stella's mother met us at the door to the ward. "She'll be happy to see you," she said.

But Stella's bruised face twisted into a pitiful mess when she saw me. "Oh, Ida, I'm so sorry. I never meant for anything like this to happen. We just wanted to have a little fun." She covered her face with her hands, and I could almost not believe this was Stella from Startown. The one with the flashy makeup and sassy attitude. She didn't seem at all like I remembered her.

I just couldn't tell her it was okay. Nothing was okay. What was I supposed to say anyway?

Laura stepped in then. "We're glad you're getting better," she said. "Things aren't the same at school without you. Patsy looks lost."

I stood there by Stella's bed and listened to them, but my eyes were on the other beds. There were four beds, and two were empty. Ellie should be in one of them. She should be on this floor getting well and going home soon. But she was upstairs.

48

IDA
November 1952

A car went by on the street and its headlights flashed across the curved white ceiling of Ellie's room. I could hear the swish of rainwater under its tires. Here in the room, the hot-water radiator clicked. It was a slow click at first, and then it came faster and faster.

"Listen, Ellie," I said. "Can you hear the sounds around you? The radiator warming the room? Rain on the window? My voice? Ellie, you must hear it. You have to know that I am here. Ellie, I need you. Squeeze my fingers if you hear me."

I'd said it so often and nothing had happened. But right in the middle of my babbling I felt a pressure on my thumb.

"Ellie! Was that you? I think it was real. Do it again. Press on my thumb. Let me know you hear me."

I waited. The radiator clicked. The clock ticked. I waited, and then I felt it again. Stronger this time. It was real! "Oh, dear God. Thank you. She hears me, doesn't she? Thank you!" I was crying and talking—first to Ellie and then to God and then to Ellie again.

"Is everything okay in here?" Nurse Jolene rushed in. "Ida, what's wrong?"

"Ellie squeezed my thumb! She hears me!"

Nurse Jolene came to my side of the bed. "Go ahead and cry," she said. "Let it out." She put her hand over mine and Ellie's. "I'm your nurse, Ellie," she said. "You're in the hospital. If you can feel our hands, if you can hear us, can you move a finger?"

At first nothing happened. But then Ellie wiggled a finger and Nurse Jolene felt it. "Oh," she said. "That's a good girl. You're gonna make it. Yes, you are. I bet you're tired from all that effort. Better rest now."

"What? You want her to sleep? But I want her to wake up."

Nurse Jolene patted my arm. "It's the middle of the night, Ida. She's not ready for much activity. Maybe you should come to the waiting room."

"Oh, please, let me stay. I promise I won't ask her to move a muscle."

"Well, if that's a promise." Nurse Jolene pulled the sheet up over my shoulder and Ellie's too. "I'll be back to run you off just before the next shift comes in."

I couldn't sleep. I tried to hold still, but it was impossible. So I paced the floor and stared out the window into the darkness. I slipped down the hall to the toilet and I itched for my sketchbook. Something to do. Some way to tell this story.

I sneaked back to the waiting room and found my sketchbook. I took it to Ellie's room and sat on the floor by the door, drawing by the light from the hall. Ellie. Her bed. High, curved ceilings. Radiators. Pipes running up the wall. The windows.

Daylight was coming into the room when I heard movement. I looked for her hand to move. I glanced at her face, and oh, my goodness—was I actually seeing what I thought I was? I went to the bed.

Ellie was looking at me.

49

ELLIE
November 1952

Ida crying.

"Ellie, you're awake! Thank God, you're back! How long have you been awake?"

How long?
What time is it? What day? Where am I?
Hospital. Did someone say hospital?

The fog was clearing. I was in bed. It was mostly dark.
Pain. In my legs. Headache.
But Ida. Stroking my fingers.
Crying.
"It's going to be okay now, Ellie. It's going to be okay."
Then why was she crying?

50

IDA
November 1952

"Why am I here?" asked Ellie.

"There was an accident. Remember?" But I could see from her face that she didn't.

"Accident?"

"It was a car wreck, Ellie. Reggie and Duncan and Stella were in the car too."

"Stella?" Ellie wrinkled her nose. "*Dear hearts. Gentle people.*" She whispered the words.

"Huh?" Now I was the confused one. A tune dropped into my thoughts—a popular song. But why would that be the first thing she remembered?

It took a few days for the memory of the accident to come to her. Everything was slow at first, but she was becoming more and more like her old self. "Where's Stella?" she asked.

"Downstairs. In the general ward. She had a concussion, broken ribs, and cuts and bruises, but she may be going home soon. Reggie and Duncan have already been released."

Dr. Johnson was astounded by Ellie's progress. He predicted she'd move to a regular ward by the end of the week. "Only two weeks in critical care, with those injuries," he said. "Remarkable!"

The whole family was in the waiting room when he told us this. We hung on to each other and laughed and cried. I felt like Ellie and I had won a race, not one of us winning and the other losing, but both of us winning together.

Nurse Jolene was standing nearby. "She had powerful love pulling her through," she said. She winked at me. So far Nurse Jolene and Ann Fay were the only ones who knew I'd spent nights in Ellie's room. I hadn't even told Vivian or Arnie.

Momma and Daddy wanted to take me home the day after Ellie regained consciousness. I was weary of the hospital but scared to leave her. "Go," said Nurse Jolene. "I forbid you to hang around this ward any longer."

I wasn't about to argue with Nurse Jolene. I trusted her even more than Dr. Johnson, who I'd known for my whole life. So I hugged Ellie goodbye, picked up my possessions in the waiting room, and rode down the elevator with Momma and Daddy.

I went to bed right after supper and slept until morning, and then I went back to school. I felt lost getting on the bus without Ellie. In all her years of school she'd only ever missed three days, before this. Other students wanted to know how she was doing. "Better," I said.

Arnie met me at my locker. And that smile—it made me cry. Maybe I wasn't ready to be back here, where Ellie had studied with him, flirted with him, hoped for him. I hadn't expected to stand there sobbing while he crammed his books into his locker so his hands would be free for holding me. I felt his chin on my head and his heart beneath my ear and I felt downright guilty. Ellie was getting better, but when she came back to school it would be me and Arnie. How would that make her feel?

Maybe like Nurse Jolene said, Ellie would think I was a godsend. But she could also hate me for all I'd put her through. Me and Arnie. I just kept thinking it was our fault.

Locker doors slammed. A voice asked, "Is she all right?"

Arnie whispered in my ear, "It's okay. Everything's gonna be okay." But Arnie was just saying what I needed to believe. Arnie never had a twin. He didn't know that breaking your sister's heart was the same as twisting a knife in your own.

51

ELLIE
November 1952

When they took me down to the general ward, Stella was there. And two other girls, a younger one named Regina and an older girl named Janice. I was glad to see Stella. Glad because nobody else could understand how that night happened. Or what it felt like to fly through the dark, out of control, thinking you were about to die.

But Stella's face was still bruised, purple and green and scarred with cuts. "Do I look as bad as you?" I asked.

"Worse," said Stella. "But it'll get better. And your hair will grow out."

I reached for that place on the side of my head where they'd shaved me. I probably looked a fright with that laceration crossing over my ear and reaching into my forehead. Would I always have scars to remind me of that night?

"Stella, what were we thinking?" I asked.

Stella was real quiet then. "I'm sorry," she said. "I was trying to get Reggie to like me. It was all my fault."

But that wasn't exactly true. Sure, Stella planned that

drive with Reggie and Duncan. And maybe she deceived us all to get what she wanted. But I wanted that joyride too. And I was even having a good time. At first.

The two of us were learning the hard way what was really important in life. I thought about the words to that song Stella had played for me on her phonograph. "Dear Hearts and Gentle People." I knew I owed my life to people like that. To Ida.

"Want to know a secret?" I asked Stella. "Ida climbed in my hospital bed with me. She pulled me out of that coma. Her voice. Her breath. Her fingers. Without her, I might have died. Every girl should have a twin sister."

"You're lucky," said Stella.

"Yeah." Whether I liked it or not, Ida had always been there. And mostly I liked it.

"We're all lucky. We could have all died. I'm sorry you got hurt the worst."

"But I'm going to walk again," I said. "You watch. If my sister could walk after polio, then I know I sure can."

"You will," said Stella. "I know you will."

Thinking about polio reminded me of Buster. I'd forgotten about him. Didn't he have it too? Or had I dreamed that? "Stella, what about Buster? Does he have polio? I feel like I've been gone for months. Whatever happened to him?"

"It's only been a few weeks," said Stella. "I think he's still in the hospital down in Charlotte. He might be there for a long time."

"Probably. Ann Fay was in the polio hospital for months."

I looked at the other girls in our ward. Regina was cutting construction-paper turkeys and taping them to the head of her bed. Those turkeys reminded me of something else. "What day is it?" I asked. "When is Thanksgiving?"

"Today is Saturday," said Stella. "Thanksgiving is next week."

"Next week?" It couldn't be. I was stuck in a hospital bed. *Does Dr. Johnson know I'm going to Connecticut with Daddy? I have to tell him. I can't miss this trip again.* "Stella, will we be out of here by next week? I'm going to New England at Thanksgiving. Did I tell you that? I have to go, Stella. I have to get out of here."

But Dr. Johnson did not agree with me. I brought it up to him the next day when he made his rounds. He shook his head. "You have two broken legs, Ellie. They need at least another month to heal. Travel is out of the question."

"But I could wear crutches."

"Using crutches requires one good leg."

"A wheelchair, then."

"Ellie, listen." Dr. Johnson used his no-nonsense voice. "This trip is for your father's peace of mind. The last thing he needs is an invalid to care for." He fastened his pen to his clipboard and turned to go. "I'm sorry, Ellie. You're young and will have more opportunities to travel." And just like that he walked out of the room.

Did he even notice that I was crying?

Laura noticed.

Her parents brought her by the hospital on their way home from church. She looked me over, and I saw her wince when she studied my face. There was a chair by my bed, and she sat on the edge of it. "I would hug you but—it looks like that would hurt." She reached for my hand. "Does it? You're crying."

"Dr. Johnson says I can't take that trip. He called me an invalid. Do I look like an invalid to you?"

Laura looked at me for a long time. Finally she said what I didn't want to hear. "Yes, actually you do."

"No, actually, I don't. '*Validus*'—what does that mean?"

"Strong."

"And '*in*' means the opposite. I am not *in-valid*. I am strong, Laura. Where there's a will, there's a way. I will find a way. Daddy can wait. We can go at Christmas."

But that night when the lights were out I couldn't sleep. Every time I closed my eyes I saw the accident. *Duncan and me in the back seat of that car. The moon out ahead of us and Reggie trying to outrun it.* Eventually I fell asleep. I think I did. But that didn't make the images and the sounds go away.

Duncan hooting. Egging Reggie on. Speed. Fear. And that car lurching out of control. Screams.

"Ellie. Wake up."

"Huh?" I felt a hand on my shoulder. In the darkness I saw a white uniform and nurse's cap.

"You were dreaming," the nurse said.

"Screaming," said Regina across the room. "My heart is going ninety miles an hour."

And mine was going at least a hundred. "I'm sorry," I said. "It was a bad dream. The accident."

It took me a long time to settle down. I was afraid to close my eyes. What if I dreamed again?

Is this what it's like for Daddy—all those nights when he hollers in his sleep? Is this what he feels? Every nerve in his body fired up? Scared to go back to sleep because he might have the bad dreams again?

Poor Momma was right there beside him. How did she feel coming out of a deep sleep with him hollering like that? It was hard enough for the rest of us, hearing it from the next room. He could be having a nightmare right that minute. Ida would be trembling and I wouldn't be there for snuggling up to.

But there was something I could do. Maybe it would help Daddy. And that would help all of us.

52

ELLIE
November 1952

I told Ida to go on the trip. It was the hardest thing I'd ever done. Well, maybe not the hardest. Because after all, I'd been through the crash and I'd somehow climbed out of a coma.

But I don't think I actually did climb out. Ida pulled me out. I owed my life to her. What was a little trip to New England in comparison? Like Dr. Johnson said, there'd be other trips. "You know where my money is," I told her. "In the bank Ann Fay brought home from Warm Springs. It's almost full."

"No, Ellie. The money you earned from Miss Pauline is yours. I can't take that. How could I ever pay you back?"

"You saved my life. If that's not enough, pay me back by going on this trip. I want you to go."

"You're lying," said Ida. "I see it all over you. Look, you're trembling. And your nostrils are flared the way they do when you're not telling the truth."

I couldn't pretend anymore. I wanted to just break

down and cry and tell her to save the money for me and maybe I could travel with it later. And I *was* crying. I could feel the tears building. I couldn't hold them back. I wiped at my cheeks with the palms of my hands. "Okay. So I'm lying. Are you satisfied? I really want to take the trip. I do. But I can't. And Daddy needs to go, and someone has to go with him. And that someone is you."

Ida squeezed her eyes shut, but the tears leaked out. I knew she felt guilty for getting this. The trip and Arnie both. It was too much for her to take from me.

I couldn't let up, though. "No one else can experience it for me the way you can!" I quoted Latin to her. "*Illis quos amo deserviam.* For those I love I will sacrifice."

Tears rolled down Ida's cheeks. She was defeated.

I felt cruel pushing this off on her. And I was mad at her for not appreciating what a gift this was. Mad at myself for the mess we were in. How did I get to be an invalid anyway?

Ida left in tears without even hugging me.

I heard Stella in the bed beside me, crying. I looked at Regina and Janice in the other beds, and they were crying too. "Stop it," I said. "Who's going to be strong for me?"

But they couldn't stop any more than I could. I pulled the pillow over my head and bit into it and nearly suffocated myself on my tears and frustration.

53

IDA
November 1952

I had a memory of Momma and Daddy standing on this same train platform right before he went off to war. Daddy's hands cradling her head. Him whispering her name. I'd never really thought before about how one train ride could change a life. A whole family. Would this one make that much difference?

The train left the station. Rocking and gentle. To the left of the train I could see the hospital where Ellie was. Hickory slipped away from us. Then Conover went by and we were in the country. To the west the sun settled pink and orange and golden over the Blue Ridge Mountains, turning Hickory into a silhouette of trees and buildings.

I reached for my sketchbook and worked fast to capture that silhouette. I sketched Jackie and Daddy sitting on a seat facing me. But Jackie was up and down, looking out the window, then talking to a skinny man with big ears that made me think of Arnie even though this man wasn't nearly so handsome.

The man pulled a stick of gum out of his shirt pocket. "You like Teaberry?" he asked.

"Oh, yes," said Jackie. He snatched the gum.

"Mind your manners," I told Jackie. He wadded the whole piece up and stuffed it into his mouth and thanked the man with his mouth full. "Manners," I said again. But it was no use. And the man didn't care.

I sketched his face and his big ears, careful to hold my paper out of his sight. And even though he wasn't there, I sketched Arnie too. Starting with the ears and building his face from memory—the dark eyes with a sparkle that never seemed to go away. His smile and his angular jawline. I missed him already. Monday morning seemed like weeks away.

Jackie couldn't wait to use the toilet on the train, and finally Daddy took him. They swayed and wobbled and hung on to the seats for balance as they moved up the aisle. I heard Jackie giggling like he was having the time of his life.

Soon after they returned, the lights in our car dimmed. Bedtime.

I wadded my scarf into a pillow and leaned my head against it on the window. A bright sliver of moon traveled alongside us. The train rattled and rocked and I felt sleep sliding over me.

I think I awoke at each station along the way and every time the train blew its horn. Jackie was curled on the seat with his head on Daddy's lap. Daddy slept sitting straight up. The chewing-gum man snored softly with his chin on his chest. His head bobbed up and down and his body swayed side to side.

Moonlight reflected off of water and I realized we were going over a swamp. It was strange to be bumping along somewhere between North Carolina and New England. And even stranger still, I realized that riding above a swamp felt safer than being in either place.

Next time I awoke, it was early morning. Thanksgiving Day. If I was at home with Momma and Ann Fay there'd be turkey roasting in the oven. And later, all the fixings with Bessie and Junior and the Hinkle sisters. I'd visit Ellie in the hospital.

But I was in the North. And Ellie probably hated me for it. The conductor came through our car, calling out the next stop. "Thirtieth Street Station."

Philadelphia, where we'd be changing trains. Daddy opened his eyes. He blinked a few times, then ran his fingers through his hair and found his hat on the seat beside him. He bounced his foot up and down, jostling Jackie awake. By the time the train stopped, Jackie was sitting up, squinting his sleepy eyes. "Stick close to me, buddy," said Daddy.

It was cold in Philadelphia and the air smelled of exhaust. People hurried past us, looking as if they knew exactly where they were going. I felt lost. *Ellie, you should be here.* I held on to Jackie's hand and inched closer to Daddy. But Daddy wasn't looking so good. He stared at the tracks below the platform. "Daddy! Are you okay? Daddy, what's wrong?" I grabbed his hand and he squeezed my fingers. His hand was trembling.

Oh, no, Daddy. Don't have one of your spells. Not here. Not now. "Daddy, we have a train to catch. Luggage to find." I saw a porter at the other end of the platform, unloading suitcases and trunks. "Come. This way." *Oh, Ellie, where are you? I need you, Ellie. I don't want to do this. I'm not the brave one.*

I tugged on Daddy's hand and dragged him and Jackie to where the porter was loading the cart. I could see the sky-blue suitcases that Laura had loaned us. The porter lifted them down for me while Daddy just watched. Dazed. "Let's go, Daddy," I said.

But where? This station was huge. "Daddy," I said. "Help me. How do we find the other train?"

I looked around. A lady was asking the porter for directions. He pointed. She thanked him and ran. We should be hurrying too. "Mr. Porter," I said, "can you tell me where to catch our train? We're going to New Haven, Connecticut."

"May I see your tickets, please, miss?"

"Daddy, I need the tickets. The tickets!" I yelled. Daddy covered his ears. I was making things worse. I reached inside his coat pocket and felt for the tickets. His heart was throbbing like a train pounding down the tracks. "It's okay, Daddy," I said as quietly as I could make myself say it. "There. I found the tickets."

The porter eyed the top ticket. "Fourth track. One, two, three, four." He pointed across the tracks, jumping his finger across as he counted. "Twenty minutes. That way." He gestured through the station and out another door to the fourth platform. "Watch for the sign. New Haven."

"Yes. Yes. Thank you. Come, Daddy. Let's go, Jackie."

"What about the suitcase?" asked Jackie.

"Oh!" Daddy had almost left his suitcase sitting by the baggage cart. "Daddy." I forced myself to speak quietly, but also firmly—like Momma—when she needed to settle him down. "You have to carry this." I held it out to him. "Follow me."

I couldn't believe I was saying this as if I knew what I was doing.

I practically dragged the two of them through the station. *Fourth platform over. New Haven signs.* Jackie walked with his eyes on the enormous ceiling and huge columns. And he ran right into a stranger. "Jackie, watch where you are going. Tell the man you're sorry. Turn here." I pushed him to the left.

"You don't have to push me, Ida."

"Apparently I do, Jackie. I have to push you and pull Daddy. Are you coming, Daddy? This way." We went through double doors to the fourth platform. According to the big clock ahead we'd used up eight of our twenty minutes. But our train wasn't there. I hurried Jackie and Daddy to the baggage cart.

"Here comes a train," said Jackie. Sure enough, way down the tracks we saw headlights.

Daddy paced the platform. I reached over and grabbed his arm. "Stay calm, Daddy. This is our train. But it's going to get louder. Brace yourself."

The train roared closer and closer and then the brakes started squealing and the engine was bearing down on us and then it whooshed into the station with a blast of wind that felt like it wanted to suck us under the wheels. Jackie grabbed Daddy's leg.

Ellie would have loved how the train made her heart race. And she would've known how to handle Daddy. But maybe I was doing okay too. I squeezed his arm. "This is it, Daddy. We'll get on this car and be on our way. Hurry. It'll be quieter inside." Daddy's face was pale. His hands still shook. He breathed short puffs of air—trying hard to calm himself.

The train was full, so we all crowded together into one seat. And maybe it was better that way except Jackie was so close. So loud and excited. Pointing and calling our attention to each tall building and high bridge.

"Hush, Jackie," I said. "Just look. Daddy doesn't need you talking to him right now."

I pulled out the sketchbook Arnie had given me. "Look, Daddy," I said. "See the pictures I've been drawing." I opened the sketchbook and started at the front. I showed Daddy the pictures I'd copied from the *Progressive Farmer* magazine. Cows, canned goods, ducks, cars, and more. I pointed out the details and told him how I made them look real. I don't think I had ever talked so much at one time, but I needed him to pay attention to quiet things. Fences and canning jars seemed to help his breathing slow down.

Eventually we were out of Philadelphia, and I realized I hadn't actually seen it. But that was okay because Daddy was calmer. We stared into the countryside and after a while I could tell we were getting close to New York City.

And then Jackie really had something to stare at. At first we saw dark shapes silhouetted against the sky. Bridges and railroad tracks crisscrossing. Miles of tall buildings. A railroad yard with dozens of tracks and hundreds of cars. And then backyards of houses all attached to each other with the train running right past their doors. Garbage cans. Clotheslines with pins dangling on them. Dogs sleeping on back stoops.

A door opened and a woman stepped out with curlers in her hair and wearing a tattered pink housecoat. She scraped leftovers into a dish for an impatient cat.

I imagined my house right that minute. Mr. Shoes curled up on Daddy's rocking chair. The rooster crowing down at Junior and Bessie's house. Everyday sights and sounds. Nothing like this. But this was okay too. Some things are scarier before you do them. Leaving home was one of them, I guess.

54

IDA
November 1952

The couple waiting by the ticket counter waved and started moving toward us. And by the time we reached them the woman was crying. "Mr. Honeycutt," she said, and then she hugged Daddy just like he was family.

The man gripped Daddy's hand with both of his. "You will never know what this means to us," he said. His Adam's apple worked up and down and his eyes glistened.

Something about that—the way they needed him—seemed to calm Daddy. I could almost see the anxiety slide off his shoulders. He put his hand on Jackie's head. "This is my son. Jackie."

"Oh! Jackie!" The woman stooped and pulled him into her arms. "Such a gift you are." Tears slipped down her cheeks and onto Jackie's hair. She pulled back and looked into his eyes. "I had a boy named Jackie," she said. She stroked his arm and repeated those words. "I had a boy named Jackie."

Things started to make more sense to me. I knew my little brother was the connection between Daddy and these people. And I knew Daddy had named him after their boy. But they weren't faceless strangers anymore. They were parents who had lost a child. Just the way we'd lost Bobby to polio.

Daddy's lip was trembling. As a matter of fact *he* was trembling all over. At home, I'd shy away whenever he showed his strong feelings. Afraid of where they'd take him, unsure of what he'd do. But I'd been there in the hospital when he first saw Ellie, and it hadn't killed me.

And I'd talked him through that bad spell on the train. So I tucked my hand around his elbow and gave it a little squeeze.

The woman let go of Jackie then. She stood and turned to me. "And this is Ellie? Thank you for coming."

"Um, I'm Ida. Ellie's twin. She couldn't come, so I'm taking her place."

"Oh, how careless of me. Yes. Your father told us on the phone that Ellie is in the hospital. How is she?"

"She's improving, thank you."

Her husband shook my hand. "I'm Abe," he said.

"Yes," said his wife. "Honest Abe. And I am Mary. We're a famous couple." She winked and laughed. "But our last name is Bedford, not Lincoln. And Mr. Bedford is a judge. Not a president."

This woman was easy to be around. And her husband was too. "Let me carry these for you," he said. He took our suitcases and led us through the station and out to the car.

Sun bounced off the white of the snow and it took a minute for my eyes to adjust. Jackie picked up a handful of snow and threw it at me. "No, Jackie!" I said.

"Jackie," said Mrs. Bedford, "we'll soon be at our house. You can play there."

New Haven reminded me of New York City except that it wasn't as big. And now I was seeing the fronts of homes. Their stoops had iron railings and the houses had steep roofs, arched doors, and windows with carved stone over them. So different from the homes in Hickory, where each house—whether a huge Victorian or a small mail-order house from Sears and Roebuck—had a separate yard. Even the mill houses weren't connected to each other the way these city houses were.

Snow was heaped onto the sidewalks and piled between cars parked on the streets. People plodded through thick snow with scarves wrapped around their faces.

I was so used to living in the country that this was a big surprise to me. Whenever it snowed we stood by the window and watched it turn the gray landscape into a world of white with deep blue shadows. And we were happy to stay home and drink hot cocoa.

After a while we left the attached houses behind. Now the streets were lined with trees. Bare limbs had snow encrusted on their upper edges. I wanted to draw it all—sidewalks, big front yards, and brick houses. Mr. Bedford turned into a driveway. "This is home," he said. "I'll let you out here by the side door."

The Bedfords' home reminded me of the Hinkle sisters'. They had a garage out back. And the house was sparkling and modern with a gas cookstove and even an automatic dishwasher. The kitchen smelled like cinnamon.

"I'll show you to your rooms," said Mrs. Bedford. "Here's the lavatory." She pushed a door open and I glimpsed a long, airy room with shiny black and white tiles on the walls.

At the next door she said, "Ida, you will be in this room. I hope you like it."

"Oh," I said. "It's beautiful." And truly it was. There was a yellow chenille bedspread and sheer curtains. And a blue and yellow braided rug on each side of the bed. I felt like I was stepping into a picture from a magazine.

"There are towels on the dresser. Refresh yourself and rest a little," she said.

"So I could take a bath? Now, in the middle of the day?"

Mrs. Bedford chuckled. "Of course. Or a shower. Please make yourself at home."

She left then, closing the door, and there I was in this room that was pretty as a painting. And for a day or two, it was all mine. I inhaled. It smelled like aged wood and furniture polish and like the lavender soap lying on the towel and washcloth.

I decided to take a shower. For the first time in my entire life I stood in a tub and turned on the water and felt it splashing down over me. "Oh, Ellie," I said. "You'd feel so rich here." How could I explain to her all that she'd missed? And why *would* I tell her? It would only add to her misery. But I knew she'd want to hear every word of it. And she would hate me for it too.

55

IDA
November 1952

The Bedfords' daughter, Margaret, came to visit. She had a boy, Roger, who was only a year older than Jackie, and the two of them played in the snow. After a turkey supper, which Mrs. Bedford called dinner, she sent the boys into the living room to watch television.

"Now, please, may I show you pictures of our Jackie?" She reached for photographs stacked on a side table—a framed family portrait and one of young Jackie in the snow with a sled. Mr. Bedford brought Jackie's high school yearbook and opened it to pictures of sports teams. Daddy could pick Jackie out of a group each time.

"You knew him well," Margaret said.

Mrs. Bedford placed another framed picture in front of us. Jackie again—this time in his army uniform. Daddy gripped that picture with both hands. He bit his lip, and I looked away from him and stared at the picture instead.

I could almost feel my hand sketching Jackie's face. Lean, with a straight nose and a cleft chin. Determined eyes. Serious mouth.

Daddy pulled the framed picture toward him and a tear dropped onto the glass. Mrs. Bedford got up, walked around the table, and slipped a tissue into Daddy's hand. Then she put her head close to his, and wrapped her arms around him from behind, and they cried together.

Margaret reached for a tissue and Mr. Bedford pulled a handkerchief from his pocket and blew his nose. All these years later, they were still grieving.

But I kept thinking that at least his death had meaning. He died fighting for freedom.

I stopped fighting back tears. Next thing I knew, Mrs. Bedford was pulling me into her hug. Daddy reached for my hand and I thought of Ellie in the hospital. Of me saying, *Squeeze my hand, Ellie, if you can hear me.* I squeezed Daddy's fingers.

After a while we all slowed up on the sobbing, and Daddy pulled his handkerchief out of his pocket and wiped at his face. He blew his nose and then he began to talk.

"He was so young—just a boy in the middle of a big war. I wanted to protect him."

"You did," said Mrs. Bedford. "He lost his earmuffs and you insisted he take yours. I didn't know then who Leroy was. But here you are, in this letter." She picked up one of the thin blue V-mails like we'd get from Daddy when he was off in the army.

"It was nothing." Daddy shook his head. "Just a pair of earmuffs." His voice broke and he bit his lower lip.

"Nothing compared to what he sacrificed for me. I failed him."

"No," said both Mr. and Mrs. Bedford at the very same time.

"Can you tell us about his last day?" asked Margaret. "We never really heard what happened. Just that he was shot while on patrol."

I thought about Ellie's accident and how we still didn't know exactly what had happened. We could only guess. What was it like for the Bedfords? Seven years without hearing the details of their son's death?

Daddy gripped that picture of Jackie again. It shook in his hands.

"We were in France," he said. "I was sick. Burning up and shivering at the same time. Jackie took me to the medic. 'You have to get well for your family,' he told me. 'I'll take your patrol.' I tried to argue. But your Jackie kept saying, 'You'd be no good to our country right now. I'm strong. I can do this for you.'

"That's what I remember," said Daddy. "And later I heard the gunfire. It was all mixed in with my feverish dreaming. But I heard them bring him in. I knew from his voice that he was in pain."

Mrs. Bedford gasped. "Oh, my poor baby."

"I rolled off that cot and pulled myself to my feet. When I got to the tent next door the medics were trying to stop the bleeding. His face. His mouth." Daddy closed his eyes and shook his head—like he didn't want to see what he was seeing. "While they worked on him, they let me hold his head."

Daddy cradled that photograph in his two hands. He pulled it to his face and sobbed. "He was like a son to me." The words came out distorted. His face was twisted too. "I'd already lost one son to polio. And then I lost Jackie too."

And now we were all crying again. It was starting to make sense the way Daddy prized our Jackie so much. How he gave him whatever he wanted and became anxious when he lost a tooth. All the while his mind was back on the other Jackie. The one who died for him in the war.

And his mind was on my other brother too—Bobby, who died from polio without Daddy ever saying a proper goodbye.

56

IDA
November 1952

On our second day in New Haven the Bedfords loaded us into the car and took us sightseeing. "I brought a camera with me," said Mrs. Bedford. "I'll take pictures, and after they're processed I'll send them to you. We *will* stay in touch, won't we, Leroy?"

"I'm not much of a letter writer," said Daddy. "Maybe Ida can write for me."

"And do send pictures of your family," said Mrs. Bedford.

She used that camera everywhere we went that day. We posed in front of a lighthouse, and she took a picture of the New York skyline from a place called Point Park.

They took us for hamburgers at Louis' Lunch. But the hamburger meat was pink and the bread was toasted and I didn't much care if it did claim to be the first restaurant in the United States to serve hamburgers.

Daddy asked if we could drive to Yale University because Ellie would want us to see it for her. On the way, he said to the Bedfords, "Your Jackie used to talk about

Yale. He said when he got back from the war he'd go there and get a degree in law. He could argue a point, that's one thing for certain."

Daddy seemed different today—freer—the way he brought up the other Jackie and talked about him without getting all teary. And I felt different too.

"He'd be in law school by now," said Mrs. Bedford. Then she turned to Jackie. "Maybe *you* will attend Yale someday."

Jackie in college? That felt so far away. But Ellie—she wanted to go. "Will you take a picture of me here?" I asked when we came to the Yale library. "It's for Ellie. She can look at me and pretend that it's her—that she's the first girl to attend Yale University."

I ran to the top step and stood the way I thought Ellie would, head high and hands outstretched to show how thrilled she was to be there. Knowing Ellie, I was sure this would be her someday. Maybe she'd even be an attorney.

It was a whirlwind day. Ellie would love it up here in the North. But people moved too fast for me. There was no time for drawing. I would just have to wait until Mrs. Bedford developed the pictures and sent them to us. Then I could draw from those.

On Saturday, after supper, the Bedfords took us to the train station. And they insisted on buying our tickets. "This visit," said Mrs. Bedford. "It means more than you can know." She dabbed her eyes with her lace-trimmed hanky. "We could never repay you, but you must let Abe take care of the tickets."

Daddy tried to argue, but it's hard to argue with a judge. Mr. Bedford simply said, "The case is closed." For a judge, he sure was a softhearted man. He reached into the pocket of his overcoat and pulled out his wallet. "I've got something special for you, Jackie," he said. He held out a baseball card with a picture of a colored man, holding a bat.

"Uh," said Jackie. He stared at the card, and I could see he didn't understand why Mr. Bedford thought it was special.

Mr. Bedford pointed to the signature on the card. "His name is Jackie. And that's a pretty good name, don't you think?"

"Yes, sir," said Jackie.

"Jackie Robinson. The first Negro to play major league baseball. That makes him one brave man. Just like my son and your father were brave. And I know you are too. Hang on to that card because Jackie Robinson is making history. People will be bragging on him long after he's gone."

"Yes, sir," said Jackie. "Now I know two famous people. Ned Jarrett and Jackie Robinson."

Mr. Bedford chuckled. "Maybe you *will* meet him someday."

Leaving the Bedfords was hard but I wanted to get home to Ellie. We found seats and were on our way.

Within minutes the conductor came through to collect our tickets. He frowned when he saw them.

"Is something wrong?" Daddy asked.

"Sir," he said. "Come with me."

Was this the wrong car? Were we in some kind of trouble?

Jackie tugged at my hand. "Where is he taking us, Ida?"

"Shh, Jackie. Be quiet." We gathered our things and followed the conductor. He led us through two cars with people staring at us as we walked past their seats. But the third car had a narrow hall with doors along the way. Most of the doors were closed, but I saw one that was open. Two people were in there sipping coffee and smoking. Laughing.

The conductor stopped at the next door. "Your compartment," he said.

"Ours?" I turned to look at Daddy, who was standing just behind me.

He shook his head. "There must be a mistake."

The conductor pointed to the tickets. "You paid for a sleeper car," he said. "I'm sorry if you didn't intend to. I'm not in a position to refund the difference in cost. Now that it's done, I think you should take advantage."

Jackie understood exactly what was going on. "Mr. Bedford paid for it," he said. "Yippee! Can we really sleep in this car?"

The conductor laughed and ruffled Jackie's hair. "You certainly can," he said. "But listen to me, young man. No snoring is allowed. You do have neighbors, you know." He grinned and pointed to the next door down.

"Yes, sir," said Jackie. He wasted no time moving in.

The conductor showed Daddy how the seats turned into bunks. "But that is for later," he said. "When you are ready to sleep I will do it for you." He showed us a button we could push if we needed anything. "I am at your service," he said as he left.

Daddy just stood there shaking his head. I knew he was having trouble believing this, and he was probably feeling guilty. "Daddy," I said. "They said they could never repay you. They wanted to do this for us. Let's enjoy it."

But honestly I could hardly believe it either. We wouldn't have to sleep sitting up. We could ride to North Carolina like rich people. Ellie would have thought she was in paradise. But she was in a hospital bed, and I was here where she wanted to be. It was hard for me not to feel guilty, too.

Jackie didn't feel the least bit guilty. He pushed that button—the one the conductor had shown him. "No," said Daddy. Jackie pulled his hand away. But it was too late. "I wonder what will happen now," Daddy said.

It didn't take long for a man to come. He was wearing a red uniform with bright brass buttons and a smart-looking cap. "How can I help you?" he asked.

"We don't need help, sir," said Daddy.

"They told me I could push the button," said Jackie.

The man laughed. "They told you just right," he said. "I shall bring you something. Coca-Cola, maybe."

"Oh, yes!" said Jackie. "Can I, Daddy?"

Daddy nodded. "And for you, Ida?"

"I'll have the same," I said. "But Daddy, you should get something."

Daddy asked for coffee. About ten minutes later we heard a tap on the door and Jackie rushed to open it. There was the man holding a tray with two glasses of Coca-Cola, one cup of coffee, and three saucers with cake.

"Cake," said Jackie. "He brought us cake!"

The man laughed. "Ah, for such excitement, I would bring much more," he told Jackie. "But first you must find the table." He showed Jackie how to fold down the table under the window. And Jackie was amazed all over again. We all were.

We sat there and drank our Cokes and ate our cakes. I watched Daddy—his eyes were closed and his head bobbed with the motion of the train. Maybe he was going to sleep. I could sleep if I weren't so interested in staying awake just to take it all in.

I pulled out my sketchbook and started drawing Jackie, sitting at that wondrous table by the window eating cake, his small hand wrapped around a glass with *Coca-Cola* etched onto the side. I did a quick sketch. Then I started filling in the details. The fringe on the curtains by the window. The white cloth napkin on the table.

The button by the door that would bring a porter who would likely give us anything we wanted. It had all been paid for already. What would that be like? To be so rich and to pay for anything you wanted?

It wouldn't take long to get used to such luxuries. But I was going home. I knew Hickory had people with money. We had judges and attorneys and doctors in our town. They probably thought nothing of traveling in a separate sleeper car. But those weren't the people I knew. I just wanted to get home to my sister—to make sure she hadn't had a setback while I was gone.

When it was time to crawl into those crisp white sheets, I rolled onto my tummy and pulled back the curtain. I stared into the darkness and waited for the lights of New York City to appear. And I declare it was a wonder to see that place at night. All I could see for miles was the outline of buildings and the sparkle of lights that seemed to have no end. It was hard to believe that down with all those lights were ordinary people like me with pets and trash cans and rollers in their hair. At night like this it seemed like a magical place where only rich people would live. And riding along in a moving bed, being rocked to sleep by a train that swayed and bobbled and sometimes clattered, that was magical, too.

57

ELLIE
November 1952

Ida and Daddy and Jackie were coming home on Sunday. I sat in the waiting room and watched for their train to come through town. But I knew I wouldn't see them until visiting hours.

When the time came, I saw Junior's car from the waiting room window. Junior dropped Ida off at the street, and she ran up the steps into the hospital. Within minutes the elevator door dinged and slid open. I was waiting on her.

"How are you?" she asked. And then she fell apart, crying all over my shoulder.

What in the world? "What's wrong, Ida? Was it that bad?"

"It was wonderful, Ellie. You should have been there. The Bedfords are so kind. They're rich, but you'd never know it from how down-to-earth they are. They loved Daddy and Jackie and they were real nice to me too. And they even bought us tickets to ride in a sleeper car on the way home."

I declare, the words poured out of her mouth until I thought she'd turned into me. And I think I was a little disappointed. As much as I wanted to hear all about the visit, maybe I secretly hadn't wanted it to be wonderful at all. How could she have had such a good time when she hadn't even wanted to go? I was trying to be happy for her. But it wasn't easy. I sat there biting my lip so hard that it hurt.

"I feel guilty, Ellie. It should have been you. You're the one who wanted it."

"Stop it, Ida. Get a hold of yourself. You're gonna make me cry." I was furious. But I forced back my angry feelings. "How is Daddy?" I asked. "Where is he?"

"At home with Momma. Catching up. He seems better. He told the Bedfords about their son and how much he loved him. I don't know if he's all better forever, but it was a good trip, Ellie. It was right for him to go. And it was right for me too. Thank you, Ellie, for making me do it."

Thank you, Ellie, for making me do it. "Yeah," I said. I hated her in that moment. First she took Arnie and then she ran off on my trip to New England. But mad as I was, I knew I'd done this to myself. I'd done something really stupid because I was angry and jealous. Ida wasn't the one who robbed me of that trip. I had stolen it from myself. And no matter how angry I felt, I couldn't take it out on her.

When she was gone I sat in that waiting room and stared out the window. A car crossed the railroad tracks up the street and then it slowed and the driver talked to someone on the sidewalk for a few minutes. People came and went from the hospital parking lot.

I couldn't just sit there day after day watching other people go on with their lives. I had to do something. *You made your bed. Now lie in it.* Nobody had said those words to me, but sometime in my life I'd heard them and now they kept running through my head.

Maybe I would go back to bed. I could put the pillow over my head and no one would know I was crying.

I wheeled my chair back to the ward and waited for a nurse to help me get in bed. I waited ten whole minutes with a pasted-on smile while I jabbered with Regina in the bed across the room. Stella had gone home, and I missed her.

Finally Nurse Little came. "Ellie, you have another visitor."

"I do?" I wasn't feeling sociable. Not at all. "Who is it?"

Nurse Little shrugged. "I didn't ask his name."

His? But who? Arnie? No. Of course not. Duncan? I didn't want to see him. The nurse wheeled me out, and there, standing by the waiting room door, grinning in that shy way of his, was Ned Jarrett. He waved, then stepped forward and shook my hand. "Ellie?"

"Yes."

He shuffled his feet a little and I saw how awkward he felt coming to visit me. I mean, it wasn't like we actually knew each other. But why was he here?

"I just bumped into Junior and your sisters," he said. "At a stop sign. Your twin told me you'd love to have a visit from a race car driver."

He glanced at the floor then and I could see how modest he was. Like just calling himself a race car driver was too braggy.

"Oh, my goodness, yes! I can't believe you came. I was ready to crawl in bed and have a good cry. Then you come along. I just can't believe it."

He laughed. And shrugged. "I'm just me," he said. "I was sorry to hear about the accident. You're as banged up as a race car."

"Yeah. The driver I was with wasn't as good as you are. But I shouldn't have been in that car in the first place."

"We all do foolish things," he said. "Thank heaven for second chances."

When he was gone that line kept running through my head. *Thank heaven for second chances.* I sat in the waiting room and watched him climb into his car and drive away. I didn't know what foolish things Ned Jarrett had done in his life or what second chances he'd had. But I'd seen him give up racing out of respect for his father and then come back strong. I'd seen No. 99 blow a radiator in one race and finish in eleventh place the next.

I didn't go to bed and cry after all. Instead I started thinking about going back to my life and what I would do with my second chance.

58

ELLIE
December 1952

Two days after Ida came home from that trip, Dr. Johnson released me from the hospital. "But this is on the condition that you behave yourself," he said. "Those casts will be on for three more weeks at the very least. You must let other people take care of you."

"Yes, sir," I said.

Momma and Daddy were picking me up on their way home from work. The nurse pushed me out to Daddy's car. "Where does the wheelchair go?" I asked. It surely wouldn't fit in the back seat.

"That chair belongs to the hospital," said Daddy. "Thanks to Miss Pauline, you've got one waiting at the house for you right now. She hasn't used hers for a few months, and she's delighted to share it with you."

"We moved the furniture," said Momma, "so you can wheel the chair around better. Jackie had a fine time trying it out."

Jackie. I hadn't seen him for so long. And when I did, I declare it looked to me like he'd grown three inches.

He hugged me so hard I didn't think he'd ever let me out of the car. And he couldn't wait until I was in the house to show me his baseball card. "Look what Mr. Bedford gave me. It's Jackie Robinson, and he's famous just like Ned Jarrett."

"Wow, Jackie!" I said. "That's really nifty."

Being home was even niftier. The house smelled like chicken and dumplings, and everything looked strangely beautiful to me. Even our shabby sofa.

They'd rearranged our bedroom—back to the way it was before Ida moved things last summer. Now there was more room for the wheelchair, and Momma had put a chamber-pot chair right by my bed because going to the bathroom on the back porch would be next to impossible. I practiced rolling the chair from the bedroom, through the living room, and to the kitchen.

Ann Fay and Ida were making supper. "Ellie, you have to set the table," said Ann Fay. She pointed to the silverware drawer.

"Yes, ma'am." I was happy to be part of things.

Over supper Momma explained how we would manage until the casts came off my legs. "Junior will bring Bessie when he picks up Ann Fay. And she'll stay until Miss Pauline or Miss Dinah can come. Most days it will be Miss Pauline because you have schoolwork to catch up on. She's eager to tutor you. Peggy Sue will drop by a few times a day to help the ladies get you on the chamber pot."

"Ugh," I said.

"Yeah, ugh," said Jackie. "That is not a topic for the supper table." And we all laughed.

The next morning when Junior picked up Ann Fay for work, he brought Bessie with him. He came inside to say hello. "I hear you have a new teacher, Ellie. I pity you. Miss Pauline used be my teacher, and I'll tell you one thing right now. That woman will make you work!"

Later, when Miss Pauline came, I asked her about it. "Junior said you were his teacher?"

Miss Pauline nodded. "What else did he say?"

I laughed. "Apparently you were hard on him."

"He had some catching up to do. Amends to make. You should ask him about that. Let's get started on your Latin."

Personally, I liked Miss Pauline as a teacher. We both loved words. And I think she was grateful that I'd kept her company last summer when she needed me. Whatever it was, the two of us got along just fine.

She didn't like talking about other things during class time, though. She was all business. By lunchtime I was exhausted. "I do believe we're both ready for a nap," she said. "When Peggy Sue comes she'll bring Bessie with her and I'll go home for the day."

I could hardly believe how Momma and the neighbors had worked out my life with friends coming and going a couple of times each day. I didn't exactly like other people helping me go to the bathroom, but I had sort of gotten used to it in the hospital.

And Peggy Sue was so cheery about it I could hardly tell she'd rather be making people look pretty in her beauty shop. Mostly she wanted to gossip about Ann Fay and Junior. "Bessie," she said, "if you ask me, that boy of yours is finally getting somewhere with Ann Fay."

Bessie chuckled. "Have mercy. I hope so. But I'm not holding my breath."

"Let's just put it like this," said Peggy Sue. "Ann Fay talks to me. And last week on the way to choir practice, I could tell she was changing her tune. I have a feeling Ellie's accident had something to do with it."

"My accident?"

"Yeah. But I'll let Ann Fay tell you about that."

"Peggy Sue, stop torturing us," I said. But she made a motion like she was zipping her lips shut, and I couldn't get another thing out of her.

That was the second time in one day somebody started to tell me something juicy and didn't finish the story. But when Junior brought Ann Fay home and picked up Bessie, I decided to at least ask what Miss Pauline meant about him making amends.

"Sounds like Miss Pauline's been gossiping," he said.

"Not really. She said I had to ask you."

Junior cocked his head and said, "I know this is hard to believe. But once upon a time, I was fourteen and foolish."

"Yeah?"

"I was mad. At my pop, who was dead. And at life, because it was so dad-gum confusing. So I quit school and . . . well, I kind of borrowed Miss Hinkle's car without asking."

"What? You stole her car?" I just couldn't believe Junior Bledsoe would do such a thing.

"I was out with Dudley Walker. Him and me together were trouble. But we got caught, and I told Miss Pauline I'd make it up to her. Thought maybe she'd have me fixing something around the house. But you know what she wanted me to do? To 'make amends,' as she calls it? She made me go back to school. So I sat at her kitchen table every weekday all summer long until she got me to the end of ninth grade." Junior went to the door between the living room and the kitchen. "You ready to go, Momma?"

When he and Bessie came back through the living room, he said, "Making amends is a good thing. Takes the selfishness right out of you. Bye, Ellie." He gave our bedroom door a little knock and called out, "See ya later, Ann Fay."

"Bye, Junior." Ann Fay answered from inside the bedroom.

It didn't take me two minutes to get my chair in there. Ann Fay and Ida were changing into everyday clothes and making plans to heat up leftovers for supper. "Wow!" I said. "I just found out Junior stole Miss Pauline's car."

Ann Fay kicked off her shoes. "That was a long time ago, Ellie. He didn't actually steal it—just borrowed it without permission. Besides, he's changed." She sounded defensive.

"Of course," I said. "I wasn't accusing him. Did you think I was? Ann Fay, are you going soft on Junior?"

"Now you're being nosy."

"You bet I am."

Ann Fay put her dress on a hanger. She started to take off her slip, but then she didn't. She plopped herself down on the bed and just stared at me there in my wheelchair.

Is she remembering when she was stuck in one of these?

"Well, if you must know," she said after a while, "I've been thinking. You almost died, Ellie. Remember? And Ida went off to the hospital and left me here alone. You've always had each other. But what about me? Don't I deserve to have somebody too?"

"Yes!" said Ida. "Why do you think I worked out that ride to work with Junior? Are you going to marry him?"

"No," said Ann Fay. "I mean, maybe. Someday. But hey, don't rush it."

"Don't rush it?" I howled at that. "He's been crazy about you forever, Ann Fay. And you've been snubbing him forever. Probably ever since he stole that car."

"Ha!" said Ann Fay. "Back then I was a pesky little kid and Junior was the one snubbing me."

Junior snubbing Ann Fay was hard for me to imagine. But then again, him stealing a car was even harder. I kept thinking about those words he threw at me just before going out the door. *Making amends is a good thing.*

That line stuck in my head like a catchy song. And that night when I was in bed and Ann Fay and Ida were sound asleep it was still there. *Making amends is a good thing . . .*

59

IDA
December 1952

Ellie screamed and it woke me out of a deep sleep. I reached for her. "Ellie, what's the matter? Were you dreaming? Wake up." She was shaking. I was too.

Ellie didn't speak. She just cried.

"Was it the accident? You dreamed about it, didn't you?"

By now Ann Fay was up, standing by Ellie's side of our bed and rubbing her back. "It's over, Ellie. You're safe in your bed."

A light came on in the kitchen and I heard footsteps. Momma. And Daddy too.

Everybody but Jackie was awake.

"Is she okay?" That was Daddy.

"I'm sorry," said Ellie. "Go back to bed. I didn't mean to wake you up. I'm just being a baby."

"Oh, honey," said Momma.

Daddy sat down on the chamber-pot chair beside the bed. "I'll hold your hand," he said. "Go back to sleep, everybody."

In the morning, he was still there—holding Ellie's hand and sleeping while sitting up. I watched him in the grayness of that room and thought how sleep made him seem younger, softer. More vulnerable. But him holding her hand that way and sleeping sitting straight up for hours made him seem strong at the same time. Like he was guarding her against bad dreams.

Guarding her. Like a soldier. That's how he learned to sleep sitting up. I'd heard him and Otis talk about being bone-tired during the war. Learning to sleep anywhere. Under any conditions.

When Ellie woke up, Daddy put her in the wheelchair and pushed her to the kitchen. It was Saturday, so Momma and Ann Fay made a great big breakfast. Ellie was her normal self. It made me think about Daddy. How he'd be extra jumpy one day and just fine the next. And I thought about how talking it out with Otis and telling the Bedfords made a big difference.

"Maybe you need to talk about it," I told Ellie.

"About what?"

"The accident. What exactly happened that night? How did you get in that car? I never really heard. Just rumors at school, and who knows if they're true?"

Ellie chewed at her thumbnail. "Could I have a cup of coffee?" she asked. "With cream and sugar?"

"Of course," Momma said.

She and Daddy jumped up at the same time. Momma poured the coffee, set the cup on a saucer, and handed it to Daddy. He brought it to the table. "Anything else?" he asked.

"Cocoa," said Jackie.

Daddy laughed. "I was talking to Ellie."

But Momma fixed cocoa for me and Jackie and poured coffee for her and Ann Fay and Daddy. Then we all sat around that table and Ellie told us what happened.

"It was just me and Stella at the pajama party. Patsy was supposed to come but I guess she got sick. Stella needed me because if I was there Duncan would come— he sort of has a crush on me—and if Duncan came Reggie would be with him. That's what she wanted all along—to go joyriding with Reggie.

"But Reggie wanted to be with Laura, and Laura refused to go to Stella's party. She doesn't like Stella."

"Laura is smart," I said.

Ellie frowned. "No comments from the peanut gallery."

Jackie busted up laughing. "Ha ha, I guess she told *you*, Ida."

Ellie ignored Jackie and kept on talking. "I didn't know about the boys coming. Honest, I didn't. Not until it was almost time for them to show up. Stella sprang it on me. And, well, I was upset about Ida and Arnie."

"What about Ida and Arnie?" asked Momma.

"He likes her," said Ellie. "He likes Ida instead of me." Her voice broke when she said it, and I could tell it still hurt. "I was upset. Real mad. And you know me—I like to have a good time. So when the boys came in the car, I decided to go along with it. After all, we were just going for a short drive."

She stopped like she wasn't sure what to say next. "But why did Reggie go along with Stella if Laura wasn't there?" I asked. "I thought he didn't like Stella."

"She led him to believe we'd be picking Laura up. She acted like I was supposed to show them where she lives. But I've never even been to Laura's house. So then Reggie started driving real fast and Stella liked it and I guess I did too. We rolled down the window and everything was going great until Reggie started showing off too much. And then a car came and I don't know—it all happened so fast. I knew we were going to crash. I saw the headlights coming and it was going to be a head-on collision and we were all going to die. But then we rolled instead. That's really all I can remember—just rolling and screaming and glass breaking and . . ."

Ellie put her head on the table and when she did she bumped the coffee, which she hadn't even touched. It splashed onto the vinyl tablecloth. "I'm sorry, Daddy. I'm sorry, Momma."

I hadn't seen my sister cry that hard in a long time. I reached over and put my arm around her, and then I felt Ann Fay and Momma there too. It was like the whole family was having one big huddle. I guess we were all crying.

Finally Momma wiped her eyes with the skirt of her apron, and Daddy pulled out his handkerchief and blew his nose. "We forgive you," said Momma.

"You're still here," said Daddy. "That's what counts."

Jackie piped up then. "And I guess you learned a lesson, didn't you, Ellie?"

"Shh," I told Jackie. "That's rude." But Ellie cracked up laughing. I guess it *was* kind of funny—the littlest one in the family doing the preaching when everybody else was just trying to be understanding.

Ellie reached for Daddy's handkerchief and wiped her eyes. "Yes, Jackie," she said. "I learned my lesson. That's one thing for sure."

It wasn't long before we saw Miss Pauline's car coming down the road. "Ellie," I asked, "is Miss Pauline planning to have school with you today?"

"No, silly. It's Saturday."

"That's Junior in her car," said Jackie.

Sure enough. Junior hopped out of the car and hurried to the front door. It looked to me like he was whistling. "He's in a good mood," I said.

Jackie ran to open the door and Junior came inside. "Whatcha doing in Miss Pauline's car?" asked Jackie.

"Important business," said Junior. "Where's Ann Fay?"

"Doing dishes."

Junior came into the kitchen. "About done with those dishes, Ann Fay?"

"Why? You need something?"

"Yep. I sure do. I need to teach you to drive. And today is as good a day as any. Sun is shining. It's not too cold. Not too hot. I borrowed Miss Pauline's Hydra-Matic."

Ann Fay turned back to her dishes. Pretending she wasn't interested. "Maybe I don't want to," she said. "And how'd you get that car anyway? Does Miss Pauline know you took it?"

"Yes, Miss Smarty-Pants. I ain't been a thief for a long time. Come on, Ann Fay. Give up and let's go."

So Ann Fay dried her hands on her apron. Pulled that apron off and threw it at me. "Guess *you'll* have to do them, Ida," she said. "Looks like I'm going for a drive."

60

ELLIE
December 1952

One week before Christmas, a package arrived from Connecticut. The mailman brought it to the door and handed it to Peggy Sue.

"It's addressed to Leroy," said Peggy Sue.

"Part of me is dying to see what it is," I told her. "And another part doesn't want to know. Ida's expecting photographs and they'll just remind me of what I missed."

"Oh, so sorry," said Peggy Sue. "But look, you need something to pick you up and today I came prepared." She reached into a basket she'd brought with her and pulled out a pair of scissors and a comb. And curlers too. Heaven only knew what else she had in there.

She pulled out a bottle. "How about a home permanent?"

Before I could say a word, she dumped every bit of that paraphernalia onto my lap and started pushing my chair into the kitchen. "Since you can't come to the salon," she said, "I've brought it to you. Your hair's growing out again where they shaved it. It's still a little short, but how about I cut all of your hair to even things up? It'll look real cute, I promise."

Really? She thought she had to talk me into this?

"Oh, Peggy Sue, I'd love it. But don't you have customers waiting on you at your salon?"

"Nope. I canceled them. This afternoon is for you."

I just couldn't believe she'd do that for me. And oh, my goodness, by the time Peggy Sue was done with me and had my hair dried and styled, you almost didn't even notice the scar coming out of my hairline onto my forehead.

She'd had to work around Bessie, who was busy baking up a storm, but the three of us joked and told stories and even sang silly songs and it was just about the best day I'd had since the accident.

"I feel guilty," I said. "Both of you have other things you could be doing right now. Instead you're looking after me."

"Don't be silly," said Bessie. "This is what people do when there's trouble. We pull together. And you look downright glamorous with your new style. Your twin might be begging for one too."

I kept turning that mirror Peggy Sue put into my hands—trying to see all sides of myself but of course I couldn't see the back of my head. So she took Momma's mirror off the wall by the kitchen door and held it so I could. "I love it, Peggy Sue. Come here so I can hug your neck!"

"You're welcome," said Peggy Sue. "I'd sure like to stick around and see what Ann Fay and Ida think of your new look, but I really do have to go." She threw her combs and curlers and scissors into her basket, and next thing I knew she was out the door.

"Whew!" said Bessie. "She's a whirlwind, isn't she?"

But of course I loved having someone as fun and energetic as Peggy Sue around. Bessie and Miss Pauline were good for taking care of me. But Peggy Sue made me feel like my old self. Sassy and confident. Gorgeous, even.

That's what Ida said I was. "Gorgeous. I might be jealous," she told me. "But Ellie, you deserve this."

We opened the package after supper. Just as I figured, the Bedfords had sent photographs. "Look at me in front of Yale's library," said Ida. "Don't I look just like you standing there?"

"No," said Jackie. "Your hair's too long. Ellie has short hair."

I laughed. "That's right, Jackie."

Truthfully, Ida really did look like me in that picture, the way she held herself so bold and confident. But I realized something else too. She looked a lot like herself. Because ever since that trip that's actually how she was.

Some days it seemed like Ida and I were swapping places. She went to school every day and came home in a real chipper mood. And I was at home, studying with Miss Pauline or sometimes with Laura or Vivian if they called or dropped in.

Stella called too, nearly every evening. And every time she told me how sorry she was. "It was all my fault," she'd say.

But I knew that wasn't true. "No, it's not all your fault," I'd argue. "It's mine too because I went along with it. And it's Reggie's for driving too fast and Duncan's for egging him on. We did it together, Stella. We're all to blame."

But she still felt guilty. Finally one day she said, "Ellie, I have something to tell you about that night."

"Okay."

"Patsy wasn't actually sick. I just wanted the four of us to have a double date. You and Duncan and me and Reggie. . . . So I told Patsy I wasn't having the party after all."

I should have been mad at Stella. But I was past that. Instead I asked, "Does Patsy know? Is she still your friend?"

Stella was real quiet on the other end of the line. Finally she said, "Obviously she knows we were together. But I haven't admitted lying to her."

"Maybe you should. Go ahead and get it off your conscience."

"I'm thinking about it," said Stella. I guess she needed a way to make things right, too, since she kept fretting about what she'd done.

"Stella, I've been thinking about making amends."

"Huh?"

"I have all these people taking care of me. And I'm just sitting here doing schoolwork and not much else. I need a project—something I can do for someone else. Want to help me? We could try to make up for all the trouble we've put people through."

"But how? What would we do?"

"I don't know, Stella. But I'm thinking. When I get an idea I'll let you know."

The idea came to me about an hour later when Ann Fay came home from work talking about polio and how 1952 was the worst year yet. "Over fifty thousand cases in the United States just this year," she said. "Dr. Sain will be sending dime cards home with all his patients."

Dime cards—little cardboard folders with slots for collecting coins. They passed them out to us every year at school, and our classes always competed to raise the most money for the March of Dimes. "That's it!" I said. "I'll raise money for the March of Dimes."

"What?" said Ann Fay.

"I need a project to work on. To make amends."

"Make amends?"

"You know. To make up for all the trouble I've caused everybody."

My mind picked up that idea and went round and round with it. If I could raise money for polio research or to buy some child braces or crutches or even one of those dad-blasted wheelchairs, maybe that would be making amends.

Stella could help me. But first I had to go back to school.

61

ELLIE
December 1952

Now that I had it in my head to raise money for the March of Dimes, I couldn't wait to go to school. But I wasn't allowed to go until after Christmas.

I had an idea, but I'd have to talk to the principal. That wouldn't be hard. Convincing Ida to go along with my plan would be the tricky part.

"Ida," I said. "You want to raise money to fight polio, don't you?"

"Of course, Ellie."

"And you'd do whatever you could to help out, right?"

Ida frowned and squinted suspiciously. "What do you want, Ellie?"

"I have this terrific idea! And I'm sure Mr. Lynn would allow us to do it. Are you ready?"

"Come on, Ellie. Spit it out."

"You're fantastic with portraits, Ida. You could sit in a public place, maybe in the cafeteria or by the trophy case, and charge to draw student portraits. All the proceeds would go to the March of Dimes."

"Uh. Ellie. I'm the shy one. Remember?"

"Yeah, I know. But I can do the talking. I'll stand in the hall with a megaphone and flag people down for you."

"I don't think so, Ellie."

"Don't answer me now. Just think about it. And don't forget, without help from the March of Dimes, Ann Fay might still be stuck in a wheelchair like this one."

"Just let me think about it," said Ida.

I knew Ida wouldn't love having all that attention focused on her, so I started thinking. What if it wasn't just *her* doing the portraits? There were other artists in the school. I just needed to find out who they were. I needed more heads to help me figure this out.

Of course! Stella. This was something we could do together. We didn't have to stop at portraits. There had to be other ways of raising money.

I called her up. "Hey, Stella. If I catch a ride to school one day this week, would you come to a meeting in the library?"

"A meeting. What kind of meeting?"

"Remember we talked about making amends? What if we asked Reggie and Duncan to help us? We could do something big—for the community."

"I guess so."

"I'll work it out with Mr. Lynn, and he can tell them."

It took a few phone calls, but once I'd explained what I had in mind, Mr. Lynn agreed to the meeting.

It wasn't that hard to convince Junior to take me to the school. He used Daddy's old truck so he could haul the wheelchair in the back. When he pushed me down the hall, I admit I looked around for Arnie. But I didn't see him.

I was sitting in the library when Mr. Lynn escorted Stella, Reggie, and Duncan in. The boys were sure surprised to see me there. "Hey, Ellie," Reggie mumbled.

"I like the hair," said Duncan.

"Thanks," I said. I almost showed him how it covered my scar, but then I thought how silly that would be. To cover the scar and then show it off.

We all had scars. You could see where Stella had gotten a gash on her chin. Reggie's arm had a long scar, and Duncan's nose was crooked. I had heard it was broken in the accident.

The boys looked uncomfortable. Duncan tapped his pencil on the library table. Reggie kept glancing at the clock and saying he was missing a test. He sat at the other end of the table from Stella and refused to even look at her.

"Ellie called this meeting," said Mr. Lynn. "So I'm going to leave you four here to talk things through."

I was ready with my clipboard and pen. I looked at each of them, one at a time. I pointed to my casts. "Do you know how many people it takes to look after me right now? I can't even get out of bed by myself. What about y'all? You're back in school. But who helped your parents when you were recuperating?"

"My grandparents," said Stella. "And people from church."

"Neighbors," said Reggie.

"My daddy's boss man," said Duncan.

"Yeah. And school friends, like Patsy and Laura and their families. What if we said thank you to the whole school? I was thinking we could go on the P.A. system and each say a word or two. What do you think? We could even apologize for causing so much grief."

"I apologized," said Reggie. "To my parents and to Duncan." He looked at me. "I'm sorry, Ellie."

I noticed he didn't mention Stella. He probably thought *she* owed *him* an apology. I saw her over there chewing the inside of her bottom lip.

"Listen," I said. "If we don't forgive each other we're just going to be spinning our wheels. I don't know about you, but I want to go places. So even though I could be mad at Stella for not telling me the whole truth that night, I forgive her. Because you know what? I wanted to be bad just as much as she did. And I was having a good time doing it, too. Or at least I thought I was."

Nobody made a sound or moved a muscle.

"Stella's been feeling real guilty, haven't you?" I said.

I saw Reggie sneaking a glance at Stella. She nodded, and when she did a tear rolled down her cheek and splashed onto the table. Stella wiped at it with her thumb and put her hand over the wet spot, but Reggie noticed. He shifted in his chair.

"Can we just agree to be friends?" I asked. "Then we can work together for a good cause."

"Like what?" asked Duncan.

"I was thinking about the March of Dimes," I explained. "My sister had polio and the community helped raise the money for her rehabilitation. We could do something like that. And the fund drive is coming up at the end of January."

Reggie leaned forward and I could tell some idea was spinning in his brain. "So this would be for Buster?" he asked. And the minute he said it Duncan straightened up too.

"Buster! Uh, sure." *Why didn't I think of that?* This was an idea we could all agree on. The whole school might get involved because polio affected someone we knew.

"What are we going to do?" asked Reggie. "Hand out dime cards?"

"That's one thing. But there're other ways to raise money. We'll meet again after I come back to school. First I have to get these casts off and learn to walk again."

Two days later, Dr. Johnson removed my casts. My legs were so pale and shriveled that it scared me to look at them. Would they even hold my weight? Dr. Johnson and his nurse helped me try them out, supporting me on each side while I stood for just a minute.

I couldn't believe how that tired me. "Your bones have healed fine," said Dr. Johnson. "But obviously you won't go dancing this evening. You'll have to take it easy at first. Slowly build your strength. By Christmas Day you may be rid of that wheelchair."

I practiced walking a little every day and I felt myself getting stronger. But whenever I was in that chair I worked on ideas for raising money. With Stella and the boys helping we could provide activities besides portraits. We could fight polio and have lots of fun at the same time.

On Christmas, when my family went to Bessie and Junior's for dinner, I left the chair at home and walked in on my own two feet. The Hinkle sisters were there already. We ate and counted our blessings, and everyone agreed that me being up and walking was the best blessing of the year.

Crowded around that table the way we were, I kept hearing that song Stella played after "Tennessee Waltz" made me cry, "Dear Hearts and Gentle People."

I'm not saying I didn't want to travel someday, maybe go to college and do better for myself, but I knew one thing: it would be hard to find anything better than what I had right there at the foot of Bakers Mountain.

I told everybody about my dreams to raise money for the March of Dimes. "I'm hoping Mr. Lynn will let us have a carnival with different booths. Like Ida drawing portraits."

"Maybe," said Ida.

"A carnival?" said Miss Dinah. "Will you have a kissing booth? They make lots of money."

A kissing booth! I'm pretty sure none of us were expecting either of the Hinkle sisters to suggest that.

We all laughed, but Miss Pauline interrupted. "Kissing booths are popular," she said. "All you need is a pretty girl with bright red lipstick. Then when the boys come for their kiss, she hands over a chocolate one."

"Oh, no," said Junior. "That's not fair."

But the truth was, everybody loved the idea. "I'll get Stella to run that booth," I said. "And Patsy too. That'll be perfect for them."

After we'd stuffed ourselves on Bessie's desserts, Junior said he had a surprise for us. He stood. "Ann Fay, you're coming with me." For once in her life, Ann Fay did not argue. "We'll be right back," said Junior, and I declare his grin was bigger than the Bledsoes' barn.

We watched the two of them go out the back door. "If you ask me," said Ida, "someone's getting ready to make an announcement."

"I'm not holding my breath," said Bessie.

Not five minutes later, we heard a car horn and we all jumped up and ran into the living room. Jackie got there first. "It's a new car!" he yelled. He yanked the front door open and burst out onto the porch. The rest of us followed him.

There in the Bledsoes' driveway sat a light blue car with Ann Fay in the driver's seat. Junior hopped out and ran around to open the door for her, and we all crowded around.

"Did you buy Ann Fay a car for Christmas?" asked Jackie. "It's an Oldsmobile, isn't it?"

"It's an Oldsmobile all right," said Junior. "But I didn't buy it for *her*. I bought it for *us*." He put his arm around Ann Fay's shoulder and pulled her close. "I couldn't afford a ring," he said. "So I traded in my stick shift for a Hydra-Matic. And then while she was busy falling in love with that car, I popped the question."

"Ring?" asked Miss Dinah. "Car?"

"We're getting married," said Ann Fay. She pulled Junior's face toward hers and gave him a kiss.

"Oh, yuck," said Jackie. "Somebody find some chocolate."

Bessie let out a big sigh of relief. As a matter of fact, I think every last one of us did. We'd been waiting for this for a long time.

62

ELLIE
January 1953

Dr. Johnson released me to go back to school in January but only for half days at first. He said I needed to break in slowly.

Junior took me to school, and when I stepped into Latin class you'd have thought I'd just won the presidential election from the way the class cheered and whistled. I wasn't ready for that. All those faces staring at me. Smiling.

Laura gave me a big hug, and just that quick I knew I was right where I belonged. Junior put my books on my desk, gave a little wave, and skedaddled as fast as he could.

Mrs. Reitzel asked if I wanted to say anything, but for once I was out of words. Finally, I said, "Thanks for welcoming me back."

She nodded and said, "Class, open your books to page ninety-eight."

I tried my best to focus on Latin, but my eyes kept wandering around the room. To the light coming through the windows. The posters on the wall. The Great Seal of the United States—*E pluribus unum*. Out of many, one. And the North Carolina seal. *Esse quam videri*. To be rather than to seem.

For some reason the sight of those seals made me feel solid. Like I belonged to something. The United States. North Carolina. And to these people right here. Some of their mothers had made food for my family while I was in the hospital. And not just for my family but for Stella's, Duncan's, and Reggie's.

The four of us met in Mr. Lynn's office during morning break. Normally I'd have been walking the halls, eating an apple, or laughing with friends by the library door. But I wasn't up for walking the halls and Mr. Lynn felt that we should make our announcement at the beginning of third period.

We crowded around the P.A. system. "Maybe I'll back out," said Duncan.

"No," I said. "Nobody's escaping." I linked my arms through Duncan's and then I looped through Reggie's arm and I guess he figured he didn't have any choice but to hook onto Stella's.

Mr. Lynn took the microphone. "Students," he said, "we have a special announcement, and I want you to pay close attention."

You could almost feel a hush fall over the whole school. The janitor stopped rolling his trash can down the hall. The secretary in the next room quit typing. Mr. Lynn set the microphone on the counter in front of us.

I started. "Hi, everybody. I'm Ellie Honeycutt." The others said their names, and then it was my turn again. "This is my first day at school for almost two months because, as you all know, I was in a car accident along with Stella, Reggie, and Duncan."

Stella spoke up. "The late-night drive was my idea. But it was a stupid idea and I regret it more than anything."

"I was driving," said Reggie. "And to tell you the truth, I was mad. I don't recommend driving while mad."

Duncan said, "We wanted to take this time to say thank you."

Then we all looked at each other, took a deep breath, and read in unison, "When we were down, you picked us up. Thank you for all your support, for food, for love, and for prayers."

I finished our announcement. "Now it's our turn to give back. But we'll need your help. The March of Dimes fund drive starts in just two weeks. And we plan on raising as much money as we can to support Buster Poovey, who is still in the hospital down in Charlotte. So please start saving your money. You'll be hearing from us again soon."

Mr. Lynn barely had that microphone turned off before we started hugging. I don't know who hugged who first, but I know from the mix of smells that all four of us were jammed together—Stella's hairspray, Duncan's aftershave, and somebody's bad breath.

The words of a cheer went through my head then. *The team was in a huddle and the captain lowered his head.* I realized something. We really were a team. And we could fight for good things. We could pull off the ideas that had been racing around in my head while I was stuck at home.

I pulled back out of the huddle. "Hey, y'all. Remember the fundraiser we talked about. We need to make plans."

"Not now, Ellie," said Mr. Lynn. "You folks need to get back to class."

"Okay," I told the others. "Let's meet during break tomorrow. I've got some really swell ideas I want to talk to you about."

63

ELLIE
January 1953

"Okay," I said, the next morning during the break. "We have about . . ." I glanced at the clock above the library check-out desk. "Eight minutes. I'm going to talk fast. See this?" I held up my clipboard. "While I was at home, stuck in that wheelchair, I had to do something. I needed to feel like I was going someplace even if I wasn't. And on top of that I was thinking a lot about making amends."

"Um," said Reggie.

"Shh. We don't have much time. Just listen. Go home and think about this. Tomorrow you can come back and argue." I held my clipboard. "Lots of the planning has already been done. I just need you to help put these ideas into action. And of course, I welcome your ideas too."

I explained to them my vision for a school day that was like a carnival. "Woo-hoo!" said Duncan. "Does that mean we get out of classes?"

"Yes. But first we have to convince Mr. Lynn. And after all, since this is for fighting polio, how could he say no? We need fundraising ideas. Everything will cost a dime. I'm pretty sure my sister will draw portraits. But we'll need more artists." I handed the clipboard to Stella. "Pass this around. If you know someone else who can draw, write their name down. And my neighbor suggested a kissing booth."

Reggie raised his hand. "Give me the clipboard," he said. "I volunteer for that one."

We all laughed. "My neighbor is a retired teacher. She's not going to encourage real kissing. She suggested chocolate ones. And I have a feeling Mr. Lynn would agree with her on that."

Reggie groaned. "Schoolteachers and principals. Always taking the fun out of life."

"Hush. We're down to four minutes. I was thinking someone could rig up a dunking booth."

"Duncan volunteers for that one," said Reggie.

"How about Mr. Lynn?" suggested Duncan.

"Write it down," I said. "Go home and write down every idea you can think of. Booths and people who can run them. Posters and people who can make them." The bell rang then. "Meet me here tomorrow. We'll gather our ideas. I'll write up the plan and we'll descend on Mr. Lynn's office the next day."

Reggie stood. "Remember when school used to be simple?" he asked. "Reading, 'riting, and 'rithmetic? Now it's the three R's and carnivals."

"Fund drives," I reminded him. "Mr. Lynn will like the sound of that better than carnival."

I headed for algebra class. My mind was racing, but my legs were failing like an old jalopy. And I had tons of work ahead of me if we were going to pull this off.

"Hey, Ellie. Want me to carry your books?"

Arnie. I stopped in my tracks. Why did his voice still go through me like a thrill and then a twist of pain? "Uh, no. That's okay," I said.

But he reached for my books and I let him take them. He was just being nice because after all he probably thought I was an invalid. "Aren't you supposed to be taking it easy?" he asked.

"Yeah. But I'm going home after third period. And then I'll take a nap."

Junior came and he carried my books to the parking lot. There waiting on us was Ned Jarrett in No. 99. "Ned and I had an errand to run," Junior said. "Hope you don't mind riding in a real live racing car."

"Are you kidding?" I was thrilled. And of course riding in that race car set the wheels in my brain to spinning—thinking about how I could get Ned Jarrett to help with our fund drive.

The next day during our team meeting I couldn't believe the ideas the team had come up with. Duncan wanted to bring his horseshoes and set up a tournament. "Good one," said Reggie.

"Another thing," said Stella. "Eisenhower is being inaugurated at the same time. Maybe we could also celebrate that. It could be a time for all of us—Democrats and Republicans—to just have a good time together. And support our new president. No competition."

"That's a great idea," I said.

But Reggie came up with the best idea of all. "That car," he said. "The one I wrecked. It's sitting at my uncle's garage. He could tow it over here and we could charge a dime apiece for people to hit it with a sledgehammer."

When he said that, Duncan roared so loudly the librarian started hushing him up. "Students, please," she said. "This is a library."

"Reggie, that is pure genius," I said. "I might just spend all my money on that." Right then I couldn't quite imagine swinging a sledgehammer, but if I could, I would sure love to give that wreck a good whack.

We took our plans to Mr. Lynn the next day. "I admire your ideas," he said. And I could just hear him getting ready to turn us down. He pulled a pen out of his pocket and tapped at the ink blotter on his desk. "But the entire student body cannot miss the whole school day. Give me a list of people who would be working the booths. They'll need to be approved for missing classes. The rest of the school can participate in your fund drive during their study hall period only."

"Mr. Lynn," said Stella. "That's brilliant. Why didn't we think of that?"

"Perhaps," said Mr. Lynn, "because you've never tried running a school before."

64

IDA
January 1953

For the last week Ellie had been back to her normal school schedule. But her mind was more on her big fund drive than it was on classes. She was constantly signing people up to run booths, collect money, make posters, and a whole lot more. But she was also being secretive about some new idea she'd cooked up.

When I glanced over her shoulder, she turned her clipboard so I couldn't see what she'd been writing. "What?" I asked.

"Sorry," she said. "For now, it's a secret."

"Then don't tell me," I said. "Never mind that I'm your twin sister. But all this stuff you're working on—aren't you worried about your grades?"

"I'll catch up," she said. "But first I need to do this fund drive."

I wasn't exactly sure how raising money was making amends for that car accident, but I knew fighting polio was a good idea. And maybe Ellie just needed to show people she'd changed. She had, for sure. I mean, she was still Ellie, raring to get someplace in this world, but she seemed more content to take it easy. Maybe she'd figured out life wasn't exactly a race and she didn't always have to be first.

She sure did like that public address system, though. It seemed like she was constantly making announcements. The next morning, when the rest of us were in home-room, she was in the principal's office again. As soon as we finished saying the Lord's Prayer and the Pledge of Allegiance, Mr. Lynn said we had a special announce-ment. Ellie came on.

"Good morning, Fred T. Foard Tigers," she said. "The March of Dimes fund drive is almost here. Friday is our school's much anticipated fundraising carnival."

"And don't forget." That was Stella's voice. "We will also be celebrating the inauguration of Dwight D. Eisen-hower, the thirty-fourth president of the United States. We'll play patriotic music and even have miniature flags for sale. All the money raised will be used to fight polio. So bring money, y'all! Ellie, is there anything else we need to say?"

"I'm glad you asked. In addition to the events we've already announced—individual portraits, a kissing booth, car smashing, and so on and so forth—we have a special guest coming to our school. This is your chance to have your photograph taken with NASCAR driver Ned Jarrett and his race car! Ned is from right here at Propst Cross-roads, and we're lucky to have him because he's super modest and doesn't like to do things in public. Except race, of course.

"So, my fellow students, I urge you to come out to the car parking lot on Friday during your study hall period and get your photograph taken with our very own local celebrity, Ned Jarrett. It'll only cost you a dime, and that will go to the March of Dimes. Drive safe, America!"

Ellie finished up just as the bell rang for first period. I gathered my books, and the whole time I was shaking my head and laughing. "What?" asked Arnie.

"Sometimes I wonder if we're really twins. Where does she get her nerve? And all those words?"

"I have a feeling," said Laura, "that back when you were learning to talk, Ellie stole half your words right out of your mouth."

We all walked down the hall and bumped into Ellie at the door to Latin class. She was smiling from one side of her face to the other. Maybe her smile narrowed up just a bit when she noticed Arnie carrying my books. But she threw her shoulders back and said, "Isn't that swell about Ned coming on Friday?"

"That was your surprise, wasn't it?" I said. "Wonderful idea, Ellie."

But I doubt she even heard me because other people were congratulating her. She was sure eating up all that attention.

"Let's go," I told Arnie. "I'm ready for my favorite five minutes of every school day. Walking to class with you."

65

IDA
January 1953

We set up the portrait event in the library.

I had four portraits to draw during first period, and it was the fastest I ever had to work. But I'd been practicing, so even though it felt like pressure I just stayed focused. Every so often Ellie would pop her head in, checking to see if we needed anything and to ask how we were holding up. She was a regular mother hen. And of course she or Stella came on the P.A. system at the beginning of every period and encouraged students who had study hall to get out and support the fight against polio.

By third period I was tired of drawing people and trying to be sociable at the same time. And by fifth, I was exhausted. I decided to take a break. After hiding in a bathroom stall for fifteen minutes, I wandered outside.

I could see Ned Jarrett out there talking to some boys. And not far away, sitting at the edge of the parking lot, was that smashed-up heap. I couldn't have told you if it was a Ford or a Chevy or something else, but I knew I hated that car. And the idea of hitting it with a sledgehammer started feeling real good. I had money in my pocket, so before I could talk myself out of it I joined the line to wait my turn.

Reggie and Duncan were collecting money and making sure people didn't take more hits than they paid for. Somebody named Gerald had the sledgehammer in hand when I arrived. He gave Reggie five dimes. "All right!" said Reggie. "Five hits on the old '48 Chevrolet for Gerald Petty!"

There were two sledgehammers on the ground. Gerald picked one up and gave it a little swing like a batter checking out bats at a baseball game. Then he dropped that one and did the same thing with the next. He scratched his head like he couldn't quite decide. And someone yelled, "Hey, Gerald, there's a line back here. Hurry up!"

So he gave that Chevy a big slug. The crowd hooted and hollered and egged him on and he made a big show of his muscles and hit it four more times. The line slowly moved forward, and finally it was my turn. I gave Reggie three dimes and he said, "Three hits for Ida Honeycutt."

Even before I hit that thing, people were cheering. I think I understood Ellie a little better in that moment. Because that applause did feel good.

It made me want to really swing at that mangled wreck that nearly took Ellie's life. To let out the anger I felt toward Reggie and Duncan, who were standing right there. And toward Stella—I'd never liked her in the first place. I picked up the nearest sledgehammer and walked around to the side of the car where I knew Ellie had been on the night of the wreck.

The sledgehammer was so heavy that swinging it nearly took me for a ride. I hit that caved-in door and the hammer just sort of bounced off. But I clobbered the car three times as hard as I could, and I felt the tears running down my cheeks when I did.

"Atta girl!" Reggie hollered. "Who thinks Ida should get bonus hits?"

Other students cheered and Duncan said, "Take a few more."

And I started to, but then the cheering got louder and someone grabbed my arm. I realized Ellie was there with tears running down her face. "Together," she said.

Two people smacking a '48 Chevrolet with the sledgehammer is kind of like running a three-legged race. It doesn't work so well, and we probably looked like a couple of fools stumbling over ourselves. But I realized I didn't care what I looked like. Ellie was with me and we were doing this together—taking out some anger and letting out some hurt and telling ourselves that we could cooperate.

But we were too tired for more than a few whacks, so we just sort of dropped the hammer and fell into each other's arms. That line of people waiting their turn came at us then. They surrounded us with hugs and sniffles and a whole lot of "Atta girls."

Finally I started pushing people away. "I've gotta go to the girls' room," I said. And I left Ellie standing there with them. Before I reached the building I could hear that car getting clobbered again.

Stella was in the bathroom at the sink, putting on makeup. She didn't notice me because she and Patsy were talking. "I don't know why I even bother," she said. "That ugly scar will be there for the rest of my life. Always reminding me."

I didn't come into that bathroom planning to forgive Stella, but watching her there, I realized I was ready. After all, Ellie wasn't the only one making amends today. Stella had worked hard on this, trying to show us that she'd changed. It probably shouldn't have taken me so long to figure that out. But this fund drive was showing me that all four of them carried the scars. And they all wanted to do something big to make amends and show gratitude.

I couldn't be angry with Stella anymore. I dried my eyes and stepped up to the mirror.

"Thank you, Stella," I said, "for helping Ellie with the fund drive. Y'all are doing a really good job. It's a big hit."

Stella stopped with the makeup sponge halfway to her face. "Thank you for saying that, Ida. I don't blame you for hating me, and . . ." Her voice broke. "I'm really glad Ellie didn't die. She's something else, isn't she?"

"Yeah," I said. "She's something else."

I splashed water over my face and dried it. "I guess I should go back out there," I said. "Ellie wants me to have my picture taken with Ned Jarrett. She's so sure he's going to be famous someday."

66

ELLIE
January 1953

The March of Dimes fund drive was a big splash, and Laura even sent a story to the *Hickory Daily Record*. Back on page eight there were two photographs and her write-up with the title DRIVE IS SMASHING SUCCESS. One of the pictures was me sitting in Ned Jarrett's car with Ned and Stella posing beside it. And the other one was Reggie and Duncan with those sledgehammers, taking a crack at the wrecked car.

Laura sure did know how to write a good story. She interviewed each of us who'd been in the accident and included quotes we'd said and what our purpose was.

We raised a total of $233.68, which the March of Dimes people said was an astonishing amount for high schoolers to manage in one day. But of course it was more than one day. It was days of planning and nights of fretting and lots of people helping.

I was in homeroom, practicing my Latin with Laura and feeling almost normal around Arnie and my sister, when Stella announced the total on the P.A. system. Our homeroom burst into applause, and I could hear other classes down the hall doing the same thing.

Then Stella said, "I have just two things to say for Ellie Honeycutt, who thought up the fund drive and organized it. Number one: Ellie, it is generally agreed upon that you should run for sophomore class president next year. And when you do, I hope to be your campaign manager."

Me? Class president? What a great idea! Other people seemed to agree, because everybody in our room clapped. "And number two," said Stella, "I have the distinct honor of announcing that you, Ellie Honeycutt, are the winner of an all-expenses-paid trip to Massachusetts this coming summer."

What? It took a minute for that to sink in. Everybody in homeroom cheered, and I finally caught on. "What?" I screamed.

Stella's voice again. "Ellie, you are asked to report to Laura Quincy for further details."

Laura. Of course. She was from Massachusetts. I ran around my desk and grabbed her hands and pulled her out of her seat and hugged her so tight I think she nearly stopped breathing.

Mr. Van Horn asked Laura to explain. "Since this has become a public matter, you may as well give *us* the details too," he said.

Laura looped her arm through mine. "You know I'm from Massachusetts," she said. "And maybe you know that Ellie was planning to visit Connecticut with her father at Thanksgiving, but then there was the accident. Sending Ida in her place was probably the hardest thing she ever did, wasn't it, Ellie?"

I nodded but couldn't speak. *Why am I crying again? Am I ever going to stop?*

"So I asked my parents if she could go on vacation to visit my grandparents with us this summer, and they said yes. Hopefully your parents will agree, Ellie."

I found my voice then. "They'll agree. I know they will. Am I really going to Massachusetts?" I squealed again and hugged Laura, and Ida put her arms around both of us. Then the bell rang, and—oh, my goodness, how was I ever going to focus on Latin after that?

All the way down the hall, people were calling out to me, "Way to go, Ellie," or "Ellie for president." It was almost too much excitement even for me.

When I watched Ida and Arnie head down the hall to their second-period classes, I knew I'd finally turned a corner, because I decided they actually looked kind of cute together.

In some ways we were like two drivers in different vehicles. Ida had art. And Arnie. But I had my voice. I could speak up and make big things happen. And who knew—next year, I might even be class president.

Both of us were going places. We just had different ways of getting there.

EPILOGUE
Ida

After Daddy came home from war
with wounds we couldn't see
and moods he couldn't predict,
I pulled back and let Ellie take the lead.

I didn't mind so much if she wanted to run on past
and steal the show from me.
I didn't need to be seen or heard the way she did.
Art was *my* voice.

But then in her race to be first
Ellie crashed
and I had to go around her—
to face scary unknowns
and accept good things that came my way.

I think we both learned
that life is not a race with one of us winning
and the other losing.
We can drive on our own separate tracks
without competing.
And when we do
We'll each come out a winner.

AUTHOR'S NOTE

Bakers Mountain Stories began with *Blue*, a book about a polio epidemic in my backyard (Hickory, North Carolina). A few years later I wrote *Comfort*, a sequel about the aftereffects of polio and war. Eventually my publisher suggested a prequel, which led to my writing *Aim*, a story of family dysfunction and of America being drawn into World War II.

For several decades I've enjoyed observing the lives and behaviors of twins in my family. So when the opportunity came to continue the Bakers Mountain Stories with *Drive*, I was eager to explore the growth of the Honeycutt twins, Ida and Ellie, who were introduced in *Aim*, *Blue*, and *Comfort*.

A Few Facts

My alma mater, Fred T. Foard High School, actually opened in the fall of 1953, but for the convenience of my story, I portrayed its beginning in 1952, the year that Ida and Ellie would have been freshmen. According to local newspaper accounts, 1952 was also the year that the Hickory Speedway opened and the local NASCAR legend Ned Jarrett ran his first race. I was delighted to include this local bit of stock car racing history and a glimpse into the life of an inspiring driver.

NASCAR

Although the prohibition of alcohol ended in 1933, many areas around the South remained "dry" for decades. But people still wanted their strong drink. Making moonshine was highly profitable, one of the few ways that poor mountain families could survive. The whiskey, made in secret, was delivered in souped-up cars by daring drivers. Lawmen were often unable to chase down those hard-driving, bootlegging boys.

Eventually all this fast driving evolved into a racing industry as drivers challenged each other to informal races. Enterprising individuals seized an opportunity to create events, draw a crowd, and charge admittance. In 1948, a race promoter and driver, Bill France Sr., saw a need to organize stock car racing under an organization with specific rules. He and other promoters created NASCAR (National Association of Stock Car Auto Racing). In June 1949, the first official NASCAR stock car race was held on a three-quarter-mile dirt track in Charlotte, North Carolina.

HICKORY MOTOR SPEEDWAY

Hickory Motor Speedway, which came to be known as the Fastest Short Track in the World, opened in May 1952. The speedway was a half-mile dirt track that presented vigorous driving challenges and developed strong skills in the drivers who ran here. From the beginning it was a NASCAR-sanctioned track, and because so many early champions drove in Hickory races it is sometimes called "the birthplace of the NASCAR stars."

"GENTLEMAN NED" JARRETT

Ned Jarrett grew up a stone's throw from Fred T. Foard High School. He entered his first race on May 18, 1952, on the day Hickory Motor Speedway opened. He finished in tenth place.

Unlike many of his competitors, Ned never ran moonshine. In fact, he gave up racing because his father was concerned that people would associate him with those illegal activities. At first Ned honored his father's request, but then one night when John, the co-owner of his car, was ill, Ned filled in for him. He took second place in that race. For a while he drove secretly as "John Lentz," but he was so successful that word leaked back to his father. At that point Jarrett's father gave him his blessing to drive, using his own name.

Although a fierce competitor, Ned was calm and respectful and became known in NASCAR as Gentleman Ned. In the course of his career he won fifty Grand National events, and in 1961 he won the Darlington 500 by fourteen laps, a NASCAR record that remains to this day.

In 1966, at the peak of his career, Ned retired from racing to spend time with his wife and three children. He continued to love NASCAR, however, and he went on to buy and improve Hickory Motor Speedway and to broadcast NASCAR events on radio and television. In 2011, he was inducted into the NASCAR Hall of Fame and has been named one of NASCAR's fifty greatest drivers.

GWYN STALEY AND JUNIOR JOHNSON

Both Gwyn Staley and Junior Johnson were early drivers from North Carolina who drove at Hickory Motor Speedway in its opening season. Staley won the first race, but Johnson threatened his leadership all season. At the end of the season they were tied for first place at the Hickory track. Junior Johnson broke the tie by winning in North Wilkesboro the following week. During his NASCAR career he also won fifty Grand National races.

Junior Johnson developed his driving skills by hauling his family's moonshine and running from the police. He was never caught delivering moonshine, but in 1956 and 1957 he served time in jail for manufacturing it.

Although less is known about Gwyn Staley, he is reported to have been on at least one moonshine run with Junior Johnson. He was killed in a NASCAR race in Richmond, Virginia, in 1958.

THE COLD WAR AND THE KOREAN CONFLICT

The United States and the Soviet Union (Russia and her satellite countries) were allies during World War II. At the end of the war, however, they disagreed on how to divide and govern the countries they'd recently defeated. As tensions increased, both superpowers began the buildup of weapons in order to protect their own interests. This escalation of tension, which involved threats and spying, became known as the Cold War.

At the end of World War II, Korea, a country formerly dominated by Japan, came under the control of the Soviet Union in the North and the United States in the South. Ideally, these two world powers would have enabled Korea to become an independent state, but the United States was committed to creating a free and democratic form of government while the Soviet Union promoted communism, a political and economic system controlled by a totalitarian leadership.

The Korean Conflict began in June 1950 when Soviet-backed Korean troops invaded the southern part of the country. The United States, in an attempt to prevent communism from spreading south, sent troops into Korea to fight communist forces. Most Americans were weary of war and not sure the spread of communism could be stopped. By 1952 the country was ready for change, and Dwight Eisenhower was elected with the hope he would bring an end to war. He did in fact negotiate a peace treaty, and the war ended in July 1953.

To this day, communist-led North Korea remains a threat to South Korea and to peace in the world.

RESOURCES

BOOKS

Driving With the Devil: Southern Moonshine, Detroit Wheels, and the Birth of NASCAR, by Neal Thompson (Broadway Books, 2009)

Hickory Motor Speedway: The World's Most Famous Little Short Track, by W. D. Washburn (Tarheel, 2003)

One and the Same: My Life as an Identical Twin and What I've Learned About Everyone's Struggle to Be Singular, by Abigail Pogrebin (Anchor/Random House, 2010)

"Then Junior Said to Jeff": The Greatest NASCAR Stories Ever Told, by David Poole, Jim McLaurin, and Tom Gillispie (Triumph Books, 2012)

NEWSPAPERS

Hickory Daily Record, March 1952–May 1953

Catawba News-Enterprise, March 1952–January 1953

Note: Websites and online statistics show dates other than 1952 as the beginning of Hickory Motor Speedway and Ned Jarrett's career. However, after interviewing Ned and reading 1952 issues of local newspapers, I can confidently state that the first race held at Hickory Motor Speedway was May 18, 1952.

VIDEOS

American Stock: The Golden Era of NASCAR, 1936–1971. Stonebridge Productions, 2004.

Greased Lightning. Warner Brothers, 1977.

Race to Live. youtube.com/watch?v= zBlTY9sR698.

1952 Grand National Daytona Race Beach NASCAR (Lloyd Moore). youtube.com/watch?v=ErW_bbkvesg.

WEBSITES AND INTERNET ARTICLES

NASCAR Hall of Fame. nascarhall.com/.

Ned Jarrett, Class of 2011. nascar.com/news-media/2013/04/10/ned-jarrett-class-of-2011.

BOOKS FOR YOUNG PEOPLE

Countdown, by Deborah Wiles (Scholastic Press, 2010)

Dwight D. Eisenhower: Thirty-Fourth President, 1953–1961, by Mike Venezia (Children's Press, 2017)

The Enemy: Detroit 1954, by Sara Holbrook (Calkins Creek, 2017)

Jacob Have I Loved, by Katherine Paterson (Harper Teen, 1980)

Top Secret Files: The Cold War: Secrets, Special Missions and Hidden Facts About the CIA, KGB, and M16, by Stephanie Bearce (Prufrock Press, 2015)

The Cold War: The Twentieth Century, by Wendy Conklin (Teacher Created Materials, 2007)

The Jarretts, by Richard Huff (Chelsea House, 2008)

THANK YOU!

I interviewed generous people while writing this story. Twins and their family members helped me understand twin dynamics. My thanks to twins Cindy King and Sandy King, Lori Smith Hatter, Lisa Smith Gerber, Alyssa Stout, Barbara Krasner, Alicia Hartzler, Paula Erickson, Lori Williams, and Miriam Moyer.

My thanks also to Teresa and Logan Gross, avid racing fans, and to Ned Jarrett, who met with me to discuss his early racing career and that of Hickory Motor Speedway.

I am grateful to Larry Mosteller and Steve Smith for help with car-related information and to Walter and Miriam King and Laura Sigmon Parker for answering medical questions. To Chuck Hostetter for helping me process my story and for attending to household tasks when I slipped back into 1952. To my children, grandchildren, and Mary Buie Schuller's fifth grade class for being my beta readers. To Carol Baldwin for providing a writing space when I so desperately needed it, for brainstorming with me, and for reading my manuscript, and insisting I remove choppy sentences! As always, I have much appreciation for my editor, Carolyn Yoder, and the team at Calkins Creek, for expressing confidence in my story and helping me bring it to publication.

OTHER
BAKERS MOUNTAIN
STORIES
BY JOYCE MOYER HOSTETTER

AIM
HC: 978-1-62979-673-4: $17.95 U.S / $23.50 CAN
PB: 978-1-68437-276-8: $8.95 U.S. / $11.95 CAN
eBook: 978-1-62979-746-5: $7.99

BLUE
HC: 978-1-59078-389-4: $16.95 U.S / $21.99 CAN
PB: 978-1-59078-835-6: $7.95 U.S. / $10.95 CAN
eBook: 978-1-62979-268-2: $7.99

COMFORT
PB: 978-1-59078-895-0: $7.95 U.S. / $10.50 CAN
eBook: 978-1-62979-292-7: $7.99